PRAISE FOR THE NOVELS
OF VICKI LEWIS THOMPSON

THE WILD ABOUT YOU NOVELS

Werewolf in Denver

"A clever, lighthearted tale.... The story line is fast-paced as the lead couple fights each other and their respective hearts." —*Midwest Book Review*

Werewolf in Seattle

"A fun frolic starring two likable protagonists ... witty." —*Midwest Book Review*

"I really love this book. Vicki Lewis Thompson did it again. She can't write fast enough for me! This is another keeper for my very full bookshelf. It will have you reading long past bedtime and still wanting more." —Night Owl Reviews

"A fun, lighthearted romance, as are the previous books in this series. It's a feel-good read that will brighten any bad mood or reading slump. If you're not sure what to read next, try this one. It's time for some fun!" —The Good, the Bad and the Unread

"A sweet romance that has humor and love throughout the entire book.... I love werewolves, love, and humor mixed together, and this series seems to have it all." —TwoLips Reviews

continued ...

Werewolf in the North Woods

"Perfect for when you need to add some romantic comedy to the daily grind. Thompson does her werewolves justice.... Sparks and fur do indeed fly." —*USA Today*

"A great read." —Bitten by Books

"Sizzling as well as howlingly funny." —Fresh Fiction

Werewolf in Manhattan

"A humorous and romantic comedy." —*USA Today*

"Enough heated sex scenes to satisfy any werewolf romance fan." —*Publishers Weekly*

"Readers will enjoy Vicki Lewis Thompson taking a bite ... out of the Big Apple." —Genre Go Round Reviews

"I loved this book and I can't wait for the next one.... A definite keeper and will be on my shelf for a lifetime." —Night Owl Reviews (top pick)

THE BABES ON BROOMS NOVELS

Chick with a Charm

"Thompson again gives readers a charming, warm, humorous, sexually charged romance with likable characters, a magical dog, and a feel-good ending." —*Booklist*

Blonde with a Wand

"Extremely readable ... terrific writing and great character development.... Readers will fully enjoy this confection." —*Romantic Times* (4 stars)

FURTHER PRAISE FOR
VICKI LEWIS THOMPSON
AND HER NOVELS

"Snappy, funny, romantic."
— *New York Times* bestselling author Carly Phillips

"A trademark blend of comedy and heart."
— *Publishers Weekly*

"Count on Vicki Lewis Thompson for a sharp, sassy, sexy read. Stranded on a desert island? I hope you've got this book in your beach bag." — Jayne Ann Krentz

"Wildly sexy . . . a full complement of oddball characters and sparkles with sassy humor." — *Library Journal*

"A riotous cast of colorful characters . . . fills the pages with hilarious situations and hot, creative sex."
— *Booklist*

"[A] lighthearted and frisky tale of discovery between two engaging people." — *The Oakland Press* (MI)

"A funny and thrilling ride!"
— Romance Reviews Today

"Extremely sexy . . . over-the-top . . . sparkling."
— *Rendezvous*

"A whole new dimension in laughter. A big . . . bravo!"
— A Romance Review

Also by Vicki Lewis Thompson

Werewolf in Las Vegas

A WILD ABOUT YOU NOVEL

Vicki Lewis Thompson

A SIGNET ECLIPSE BOOK

SIGNET ECLIPSE
Published by the Penguin Group
Penguin Group (USA) LLC, 375 Hudson Street,
New York, New York 10014

USA | Canada | UK | Ireland | Australia | New Zealand | India | South Africa | China
penguin.com
A Penguin Random House Company

First published by Signet Eclipse, an imprint of New American Library,
a division of Penguin Group (USA) LLC

First Printing, March 2014

ISBN 978-0-451-41568-4

Printed in the United States of America
10 9 8 7 6 5 4 3 2 1

To those whose dedicated study of wolves has given us a better understanding of these magnificent creatures.

ACKNOWLEDGMENTS

As always, I'm grateful for the cheerful encouragement and editorial skill of Claire Zion and the invaluable support of my assistant, Audrey Sharpe. I'm also blessed with three amazing plotting partners—Rhonda Nelson, Andrea Laurence, and Kira Sinclair—who've turned out to be extraordinary travel partners, too. Now I can finally say . . . We'll always have Paris!

Chapter 1

Everyone in Vegas who'd heard about tonight's poker game said Luke Dalton was crazy. As he sat across the table from Benedict Cartwright in a staged venue that provided room for two hundred paid spectators, Luke briefly questioned his own sanity. But regardless of the game's outcome, the status quo would change, and that was all he cared about.

He'd challenged Benedict to this winner-takes-all poker game — the deed to Luke's Silver Crescent Casino against the deed to Cartwright's neighboring bar, Howlin' at the Moon. The casino was worth twenty times more than the bar, but the Moon was a Cartwright family treasure, a Vegas landmark built thirty years ago by Harrison Cartwright, Benedict's late father.

Luke lived in the Silver Crescent's penthouse, which meant he had to lay eyes on that damned bar every single day and be reminded that Harrison Cartwright had driven Luke's dad, Angus, to his grave at the young age of fifty-six. Angus had died on Christmas Day, thrusting

Luke abruptly into the position of CEO of Dalton Industries.

The feud between Angus and Harrison must have taken its toll on both men, because Harrison had died a week later, on New Year's Eve. For three long months Luke had struggled with the pain of living next to a Cartwright property. Tonight he'd either win it—and then maybe even bulldoze the building—or he'd lose the Silver Crescent and change his place of residence. Either way worked for him, but he'd prefer to win.

They'd been at it for almost two hours, with the piles of chips shifting back and forth across the table. Cartwright, whose blond good looks made him a favorite with the ladies, had just won a hand that put him up a little. But he looked tired.

Luke experienced an unwelcome flash of empathy for the guy who'd also just lost his dad. Benedict's twin brother, Vaughn, older by two minutes and a born leader, had inherited the bulk of the Cartwright holdings, which had surprised no one. Benedict, the happy-go-lucky brother, had been given the bar, which also had surprised no one.

Benedict was a natural at bar ownership, and business was booming. But he'd also eagerly accepted Luke's challenge, which made Luke wonder if Benedict was sick of looking at the Silver Crescent and being reminded of the feud that had likely hastened his own father's death.

It hadn't always been this way between the two families. Angus Dalton and Harrison Cartwright had once been best friends who'd enjoyed weekly poker games. Their fortunes had grown and so had the stakes. They'd started betting real estate.

They'd regularly traded Vegas properties, and neither had seemed to worry about it much. The families had socialized. As a teenager, Luke had shot hoops with Benedict and Vaughn.

But one night, Angus and Harrison must have become bored with their usual wagers. That's all anyone could figure, since Harrison had taken a dare and bet his premier holding, the Silver Crescent. He'd lost.

Harrison Cartwright had loved that casino more than any of his establishments except for Howlin' at the Moon. For the first time in their long history, Harrison had accused Angus of cheating. Enraged by the accusation, Angus had vowed never to play with his old rival again, which meant Harrison couldn't win back his beloved casino.

What followed had become Vegas legend. Harrison had tried every trick in the book to avoid turning over the deed. The legal battle had been long and costly on both sides. In the end, Angus had been awarded the casino and had asked the judge to throw in the bar, too, as compensation for his pain and suffering. The judge had refused.

As the dealer shuffled the cards in preparation for the next hand, Luke glanced toward the group of onlookers who supported him, which represented about half the crowd. His little sister, Cynthia, had shown up. Although he appreciated the support, he couldn't look at his brilliant, beautiful sister without gnashing his teeth. She should be finishing her final semester at Yale right now.

He understood that grief over their dad's death had sidelined her, but he couldn't even get her to promise she'd go back in the fall. She was on track to graduate magna cum laude, for crying out loud.

Yet she was determined to abandon her studies and become a showgirl. On top of that, for the past month she'd been hanging out with Bryce Landry, a high-stakes gambler from 'Frisco. Landry was with her now, in fact. Whenever Luke thought about his little sister throwing away a promising future, he felt sick to his stomach.

He had no clue how to convince her to finish school, either. His mother was no help. Her grief had been so profound she couldn't bear to stay in Vegas, or even in the States, so she was currently living in Provence.

The only good news was that Cynthia had set her heart on being a showgirl at the Silver Crescent. Specifically, she wanted to dance with the Moonbeams, an ensemble created by Luke and Cynthia's mother years ago. Cynthia's sentimental streak was a mile wide, apparently.

In any case, he'd be the one to hire her. She wasn't happy that he'd refused, but at this point, it was his only line of defense. If he lost the Crescent tonight, the Cartwrights might discontinue the Moonbeams show, but even if they kept it, chances were slim they'd hire a Dalton.

Taking a slow, even breath, he scooped up his hand and glanced at it. He kept his expression blank as the betting began. Nothing in his behavior indicated that the hand he had been waiting for had finally arrived. He had aces over kings. Even better, the cards in his hand denied Cartwright the possibility of a royal flush.

He reeled his line out slowly, raising the bets at a steady pace. Finally Luke shoved all his chips to the center of the table. "All in." Benedict Cartwright was going down. The sharp pang of empathy struck again. He forced himself to ignore it.

Only a slight twitch in Benedict's right eyelid betrayed his nervousness as he pushed his chips forward. "Call." He laid out three queens and two kings.

Not bad. But not enough. Luke laid his cards on the table. Howlin' at the Moon now belonged to the Dalton family.

For one long, agonizing moment, his gaze collided with Benedict's. The shock and pain in his adversary's eyes was tough to see, and Luke looked away again. He didn't want to know how bad this was for the guy. But he was afraid that look of devastation would haunt him, at least for a while.

After a collective gasp from the crowd, the mood shifted. Some cheered and others cursed and called for a rematch. Luke shook his head. He had what he wanted, a change in the status quo.

In the midst of the chaotic scene, he heard something odd—a distinct and very canine snarl. Maybe someone had brought a service dog into the room, but he couldn't see an animal anywhere. Yeah, maybe he was going crazy, after all.

After her flight from San Francisco landed at McCarran, Giselle Landry hopped the trolley for an open-air ride to the Illusions Hotel and Casino at the far end of the Strip. The werewolf-exclusive establishment had been the Cartwright pack's flagship property ever since Harrison Cartwright had lost the Silver Crescent to a human named Angus Dalton in a poker game.

A hotel for werewolves in the heart of Vegas had been a daring idea when Harrison had built the Silver Crescent years ago. The other two establishments in the country that catered exclusively to Weres were in more remote areas. One was a resort on an island in Puget Sound, and the other was outside of Denver, a sprawling lodge where Giselle had attended WereCon2012.

Everyone in the werewolf world had understood the significance of losing this urban hotel, but the humans hadn't realized that major panic had ensued. The hotel had been designed for Weres, complete with werewolf-friendly entrances and exits that would make no sense to a human guest. When Harrison Cartwright had owned the Silver Crescent, humans who tried to book a room had been told the hotel was full. Humans could gamble in the casino, but only registered guests could enter the hotel lobby.

While Harrison had fought the deed transfer in court, werewolf crews had reconfigured the rooms, doors, and elevators so that human guests would never dream it had been anything other than a normal Vegas hotel. Humans had no idea that werewolves lived and worked among them and had vast financial holdings in all major cities in the world. Giselle didn't believe they ever should know, although a faction in the Were community was pushing for a full reveal.

With help from a team of lawyers, Harrison had stalled long enough that the renovations had been completed by the time the court awarded the Silver Crescent to Angus Dalton. Most important of all, the underground tunnel to Howlin' at the Moon had been blocked off.

Giselle had been in touch with Angus's son Vaughn for the past several weeks as she'd debated whether to come to Vegas. Once she'd made the decision, he'd offered to send a limo to the airport to pick her up, but she'd opted for the trolley. Between the open car and the overcast sky, maybe she could pretend she was still in her City by the Bay instead of in Vegas looking for her AWOL brother, Bryce.

But Vegas would never pass for 'Frisco. Instantly she was

immersed in the jaw-dropping excess that had produced a giant black pyramid, replicas of the Statue of Liberty and the Eiffel Tower, and a sprawling Roman palace. The trolley rolled by the forty-story Silver Crescent, a glittering tower of reflective glass with hundreds of quarter-moon windows lining the facade and giant chrome quarter-moons on either side of the gleaming entrance.

The hotel dwarfed the one-story, rustic bar sitting next to it. But Howlin' at the Moon had a worldwide reputation among Weres. The legendary watering hole had served drinks and bar food to world-famous shape-shifters for more than thirty years.

But the bar wasn't famous because of its refreshments, excellent though they were. Howlin' at the Moon sat above a top secret Were playground, Harrison Cartwright's proudest achievement. He'd claimed to be excavating the site four stories deep so that he could put in a foundation that would support a hotel someday if he took the notion to build one there. Instead, werewolf-only crews had created a subterranean, climate-controlled world that included evergreens, steep trails, rocky outcroppings, waterfalls, bubbling streams, and a moon that cycled through phases in sync with the real one. Powerful lights kept the plants and trees growing, and heavy-duty pumps moved the water in an endless loop.

Harrison had been hailed as a genius for creating a secure place for werewolves to run in the heart of Sin City. The stark landscape surrounding Vegas offered precious little cover for a wolf. Anyone spotting one or more of the large animals would most likely alert wildlife experts, destroying any hope of secrecy. Besides, the playground was climate controlled, a real plus for a discriminating wolf wearing a thick fur coat.

Giselle had seen the place once. She and two of her female Were friends had gone on a road trip that included one night at the Silver Crescent in Vegas. After checking into their room, they'd all shifted and used the special paw controls on the elevators to access a tunnel connecting the hotel with the bar.

They'd arrived in an anteroom one level below the bar. Lockers lined the walls, which had puzzled Giselle at first until she realized that bar patrons who wanted to use the playground would need a place to shift and store their clothes. Harrison had thought of everything.

She and her friends had pushed through a revolving door at the far end of the locker room and had stared in amazement. They'd entered another world, one bathed in moonlight, scented with evergreen, and filled with the sounds of rushing water and the hoots of an owl.

Once they'd recovered from their sense of awe, they'd romped through that pretend forest, howling and yipping like teenagers. She smiled at the memory of it and wondered if she'd have time to go while she was here. What a great way to release some of the tension created by her brother's dereliction of duty.

The trolley moved on, gliding past rippling neon and flashing billboards promising riches beyond compare. A river of pedestrians seeking those treasures eddied in and out of the elaborate pleasure domes lining the busy thoroughfare.

Giselle searched their faces, as if she might spot Bryce in the crowd. His hair, dark red like hers, made him fairly easy to see, especially because he was tall. He was here somewhere. He'd said so, and although he could be a royal pain, he didn't lie. He'd texted every few days to let the family know he was okay, but he'd ignored all requests, or demands in the case of her father, to return home.

She'd decided not to let him know she'd flown down. Not yet, anyway. He wouldn't be happy that she'd come to drag him back, and ideally, she'd like to make her plea in person rather than over the phone. Maybe she could arrange to run into him and catch him off guard.

Whenever she thought of Bryce, she alternated between being worried and being royally pissed. Although she was familiar with his pattern of going along with the program until something hit him wrong and he bolted, this particular incident had lasted way too long—more than seven months, in fact.

He had to know how severely his juvenile stunt had impacted her and the rest of his pack. He was slated to be the next Landry alpha and had duties as a result. Giselle had ended up covering for him in addition to handling her job as the pack's chief financial officer. She wanted him home, preferably before he did something terminally stupid.

She wasn't terribly surprised that he'd left. At first the plan to mate with Miranda Randolph, heir to the Randolph winery fortune, had been his idea. But the two packs, especially the two sets of parents, had jumped in and taken over. Whenever Bryce felt pushed, he simply abandoned the field.

Giselle had to figure out a way to coax him back, even if the Miranda situation was ruined forever. Members of the Landry pack, including their parents, were talking about making Giselle the next alpha, and she didn't want it. The political maneuvering required of an alpha didn't appeal to her at all. She'd much rather crunch numbers than settle pack disputes, which meant she had to find Bryce.

According to Vaughn, Bryce wasn't staying at Illusions or frequenting any of the usual werewolf haunts, including Howlin' at the Moon. That probably meant he was spending all his time with humans, and that worried Giselle more than anything else. She prayed he hadn't embraced the new and dangerous idea of Weres mating with humans.

After leaving the trolley and entering the soothing ambience of the Illusions lobby, she registered and surrendered her suitcase to the bellman. She'd brought a small one, figuring she wouldn't be there long.

Giselle's nose told her the area was human-free, which probably meant no humans were allowed through the front door. If so, then only Weres would be able to enjoy the three-story atrium filled with evergreens and a babbling brook. In some ways the lobby echoed the playground underneath Howlin' at the Moon.

Giselle didn't have time to stand around and admire the beauty of it, though. She was a werewolf on a mission. Once in the elevator, she called Vaughn, whose office was on the top floor of the building.

"Welcome to Las Vegas, Giselle. The front desk notified me that you'd checked in." Vaughn had the quiet authority of a seasoned alpha, although he couldn't be much older than Giselle, who'd just turned twenty-eight. He'd assumed his father's role with confidence. He'd chosen a suitable mate years ago, and now a baby was on the way, a grandchild that poor Harrison would never see.

"I have checked in," Giselle said. "Are you free to see me?"

"Absolutely. Come on up whenever you're settled. Is the suite okay?"

"I'm sure it is, but I haven't been there yet. I'm in the elevator headed for your floor."

"Okay, good. We have a lot to talk about. Have you had any texts from Bryce today?"

"No. Has something happened?" Her heart rate picked up.

"He was seen at a poker game last night."

She sucked in a breath. "Where?"

"I'd rather tell you about this in person."

"I'm nearly there."

A few minutes later, a receptionist ushered her into Vaughn's office. It looked more like a mountain hideaway than command central for Cartwright Enterprises. Beamed ceilings sheltered rustic furniture created from peeled logs, and a gas fire flickered on a stone hearth. A wall of windows looked out on the Strip, but otherwise, the room could have been part of a ski lodge in Aspen.

Vaughn came around from behind his hand-carved desk. "It's great to finally meet in person." He took her hand in both of his. He was a good-looking Were with dark brown hair and the kind of solid build typical of strong werewolf males.

"Same here. I appreciate your support in this, Vaughn, especially because you must have a ton of issues you're dealing with."

"Yeah." His smile was tinged with sadness.

She gazed at him with sympathy. "Your dad was so young."

"Yeah. Only fifty-seven. I keep expecting him to come walking through that door."

"Was this his office?"

"Yes, and I always loved it, so I've kept things the way he had them." He gestured to a couple of overstuffed easy chairs in front of the fireplace. "Please have a seat. Can I get you anything?" He walked over to a wet bar along the wall next to the windows. "Wine? Mixed drink? Something to eat?"

"Nothing for me, thanks." She settled into a comfy leather chair.

"You're sure?" He sounded disappointed.

She glanced toward the wet bar, where he was in the process of returning two glasses to the shelf. "I'm sure, but if you want something, go ahead."

"Guess I was hoping to have somebody to share a drink with." He turned. "Shana can't because of the baby, and it's been a rough twenty-four hours."

She realized then what she might have noticed right away if she hadn't been so caught up in her own problems. Despite his crisp white dress shirt, his Ralph Lauren tie, and what were probably designer slacks, Vaughn Cartwright didn't have it together this afternoon. His hair was mussed, and without the smile he'd given her earlier, she was able to see the anxiety lurking in his gray eyes.

"What's happened, Vaughn?"

Vaughn rocked back on his heels. "Well, that wasn't just an ordinary poker game last night. It was a special event between two players, one of them being my brother, Benedict, and the other being Luke Dalton."

"So it was a Cartwright-Dalton rematch?" Now she knew why Bryce had been there to watch. He loved to gamble, and he'd been fascinated with the Cartwright-Dalton feud.

"Exactly. Dalton put the Silver Crescent on the line, and Benedict thought he could win it back."

"Would that even be worth doing? I can't imagine the cost of renovations to create what you had there before."

"Yeah, it would be pricey, but we'd make it back in no time by restored access to the Moon and the playground. But that's a moot point. Instead of winning the hotel, my brother lost the bar."

"He bet the Moon? How could he? You're the alpha! Surely you wouldn't let—"

"He inherited it." Vaughn sounded exhausted. "Unfortunately, it was his to lose. I got pretty much everything else, but my dad willed the bar to Benedict, who really is a natural at running it. Or was. Now it's owned by a human."

"What about the playground?"

He blew out a breath. "Handled as best we could. The transfer of ownership didn't take place until this morning. We had crews working all night. They drained the water, turned off everything except the automatic lights for the plants and the drip system, and reconfigured the entrance. Now it looks like a blank wall instead of the door that used to be there."

"Will the plants be okay?"

"Should be. I certainly can't let them die. For one thing, it would make one hell of a mess under there."

Giselle couldn't even imagine. "Can you buy it back?"

"Not today, but I plan to keep trying. I spent the entire morning over at the Moon making offers that would give my CFO cardiac arrest if he knew. Dalton wouldn't budge. He said that having a Cartwright property next to the Silver Crescent was too painful for him after his father's death."

"I suppose it was."

"Oh, I don't doubt it. Benedict hated seeing a Dalton property next to the Moon. He thought he'd win and we'd get the Silver Crescent back."

"This is horrible, Vaughn." She wondered how this would affect the alpha's relationship with his twin brother. "Where's Benedict, now?"

"I don't know. He supervised the work last night and let me know it was secure, but I haven't heard from him since. Turns out I'm not the only one with family issues, though. Before I left the bar this morning, Dalton's little sister, Cynthia, showed up and they got in a huge fight. She told him she was disappearing for a while so she could spend quality time with her new boyfriend, who happens to be someone you know and love."

"Good Lord." Giselle squeezed her eyes shut. "Are you saying the new boyfriend is my brother?"

"'Fraid so."

She groaned and let her head fall back against the plump chair cushion. "I'll take you up on that drink, Vaughn. And forget the girly stuff. Give me a Scotch on the rocks."

Chapter 2

After the embarrassingly public fight with Cynthia, Luke retreated to the office of his recently acquired bar and shut the door. She'd obviously thought that after he won the bar he'd be in a celebratory mood and would magnanimously agree to hire her as a Moonbeam. She'd figured wrong, but arguing with her had taken the shine off his poker victory. She was basically the only family he had left, and he yearned to make peace with her. But she seemed determined to ruin her life, and he felt an obligation to try to prevent that.

She'd never totally cut out on him before, and he hated the feeling of being disconnected without any idea of where she was. But he dared not follow his first instinct and scour the town looking for her.

She hadn't said where she was going, obviously on purpose, but he didn't think she'd leave the city. She'd always preferred her hometown to travel. She hadn't liked being so far away during her college years, and she'd flown home every chance she got.

If he went looking for her, though, and she realized he

was after her, she might take off for parts unknown, especially if Landry was encouraging her. Worry sat like a cold, hard lump in his stomach. She was twenty-two, an adult, but when he thought of the bad decisions he'd made at that age, the knot of worry got bigger.

He'd lost his father and felt as if he'd lost his mother, too, now that she was living in France. He couldn't lose Cynthia. He'd ask Owen Banks, his chief of security, to keep track of her.

Owen looked like a nerd with his thick glasses and supershort haircut, but he had the mind of a CIA operative. Unclipping his cell phone from his belt, Luke speed-dialed Owen.

"What's up, boss?" Owen insisted on calling Luke that, despite many conversations in which Luke had suggested Owen use his first name instead.

Luke filled him in. "I want to know if she leaves town, either driving or flying, but I don't want her stopped. Only followed."

"Do you know if she's in her Corvette?"

"Damn it. No, I don't." Luke squeezed the bridge of his nose. "And if she's in Landry's vehicle, he probably has a rental."

"No worries, boss. Regardless of what they're driving, I'll find them and keep you posted."

"Thanks." Luke thought of something else and wished he hadn't. But he should consider all possibilities. "Better alert all the wedding chapels, too. If she comes in with Landry, they need to stall as long as possible. I *will* interfere if she decides to go that far." Technically he couldn't stop her, but he could make a hell of a protest.

Cynthia had met the guy a couple of months ago at a local gelato shop, of all places. They'd hit it off, and Luke had made it his business to find out what he could about Bryce Landry. The details were sparse. Landry came from a wealthy family in San Francisco and spent most of his time in Vegas playing high-stakes poker. Luke had no quarrel with that lifestyle—Vegas depended on men like that to keep the lights on—but that didn't mean Luke thought a high roller was the right choice for his sister.

"Got it. Talk to you soon." Owen disconnected.

Luke laid the phone on the battered wooden desk and sat back in the worn leather desk chair with a sigh. He should have seen this coming, but he hadn't. Cynthia might have hoped he'd be toasted after his success, which could make him easier to convince about the showgirl thing. Curiously, he hadn't been as elated about winning the bar as he'd expected to be, and he hadn't touched a drop of liquor all day. So he'd been stone-cold sober when she approached him. Good thing. He'd needed his wits about him.

Of course she'd asked him for the hundredth time to let her perform with the Moonbeams. Even though she could have signed on with any of the casinos just to spite him, her only goal was performing with the signature act created by their mother, Felicia. Felicia had been a dancer before her marriage to Angus, and afterward, she'd supervised the hiring and helped with choreography. Luke could understand that Cynthia had been starry-eyed at fifteen, but he'd expected that by now she would have grown out of it. Instead, they'd had a blowout fight when she arrived after the poker game and he'd refused her request again.

Although he was only eight years older than his sister, sometimes he felt a hundred years older, and this was one of those days. He had to be both father, mother, and brother to her, and he was doing a piss-poor job of it. Although he couldn't blame his dad for dying, he wished his mom had stuck around to help deal with Cynthia.

No, no, he didn't. Not really. Felicia Dalton had never been particularly maternal. She'd loved her husband passionately, and Angus had spoiled her rotten. Her grief when he died had threatened to suck both her children under. Luke had been secretly relieved when she'd decided to move to a little cottage nestled among fields of lavender in Provence. A couple of her friends had already flown over for visits. He'd been way too busy to go, but Cynthia kept saying she would.

She hadn't, though, because she really did avoid travel as much as possible. A few weeks ago, he'd called his mother and asked her to talk Cynthia out of her obsession with the Moonbeams, but his mother couldn't see the problem with letting her do it. Sometimes he wondered if he should just say to hell with it and put his sister in the Moonbeams' lineup. He tried to imagine himself giving up the struggle, and it hurt his soul. He'd think of his dad, who'd been so proud of announcing that his daughter was attending Yale. He hadn't cared that she hadn't chosen a profession yet. She was one smart cookie, he'd say, and he'd had every confidence she would pick an exciting career in her own time.

Well, she had, and performing with the Moonbeams was it. She'd admitted today she'd only attended Yale to please their father. She'd always planned to follow in their mother's dancing footsteps.

But he had to believe she wouldn't have pulled this disappearing act if she hadn't fallen in with Landry. The more he thought about it, the more he became convinced that the guy was encouraging her to push the envelope. Otherwise, why disappear with him? Why not go alone? Landry appeared to be an accomplice of some kind, and if he was, then he'd just made an enemy of Luke Dalton.

A knock sounded on the door. "Luke?"

He recognized the voice of Chuck Stevens, a friend since grade school and his CFO for Dalton Industries. Chuck had tended bar all through college, and he'd offered to oversee the operation this first day. "Come on in, Chuck."

Chuck opened the door and stuck his head in. "Sorry to bother you. I figured you came in here to be alone."

Luke waved a hand. "I could probably use some company. What's up? Are we running out of booze already?"

"Nah. Still plenty. But ... uh ... somebody's here to see you. I'm not sure if you want to see her, though."

"Cynthia?" Luke leaned forward so fast the chair creaked.

"No, sorry. This lady's name is Giselle." He paused. "Giselle Landry."

"Landry." Luke gazed at his friend. "Is this some weird coincidence?"

"No. She's Bryce Landry's sister."

Luke stood. "Good. This is good. Maybe she'll have some insights into the situation."

"Well, shoot." A tall redhead with green eyes walked into the office. "I was hoping *you'd* have some insights."

Luke stared at her. He was very afraid his eyes had widened, but he managed to clamp his jaw so it wouldn't drop. As he took in the sight before him, all rational thought ceased. This Giselle Landry had to be the most beautiful, sexy woman he had ever seen. She was exactly his type—long legs, adorable freckles, and fiery hair.

Looking at her, he felt a wave of desire that almost knocked him over.

But one Dalton mixed up with a Landry was more than enough. He wasn't about to make it two for two.

Giselle hadn't thought to ask Vaughn to describe Luke Dalton. Vaughn wouldn't have given her any significant information, anyway. He'd probably have said Dalton had dark blond hair and blue eyes. He might have mentioned that the guy was about six-two.

Those facts wouldn't have prepared her for this man with broad shoulders, a chiseled jaw, and the mesmerizing gaze of a movie star. His slightly unkempt, almost shaggy haircut only added to his sex appeal. A cotton dress shirt, open at the throat, and a snug pair of jeans signaled his disinterest in traditional business attire. This was the kind of guy who could, if he chose to, use his looks to get anything he wanted from a woman. And possibly from a Were who wasn't against Were-human sexual connections.

Which she was. She didn't allow herself to be attracted to human males because she was opposed to cross-species mating, so why even go there? Her libido might not like that restriction, but too bad.

The guy who'd brought her into the office glanced at Luke. "Holler if you need anything."

"I will, Chuck. Thanks. Close the door on your way out."

"Right." Chuck pulled the door shut behind him.

After it clicked into place, Luke leaned his palms on the surface of the desk, which made his shoulders look even more muscular. "So you don't know where your brother is right now?"

"I assume he's with your sister." She noticed he hadn't asked her to sit down. "Where is she?"

A trace of vulnerability touched his blue eyes. "I don't know." Then he covered that immediately with bravado. "But my people are on it."

"I see." She wasn't fooled. Worry for his sister was tearing him up inside, but he didn't want her to know that. "Do *your people* have a plan of action, then?"

"Of course." His gaze didn't waver.

She doubted that he had everything under perfect control or he wouldn't have made his earlier comment about hoping she'd have some insights. But he was a poker player, and a damned good one, apparently. Aside from that first unguarded comment, he wasn't going to let her see him sweat.

The truth was that she needed this guy and *his people*, whoever they might be. Although Vaughn was sympathetic to her situation, Bryce had hooked up with a Dalton. At this point, no Cartwright, including Vaughn, was particularly enthusiastic about saving Bryce from himself, and they were thrilled that Luke's little sister was causing problems.

Giselle decided diplomacy might be the right way to go. "Look, you obviously have resources and connections that I lack. I'm very eager to find my brother and convince him to come back to San Francisco with me."

"Then our purposes are aligned, because I want him on the next plane bound for 'Frisco. I think he's responsible, directly or indirectly, for this latest move of Cynthia's. He's a bad influence on my little sister."

Diplomacy might not be the answer, after all. "It takes two to tango, Mr. Dalton."

His glance was assessing. "Do you tango, Ms. Landry?"

"Some."

"Then you're aware that the man leads and the woman follows."

He'd hit upon one of her pet peeves about ballroom dancing, the tango included, but she managed a comeback anyway. "That presumes she already knows the steps."

His gaze locked with hers. "Ah, but an experienced male dancer can encourage an inexperienced female dancer to try things she'd never attempt on her own. How old is your brother, Ms. Landry?"

"Thirty."

"What a coincidence. So am I. So I can speak with some authority when I say that your brother's experience with the dance between a man and a woman is far greater than that of my little sister, who is only twenty-two. He has an unfair advantage."

Giselle fought to control her temper. "My brother would never try to convince your sister to do something she didn't want to do. If she's pulled a vanishing act, then it was entirely her—"

"Who told you that?"

She'd prefer not to reveal her connection to the Cartwrights, but neither did she want to get caught in a lie. And Luke Dalton had *people*, so eventually he'd learn where she was staying and figure it out. But she'd postpone that moment as long as she could. "It's all over town," she said.

"Is that so? When did you arrive?"

"Today."

"Then you must have been swinging on that grapevine from the moment you hit the tarmac at McCarran. Come on, Ms. Landry. You have a connection here in town, somebody who gets the local dirt and filled you in. Who is it?"

"I'd rather not say."

"That's up to you, but I'll find out sooner or later. You've implied that we might want to join forces, and being evasive with information isn't a good way to build trust."

That made her laugh. "You aren't about to trust me. You're convinced my brother's leading your sister astray, so don't make it sound like we're going to take some Fellowship of the Ring oath of solidarity."

A flash of amusement transformed his hard features for a brief moment and gave her a glimpse of someone else, someone she might like much better. But then it was gone and the poker face reappeared.

"All right." His tone was mild, but the look in his eyes was intent. "Maybe it doesn't matter how you found out about my sister's plans."

Oh, yes, it does. But if he was willing to let it drop, great. Time to go on the offensive. "Why did she decide to disappear?"

That seemed to take some of the wind out of his sails. He started to sit down and stopped himself, as if only then realizing that she remained standing. "Please, sit down. I should have invited you to do so earlier."

"Perhaps you weren't sure whether you would end up having me thrown out."

He sighed and gestured to one of two upholstered chairs in front of his desk. "I would like to think I haven't descended to that level."

She took the right-hand chair. "What level?"

"Throwing a woman out of my office."

Her feminist instincts wouldn't let that pass. "Have you ever thrown a man out of your office?"

"Once or twice. But—"

"Then if I offend you, feel free to throw me out. I'd consider it a matter of principle and would be upset if you didn't."

He stared at her as if she were speaking in tongues.

She groaned. "Lord help me, I'm dealing with a throwback. I should have realized it when you started describing the whole dancing routine. You truly believe that men were created to lead and women were created to follow, don't you?"

His poker face disappeared. "No, damn it! I was just trying to explain how a guy of thirty could easily influence a young woman of—"

"Have you seen the research on maturation, Dalton? Females mature *much* faster than males. I'd say a twenty-two-year-old female is operating about even with a thirty-year-old male, if not slightly ahead of him."

Abandoning his stoic expression completely, he leaned across the desk and pointed a finger at her. "Screw your research. I know my sister, and she's not all that worldly. She may be a semester away from graduating magna cum laude, but she doesn't know squat about—"

"Magna cum laude?" Giselle realized she might have to take this potential matchup more seriously. Bryce loved brainy females. "From where?" She hoped it was some no-name college with a total enrollment of five hundred.

"Yale. But that's beside the point."

"Actually, it's not beside the point at all." Giselle became more worried by the second. "She must be very goal-oriented."

"Trust me, she is. Her goal used to be graduating with honors from Yale so she could make our father proud.

Now that he's gone, she doesn't want to go back. She says that was his dream for her, and even attending classes there now would be too sad and painful."

"Poor kid."

"That's what I thought, too! I was ready to cut her some slack. I figured if she gave it a few months, she could manage to go back for the fall semester. She was so close! But she said no, she wasn't going back at all."

"She could change her mind."

He shook his head. "I doubt it."

Giselle made a calculated guess. "You're thwarting her new goal, aren't you? And that's why she's disappeared."

He looked as if he'd been Tasered. "My God." His voice dropped to a whisper as he stared at a point beyond her left shoulder. "That's it." Slowly his gaze returned to lock with hers. "Thank you."

She shrugged. "Good guess."

"Brilliant guess. You don't even know her, and you've hit upon the most important part of her personality. What are you, a shrink?"

"Accountant."

His eyebrows lifted. "No kidding? You don't look like—"

"Spare me. Accountants aren't all skinny nerds. And they're definitely not all male." Hacking her way through this guy's jungle of stereotypes would take some effort, but he had resources and it was clear his sister could pose a real threat to the future serenity of the Landry pack.

She was also in desperate need of more information about said sister. "Out of curiosity, what are you denying Cynthia that she wants so desperately?"

He sighed and leaned back in his chair. "Okay, some

background. Here's this kid—smart as a whip, straight-A student, and my dad doted on her." He picked up a pen and laced it through his fingers. "She got into Yale, and he busted his buttons over that. Told all his cronies she'd be president someday." He worked the pen through his fingers as he talked.

Giselle wondered if he even knew he was toying with the pen, but he had amazing dexterity as he wove it endlessly through his fingers. She found that sexy as all get-out. She brought her attention back to the subject, his brainiac sister.

"Turns out she doesn't want to be president. Or a molecular biologist, or a corporate lawyer, or an astrophysicist." He tossed the pen on the desk. "She wants to be a showgirl. She wants me to give her a job dancing at the Silver Crescent."

"And she's no good." Giselle pictured a bookworm who secretly longed to be onstage wearing glamorous outfits but had no natural rhythm or coordination. If that were the case, then Cynthia wouldn't be Bryce's type after all. He liked a female with brains, but he wanted her to be poised and confident, too. Maybe Cynthia wasn't the threat Giselle had feared. Perhaps Bryce only felt sorry for her.

"Oh, no, she's a great dancer. But I thought it was a hobby, something she did for exercise."

"So what's the problem? Is she too fat? Too unattractive? Too short?"

"She's beautiful." Luke grabbed his phone off the desk and clicked it a couple of times with his thumb before turning it to face Giselle. "That's her."

Giselle looked at the smiling blonde on the screen

and saw her worst nightmare. All that and outstanding grades from an Ivy League school? Bryce probably thought he'd hit the jackpot.

"You haven't mentioned your mother. Is she alive?"

"She lives in France." He said it as if France might as well be Mars.

So Luke had no support or guidance from that quarter. He was fighting this battle alone, and that touched her. She'd just seen how Vaughn had been emotionally rocked by the unexpected loss of his dad, but at least he had backing from his mother and his mate.

Luke didn't have that, and yet his sense of responsibility toward his immediate family seemed as strong as any Were's would be. When Cynthia had chosen to disappear, Luke's protective instincts had been thwarted. Giselle understood his visceral response to the situation. It was werewolf-like in its intensity.

Giselle contemplated the situation. Cynthia wanted to be a showgirl, and from the looks of her, she could handle that job just fine. Her older brother, however, couldn't. By objecting to her plan, he'd sent her into rebellion mode. Cynthia and Bryce could easily have bonded over the subject of dealing with unbending family expectations.

Giselle couldn't decide where to start to untangle this mess. "It's obvious that you don't want your Ivy League–educated sister to become a Vegas showgirl." He had no right to meddle in her life to that extent, but Giselle decided not to mention that. She didn't think Luke would take it well when he was so upset.

"Damn straight. One of the last things my dad said to me was, *Watch out for my little girl.* If I put her in the chorus line at the Silver Crescent, he'd be spinning in his grave."

Dear God. A deathbed promise, no less, one that Luke was taking to heart. It made him even more appealing to her. She was certainly vulnerable to pressure from her folks.

Luke was convinced he was doing the right thing. She had a fair amount of sympathy for his position, despite his somewhat patriarchal mindset. The poor man had no idea that letting his sister try the showgirl option would have been the safer bet than forcing her into this rebellion. Because he'd denied his little sister, she'd hooked up with a werewolf.

Chapter 3

Luke couldn't deny that Giselle impressed him with how quickly she'd hit on the main issue with Cynthia. Although he had plenty of eyeballs to keep track of Cynthia's whereabouts, they were all guys. They thought like guys.

Now he realized he could use a woman's perspective. And as he'd said earlier, he and Giselle wanted the same thing. Or almost the same thing. They both wanted to separate Cynthia from Landry and get his ass back to 'Frisco.

After that, Luke still had to derail Cynthia on this showgirl thing. Because Giselle had figured out the problem right away, she might have some ideas for changing Cynthia's mind. Giselle had pegged her as a goal-oriented person. All he had to do was subtly direct Cynthia toward a more suitable goal.

His cell phone pinged, signaling a text. He picked it up, checked the screen, and glanced over at Giselle. "We might have some news."

"That would be great."

He read quickly. "According to my guys, Cynthia's Corvette and Landry's rented SUV are parked side by side in a public lot near the Strip. Either they've rented a different vehicle or they're on foot. My guys are checking the rental agencies."

"The rental agencies will give them that kind of information? I thought that was against the law."

He looked up from his phone. She really was a straight arrow. He'd have to keep that in mind. "Technically, that's true."

"But they'll bend the rules for Luke Dalton?"

He shrugged. "Depends on who's working the desk. My dad knew a lot of people in this town, and he made sure they understood that I'd be stepping into his shoes someday. I didn't expect to have to take over this soon, but they're treating me the way they would have treated him, and I appreciate that."

"How old was your dad when he died?" Her tone was gentler than it had been a few minutes ago when she'd chewed him out for his views on men, women, and dancing the tango.

"Fifty-six." His chest tightened. His dad had loved contemplating the grandchildren he'd have someday. Luke had figured he had plenty of time to give him some.

"Not very old."

"Nope. It was his heart. I lay a lot of the responsibility for his condition at Harrison Cartwright's feet."

"He also died young."

"Yeah, but he's the one who created the problem. If he'd turned the deed over right away instead of making my father get lawyers involved, they might both be alive today."

"Have you asked her why she wants to be a show-girl?"

"No." But as he looked into Giselle's green eyes, he realized that would have been a good move. Yeah, he really could use the female perspective as he worked through this problem. "I just assumed it's because our mother was a dancer and Cynthia always thought that was cool. So what? It's still a terrible idea."

"Your mom was a dancer?"

He nodded. "My father saw her performing at the Sahara thirty-two years ago, and that was it for him. He never looked at another woman. She never looked at another man, either. They were crazy about each other."

Giselle's expression softened. "Is it any wonder your sister wants to be a showgirl after hearing a romantic story like that? If she wants a guy like your dad, she's not going to find him working in a microbiology lab."

"You think that's her motivation? To find the man of her dreams?" Luke hadn't thought of that. Cynthia probably wouldn't want to hook up with a nerdy scientist or lawyer. She'd want a charismatic gambler like her dad had been. Unfortunately, Bryce Landry fit that profile.

"I have no idea if she's hoping to re-create what your parents had. As smart as she is, that's probably only a small part of her thinking. But you would know for sure if you asked her."

"Which brings us back to the *so what* part of this discussion. No matter what her motivation is, being a showgirl is still a lousy idea. She could attract a psycho stalker just as easily as Prince Charming. Easier, actually."

"But she wants to work in your casino, which means she's putting herself under the protection of you and your staff. That's extremely smart, don't you think?"

"I've thought of that, and I swear it makes me break out in a cold sweat. What if she's counting on the Silver

Crescent being a safe environment and then one night it's not?"

"You say that because you're paranoid."

"Damn right I'm paranoid. Vegas has its share of strange people. If you had a sister, would you want her putting herself on display for any weirdo who happened to be in the audience?"

She gave him a smug little smile. "I'd want her to do whatever made her happy."

"Oh, bull. You're here to drag your brother back home, whether he likes it or not. Why is that? Maybe he's perfectly happy where he is. I wouldn't doubt it, now that he's met my sister. In fact, I'd bet he is happy, or he'd be coming home of his own accord."

She lowered her lashes and her cheeks grew rosy.

Damn, she was sexy. He really would have to watch himself around this woman. He'd already caught himself admiring the cut of her emerald-green T-shirt, which gave him a tantalizing glimpse of cleavage. Her designer jeans fit her well, too, and he was pretty sure she was wearing leather boots. She'd come in carrying a fringed leather jacket, which she'd laid across her lap when she'd taken a seat.

She had the kind of style he admired, and that was dangerous. More than that, she challenged him to question his assumptions. Irritating as that could be at times, he kind of liked it, too. Cynthia used to debate issues with him when she'd come home on vacation, and he'd enjoyed the mental exercise.

But now wasn't the time to become interested in a woman, especially not this one. He couldn't afford to be distracted. Too much was at stake, and besides, she had insights he needed. He didn't want to miss those insights because he was caught up in her as a person.

She met his gaze with a reluctant sigh. "You have a point. My brother's not living up to the role I envisioned for him, either. But I promise you that if I have a chance to ask him why he's acting this way, I will ask. I don't know how we can judge someone's behavior without finding out their reasons."

"Bravo, Dr. Phil."

"Bite me, Dalton."

He laughed. "Don't tempt me." But she already had, and she wasn't even trying. If she put effort into the task, he would be in big trouble.

His cell phone pinged again, and he picked it up to read the text. "Apparently, they didn't rent anything. Owen's reminding me that Cynthia has friends in town who might loan her a car."

"Who's Owen?"

"Owen Banks, master of intrigue, head of security. He lives for this kind of stuff, and I hardly ever give him enough of it." Another ping. "Well, there you go. He's done a rundown of Cynthia's friends, and all of them are still in possession of their cars."

"He knows all her friends? Are you telling me she's been under this kind of surveillance all her life?"

He glanced up, surprised at her horrified tone of voice. "Yeah, probably. My dad was very protective. Why?"

"Because . . . if I were Cynthia—and thank God I'm not—I would deliberately disappear, too! The poor girl's not allowed to breathe without being monitored by her father's henchmen, who are now your henchmen."

He bristled. "I think *henchmen* is a little harsh, don't you? These are security people. My family has a lot of money. That draws criminal attention, especially in Vegas. We've always been at risk for things like kidnapping and ransom. Understandably, we want to avoid that."

"I hope you're not lumping my brother into that *criminal element* category." Her green eyes snapped with indignation. "She went with him of her own free will. And he would never—"

"Easy, Giselle. Easy." The fire in her eyes was compelling. "I never meant to imply that your brother was a criminal. I had my people do a preliminary background check on him a couple of weeks ago, and I'm not worried that he's after Dalton money."

"I see." She narrowed her eyes, obviously not happy that he'd had her brother investigated.

"You don't have to look like that. I didn't pry into your family secrets. In fact, I didn't pry into your family at all. I just made sure he didn't have a police record or mountains of debt. It's the sort of thing my father would have checked. You can't blame me for that."

"I suppose not."

"So he's not a fortune hunter, but he's still a bad influence on her."

Her indignation returned. "You don't know that! I refuse to let you make my brother out as the villain in this scenario. He just happened to be around when she felt like giving you grief."

"So, he could have talked her out of doing it!" Luke felt his control slipping.

"Why? I wouldn't have! She's twenty-two, and you're trying to engineer her future."

"I am not." He felt a headache coming on. "I'm trying to keep her from making some really bad choices."

"What's the difference?"

"There's a *huge* difference! She has hundreds of choices left, all kinds of options open to her, and money to finance them."

"Except the one choice she wants."

"It's a horrible choice!" A light on his phone blinked. "Hang on a minute. She's sent me a text."

"Cynthia?"

"No, Madonna." He heard the sarcasm in his voice and sighed. "Sorry. Yes, Cynthia. When she's happy with me, she calls, but when she's mad at me, she texts."

"Probably because she knows you don't like it."

"Could be." He read the message through twice and swore under his breath.

"What does she say?"

"God knows. Makes no sense to me. Here, I'll read it to you: *She who pulls the sword from the stone claims a power all her own.* Then she has a four-digit number." He glanced up at Giselle. "What the hell is that all about?"

"She's sending you a riddle."

"A *riddle*?"

"Sounds like it to me. She's inviting you to solve it."

"Why?" He was completely at sea.

Giselle took a deep breath. "Well, I'd only be guessing."

"Please, guess away. Cynthia's never sent me a riddle in her entire life."

"First of all, I think it's encouraging that she's communicating with you."

"You call this communicating? I call it trying to screw with me."

Giselle smiled. "Maybe that, too. But at least she reached out, and . . . I know something about this riddle business."

"That makes one of us." He had a sudden suspicion. "Why do you know?"

For the first time since she'd come into his office, she looked uncomfortable. "Bryce and I used to play riddle games all the time when we were kids."

"Aha!" He pointed a finger at her. "And you were so sure he wasn't influencing her. Now suddenly she's sending me riddles, which she's never done before. Where do you suppose she got that clever idea, hmm?"

"From him. It's exactly the sort of thing Bryce would do. But maybe he's convinced her that she needs to keep in touch with you and this is a way that appeals to her. You said she's smart."

"Oh, she's smart, all right."

"So is my brother. But what if he's trying to help straighten this out between you two? Wouldn't that be a good thing?"

"Not if I have no effing clue what she's talking about! This isn't communicating. It's taunting."

"But if we solve the riddle, we might be getting somewhere."

"All right." He crossed his arms and leaned back in his chair. "Go ahead, Ms. Riddle Expert. Solve it." He waited for her to admit she had no clue, either.

Instead she brightened. "She's talking about Excalibur. That's what the sword-in-the-stone reference is about. What if the number is a room there? What if the two of them have checked in and that's where they are?"

Luke shoved out of his chair, refusing to admit how surprised he was by the ease with which she had cracked his sister's code. "I don't like the sound of that. I don't like it at all. I know what goes on in hotel rooms."

"Luke, she's twenty-two. She's been away at college. Surely you don't think she's still a—"

"I don't want to discuss it. But I am going over to Excalibur to see who's in that room. Are you coming with me?"

"Sure." She stood and put on her leather jacket. "We'll go on my motorcycle."

That brought him up short. "Your what?"

"I rented a Harley to get around while I'm here. It's what I'm used to back home, and it's parked in Howlin' at the Moon's patrolled lot. Or did you want to walk?"

"No. Takes too long. The valet can bring my car around."

"We'll get there faster on my Harley. The rental company insisted on giving me an extra helmet. They seemed to think I'd have a passenger sooner or later while I was here."

Luke hesitated. He wasn't in the habit of surrendering control of his transportation.

"Cynthia won't expect you to be riding around on the back of a motorcycle."

He had to admit he liked the way she thought. "Okay, yeah. That's a good point. She's not the only one who can play games." He grabbed a denim jacket from the coat tree by the door and followed Giselle out of the office.

As they walked together through the noisy bar toward the front door, Luke stopped to fill Chuck in on the proceedings. Chuck agreed to monitor the bar situation while Luke was gone.

He turned back to Giselle and discovered that she

was inspecting the decor with obvious interest. "Ever been in here?"

"Years ago with some friends. You must be happy about owning such a Vegas landmark."

"I expected to be happier about it." He surprised himself by saying that.

"You mean because of this business with your sister?"

"That doesn't help, but after all the drama of the poker game, the actual ownership of the bar turns out to be anticlimactic."

"Maybe it hasn't sunk in, yet."

"Maybe that's it." He started toward the double front doors with their oval insets of etched glass. Giselle walked beside him, and he couldn't help noticing that they moved with a similar rhythm. She was tall, about five-eight without the two-inch heels on her boots. But he was taller by about six inches.

He'd always liked that ratio. Any woman who was shorter than five-eight seemed small to him, probably because his mother and Cynthia were also around five-eight. In any case, he liked having some height advantage when he dated someone.

Not that he was dating Giselle or ever would. He'd help her corral her brother, and that would be the end of that. She'd called him a throwback, and that wasn't so far off. He still believed in protecting those who were smaller and weaker than he was. The meant all children and most women. It definitely included Cynthia. He was still debating whether it included Giselle, especially after he saw the motorcycle. Any woman who blew into town and rented a black Harley might not need his protection.

As he strapped on the helmet and goggles she handed him, he admired the practiced way she tucked her hair under her helmet, adjusted her goggles, and climbed on the bike. Okay, he admired her ass, too. Was that a crime? Not in his world.

"What about you, though?" he asked as he swung up behind her. "Won't your brother suspect you're on a motorcycle, if that's what you always drive?"

"Bryce doesn't know I'm here." She started the engine.

"Ah." He'd assumed she would have warned him that she was on the way. Knowing she didn't telegraph her punches was valuable information and increased his respect for her. "Planning to sneak up on him, are you?"

"I guess you could say that. Ready?"

"Anytime you are." Now was not the time to admit he'd never been on a motorcycle before. All his buddies had either owned one or had at least ridden on one, and somehow he'd missed the experience. Once the teenage years had passed, he'd lost the urge to try it. But it couldn't be that hard.

"You might want to hang on."

"I'll be fine."

"If you say so." She zoomed into traffic and he damned near fell off.

Grabbing her around the waist, he straightened. Holy hell, but the woman could drive this sucker. He wouldn't say she took unnecessary chances, but she did some impressive maneuvering through traffic.

It was an exhilarating ride, but if he hadn't been holding on to her, he might have been left somewhere in the middle of the road. To be fair, she'd warned him, and he'd been too macho to listen. He might not want to make that mistake again.

Chapter 4

After parking the bike, Giselle finger combed her hair as she walked with Luke through Excalibur's lobby toward the elevators. Her Were senses were on overload. She'd forgotten that regular casinos were extremely loud and exceedingly smelly. Humans loved their perfume and shaving lotion, and for some reason they loved it more in Vegas than anywhere else. She'd forgotten that.

The only time she'd visited, she and her friends had stayed at the Silver Crescent, so they'd been surrounded by other Weres, who used only light scents if they used any at all. The slot machine noise had been muted there, too. Now that she stood in front of the elevators at Excalibur, she remembered touring the Strip with her buddies. The noise and heavy perfume had driven them out of each casino after only a few minutes.

Now she was about to step into a crowded elevator, something she avoided even in San Francisco, although the humans didn't seem as fragrant there. Maybe the cool breezes blew it all away. Not so in Vegas. Taking a deep breath, she held it as she got on the elevator with Luke. Then she prayed for a fast elevator that didn't stop at every floor. Her prayers went unanswered.

Eventually she had to breathe or pass out, and when she sucked in a lungful of whatever all the humans had splashed on themselves or sprayed in their hair, she grew dizzy. She must have staggered, because a strong arm came around her shoulders and supported her against an equally strong body. Taking shallow breaths, she gazed at her feet and leaned against Luke.

That sensation almost made up for the smelly elevator. She'd bet good money that he had a top-notch workout room at the Silver Crescent and he paid regular visits to it. Because she hung out with werewolves, she was used to well-built males. Weres seldom allowed themselves to get soft.

But she couldn't help being a little fascinated by the muscle definition on this particular human. She didn't often have a chance to check out that kind of thing. Maybe she could consider it research.

Weres liked to imagine that they were physically superior to humans, and most times that was true. But Luke Dalton rivaled the physique of the male Weres she'd known. Not only that, he smelled good. In this swampland of artificial smells, Luke gave off a clean, refreshing scent with a subtle underlying note of male musk.

She blinked. Unless her nose was mistaken, and it never was, Luke was more than a little sexually aroused. She'd detected his interest from the moment they met, but it was far more pronounced now. How interesting. She should ignore that fact, because she had similar chemistry going on, although his human sense of smell wouldn't be able to detect it, especially with the olfactory disaster going on in this elevator.

When they finally reached their floor, Luke guided her out. Her legs wobbled, but he supported her by keeping his arm firmly around her shoulders. "You okay? You're almost the color of your shirt."

How romantic. But then, she didn't want romantic. She wanted someone to help her with the business at hand, which was locating her brother and his sister. "Sorry. I get a little overwhelmed in crowded spaces."

"That's okay. Take your time. If they're here, they won't get by us. Well, unless they take the fire stairs, and if they're willing to hike down that many floors, then I say let 'em."

She nodded as she drew in relatively fresh air, at least compared to the elevator. The hallway wasn't so bad. The carpet was new and stank to high heaven, but she could deal with a single smell better than fifteen competing ones.

"I admit I'm not a fan of crowded elevators, myself." He rubbed her upper arm with gentle strokes. "We probably should have skipped that one and taken the next. We don't even know if they're here."

His touch, combined with his rich baritone, temporarily mesmerized her. In her vulnerable state, she had the strongest urge to turn in his arms and snuggle against his broad chest. She could verify for certain now his first instinct was to protect, a trait he shared with werewolves. She shouldn't be looking for reasons to like him, but she couldn't seem to help herself.

Obviously his protective instinct could get out of hand and lead to controlling behavior. That's when she remembered why they were standing in this hallway. Luke wanted to keep his little sister from getting involved with her big brother.

Exercising great willpower, she extracted herself from the support of his steady arm. "Thanks. I'm better now."

"When we go back down, we'll wait until there's an empty elevator, or one with only a couple of people in it."

"I'd appreciate that." She allowed herself to look into those sexy blue eyes and smile at him. After all, that was the polite thing to do after he'd kept her from fainting in public.

"No worries. Of course, we may have your brother and my sister with us, but that won't be the same as an elevator crammed with strangers."

"You think they'll just agree to leave with us?"

He shrugged. "Maybe not, but I can dream, can't I? And after we all ride down in the elevator together, we'll go somewhere quiet for a drink and talk everything out. Cynthia will agree she should finish school, and Landry will agree to do . . . whatever it is you want him to do."

"He's eventually supposed to take over as the CEO of my family's business." It was a close enough approximation of the truth.

"I'd think they'd rather have you do it." He regarded her with open admiration. "You're smart and obviously capable."

"Thank you." She was delighted to hear that he didn't think all CEOs should be male. Maybe his attitudes weren't quite as retro as she'd assumed. "It's been discussed, but I don't want to. I'm actually happier as the CFO. I like keeping track of the money."

"Excuse me for saying so, but your brother doesn't seem to want to do it, either."

"I know it looks that way, but he'll get over this. It was

a bunch of things at once, and he doesn't like to be rail-roaded." She gazed at him. "Much like Cynthia."

"And that's why they're not good for each other. Left to her own devices, Cynthia won't leave Vegas. She's bonded to the place. But I'm afraid they'll whip each other into a frenzy of resentment and book a flight to New York so she can get a job on Broadway."

"That wouldn't be the end of the world, Luke."

He just looked at her.

She didn't need much imagination to read his mind. If Cynthia ended up on the other side of the country, in a big city where he had no "people" to keep an eye on her, he'd worry himself to death. He had to get over that kind of thinking, but he'd been in charge of the family for only a few months. He had a lot to learn.

In sympathy with his angst, Giselle tossed him a life-line. "I might be more worried about her jetting off to New York if she hadn't texted you a riddle. I doubt she's going anywhere at the moment."

He sighed. "Ah, yes. The riddle. I guess we might as well go find out if you solved it or not."

"Might as well." After they figured out which way the rooms were numbered, they turned to the right and started off down the hall. They didn't speak, as if in silent agreement not to give themselves away as they ap-proached the door.

Giselle didn't know Cynthia at all, but she had a fair idea of what motivated her. She wanted to guide her own destiny instead of being controlled by the expecta-tions of others. That was exactly what Bryce wanted, too.

Giselle hoped they both had the good sense not to text what room they were in and then proceed to get it on while they waited for Luke to solve the riddle. An embarrassing scene wasn't going to help. Giselle knew that for sure, even though she didn't know yet what would help, or whose side Bryce was on.

Giselle slowed down as they approached the room. Luke pointed to the security latch propping the door slightly ajar. If Cynthia and Bryce had rented the room, they'd deliberately left it open.

When Luke held up his hand like an infantry patrol leader signaling a halt, Giselle had the urge to giggle. She never giggled. She wasn't the giggling type. But this was turning into a melodramatic cloak-and-dagger affair that she suddenly found hysterical.

She supposed all the drama was appropriate. They were in Vegas. In an arena somewhere below, knights jousted on horseback. Down the road at Treasure Island, two ships fired broadsides at each other, and across the street a gondola was gliding down a canal that looked astoundingly like one in Venice.

Luke put his ear to the crack in the door, and Giselle stood quietly listening. She heard nothing.

If her nose hadn't recently been assaulted by all the human-induced fumes in the elevator, she might have been able to tell whether a Were was on the other side of the door. But between her nose overload and whatever glue was off-gassing from the new carpet, she was fairly useless for nose patrol.

Stepping back from the door, Luke let out a breath. "I don't think we have to worry about being quiet. Nobody's in there."

"There's one way to be sure."

He glanced at her. "Maybe I should go in first, just in case."

"Just in case what? That they're lying there naked and asleep? Or worse yet, naked and quietly smiling at us?"

Luke's expression became thunderous with disapproval. "I don't care if they're smiling, but they damned well better not be naked."

"If Cynthia knew for certain that she'd get that reaction from you, she'd definitely be naked. You need to lighten up, Dalton."

He rolled his eyes before stepping toward the door and knocking. "Cynthia? You in there?"

Silence.

"Okay, I'm going in."

"I'll cover you."

He turned back to her with a grin.

"Just kidding." She returned his smile. "I've always wanted to say that, but I'm not armed."

"Didn't think so." Turning back to the door, he pushed it open, stepped inside, and was immediately soaked with water. "What the hell?"

Giselle clapped her hand over her mouth. It wouldn't do to laugh, especially when that stunt had Bryce written all over it. She remembered the first time he'd seen it done in a movie when he was twelve.

He'd spent months perfecting the technique of balancing a bucket of water over a doorway, tying a string to the knob, and carefully exiting the room. The first person through the door would get doused. He'd quit doing it when their folks threatened to permanently ground him, but obviously he hadn't forgotten how.

"Cynthia! That wasn't funny!" Bellowing and dripping, Luke stomped the rest of the way into the room. "You'd better *not* be here, damn it!"

Stepping over the damp carpet, Giselle glanced down

at the hotel ice bucket upended on the floor. She knew Cynthia and Bryce had left. She'd watched her brother create this booby trap countless times, and the last part involved closing the door very carefully.

"Good thing there are towels in this room. At least I can dry off. I suppose I should feel lucky it was only water. Could've been tomato juice or maple syrup." He continued to rave on as he walked into the bathroom and flipped on the light.

"Better not be hiding in the shower!" he called out. That was followed by the squeak of shower rings being pulled along the metal rod. Obviously he'd had to check.

Moving into the room, Giselle scanned it for any other booby traps. "Someone left an envelope on the bed."

Luke came out of the bathroom, drying his wet hair with a towel. "Oh?" He draped the towel around his neck in a typical male gesture. "Maybe they left us a note."

"Must be a really big note."

His eyes widened as he spotted the large manila envelope lying precisely in the middle of the bed. "My name's on it, and that's her handwriting." He finger-combed his wet hair. "After the bucket of water, I'm not sure whether to pick it up or not."

"It looks harmless enough." Giselle was dying of curiosity.

"It does. Oh, what the hell." He grabbed the envelope, and when nothing happened, he blew out a breath. "Sometimes an envelope is just an envelope." Prying open the flap, he pulled out a glossy studio shot of a little blond girl in a pink tutu. "Oh, shit." There was a definite catch in his voice. "I should've guessed it would be something like this."

"How old was she in that picture?"

"Three, maybe four." He cleared his throat. "Her age is probably written on the back." He flipped the picture over. Someone, probably his mother, had written Cynthia's name in a flowing script and underneath had added her age, three and a half. Below that, in a much bolder hand, someone had scribbled, *You're all wet, Luke Dalton.*

Giselle pressed her lips together to keep from smiling.

Apparently Luke could tell she thought it was funny. "Oh, yeah, that's hysterical."

Giselle met his gaze. "It's clever, pointed, and harmless. And it communicates that she still wants to engage you in a discussion of sorts. If she was determined to defy you and risk causing a permanent rift, she could have gone up to Reno and landed a job up there, or taken off for New York."

"I guess." He tucked the picture carefully back in the envelope as if to make sure he didn't damage it. "I wonder if she swiped any more of these."

"Where would she swipe them from?"

"The family photo gallery in the penthouse of the Silver Crescent. She has a key."

"Your family moved to the Crescent?"

"Yep. My father, mother, and Cynthia all lived in the penthouse. They wanted me to live there, too, but a twenty-three-year-old usually doesn't care to stay in a bedroom down the hall from his folks. We compromised, and I took an apartment one floor down. After Cynthia turned eighteen, she insisted on having the same arrangement I had."

"Is the penthouse vacant now?"

"No, I live in it. My mom insisted that she wanted me

to since she's now in France. It's a beautiful place, and it shouldn't stand empty. Anyway, my father dedicated an entire room to professionally framed pictures of all of us at various ages." He held up the envelope. "She would have had to cut the backing off to get this out. I hope she didn't do that to the whole batch."

"How many had to do with dance?"

"A lot. She took lessons until she left for college."

Giselle wondered if he realized that this was more than a hobby for his sister. She'd been dancing since she was three, and now that her father wasn't around to disapprove, she had only to get past her big brother to have the career she'd dreamed of her whole life.

"That's going to bother me, wondering about those pictures." He looked over at Giselle. "Would you mind if we went over to the penthouse to check?"

"Fine with me. Unless we get another riddle, we don't know what to do next, anyway."

"I know what to do next—eat. I'm starving. How about you?"

Now that he'd mentioned food, she realized she was hungry. "Sure, that sounds good."

"Excellent. I'll call Mr. Thatcher and have him bring us something from the main kitchen." He pulled out his phone again.

"Who's Mr. Thatcher?"

"Our very English butler. He's been with the family for years. What would you like for dinner?"

"I'm not picky. Anything."

"But you're from 'Frisco. Lots of vegetarians up there. Are you a vegetarian?"

"No."

"Vegan?"

"Nope. I'm a carnivore. I promise you."

"You're doing it again with the little smile. Did I say something funny?"

"Not everyone from San Francisco is a vegetarian, you know."

"Guess not. You're okay with steak, then?"

"Absolutely."

"Do you like it rare, medium, or well?"

"Definitely rare."

"Good. Me, too." He placed his call to Mr. Thatcher and ordered two steak dinners with all the trimmings, a bottle of red wine, and two pieces of chocolate cake for dessert.

It was a meal fit for a Were, and Giselle could hardly wait. Plus she wanted to see how the Silver Crescent had changed since she was last there. She and her friends must have been guests right before the Crescent became involved in the Cartwright/Dalton legal battle.

"Okay." He disconnected the call. "We're out of here. Wait. Hold on a minute. Let me leave a tip for the maid." He dug in his back pocket for his wallet.

"But the carpet will dry and the room was barely used at all."

"Doesn't matter. They count on these tips, and if this room is easy to clean, the next one might be a total disaster. It's a tough job. They earn their money."

"You're right. They do." She liked the fact that he thought about the maids and thanked them. She was starting to like too many things about Luke Dalton, and that wasn't a good idea. No matter how much he appealed to her, he was still very much a human.

Chapter 5

"I'm grateful for the private elevator," Giselle said as they rode up to the Silver Crescent's penthouse. "And the wood paneling is gorgeous."

"You can thank Harrison Cartwright. I don't know if he had a private elevator when the building first went up, but he installed all new elevators throughout the building before he finally turned it over to my dad. If he went to that kind of expense, he must have thought he'd get to keep it, after all."

"Are all the elevators this nice?"

"Not quite. This one has genuine hardwood. The others are laminate."

"I know you don't think much of Harrison Cartwright, but he had good taste."

"Can't argue with that. Wait'll you see the view from the penthouse." The thought came to Luke that he'd never brought a woman up here.

Well, that would be because he hadn't become involved with anyone since his dad died. Duh. Too damned busy. But he certainly *intended* to bring women up here at some point in time, when his life settled down and his sister stopped giving him fits.

With his mother's blessing, he'd renovated the master bedroom and bath so it no longer resembled his parents' bedroom. He was happy with the way it looked, although he wouldn't be showing it off to Giselle.

But how ironic that the first woman he invited here was one he had no intention of sleeping with. The only people who had seen the final result had been Cynthia and Owen. His sister had liked it okay but thought it needed more color. She'd compared the suite to a hospital room, which wasn't the effect he was going for.

Then Owen had seen it the day he'd supervised an update of the penthouse security system. Owen, a guy of few words, had said it was "nice." That didn't tell Luke a damn thing. Owen wasn't exactly Martha Stewart, but Luke would have liked a little more commentary.

When it came to color, he was no expert, so he'd stuck with white. Even that had been trickier than he'd thought. Who knew there were so many shades of it? But he'd found one he liked called "linen," and then he'd matched everything to that.

The suite resembled his image of heaven, with the pillows and quilts reminding him of fluffy clouds. He'd found some pictures of Greek temples, also white, and put those on the walls, which were also white. It all blended in beautifully. But it might be too monochromatic. He just wasn't sure.

They stepped off the elevator, and he used a card key to open the black enamel, silver-edged double doors into the foyer. Then he moved back and let Giselle go in ahead of him. He did like the way she moved.

He wondered if she'd taken dancing lessons as a kid

and maybe dreamed of making it a career. That would explain her defense of Cynthia. Maybe he'd ask her some-time.

They walked through the elegant foyer with its chrome tables and quarter-moon mirrors on either side. Fresh flower arrangements provided by his staff per-fumed the air.

He left the envelope containing Cynthia's picture in the foyer. He'd deal with it later. Right now he was inter-ested in Giselle's reaction to the penthouse. This was his home now, and he realized that he wanted her to like it. Why he even cared about her opinion was a question for another time.

He'd kept the living room decorated exactly as it had been when his parents had lived there. Muted lighting revealed soft leather sectionals in butter yellow. Pillows in every color of the rainbow were scattered around. Maybe that's what Cynthia had meant. He needed some of those little square pillows in his bedroom.

The open floor plan included a linen-draped dining table on the left side of the room. Not long ago he'd taken out the two leaves to create a cozier setup. He didn't intend to hold the kind of large-scale dinner par-ties his parents had enjoyed.

The kitchen was through an arched opening to the right, and the bedrooms were also to the right down a long hallway. Most first-time visitors missed those details.

Usually they were captured by the floor-to-ceiling windows that provided an unobstructed view of the Strip. His father had said the panoramic vista was worth all the effort of winning that lawsuit. Luke didn't agree, considering it had shortened his dad's life, but the view was spectacular, especially now that the sun had set.

The windows lined the west and north walls. Unless he was there to deal with the shades, a maid came in and raised them on the west windows just before sunset, so that even as you walked into the room you could watch the sun go down. He and Giselle had missed that show, but it didn't matter. Looking north was a nonstop extravaganza.

In the foreground jutted the skyscrapers of Manhattan, with the Statue of Liberty and the Coney Island Cyclone roller coaster looping through the buildings. Beyond that, the distinctive Eiffel Tower spire glittered against the night sky. Across the way, streams of water jetted upward from the dancing fountain fronting the Bellagio.

Giselle walked toward the window. "That's quite a view, Dalton."

He came up to stand beside her. "My father never got tired of looking at it. Here, let me take your coat." He helped her out of it before removing his still slightly damp denim jacket. He laid them both over the back of the sectional.

"I'd forgotten how over-the-top Vegas is."

"That's what fantasy is all about—going over-the-top." He studied her profile. She had a high forehead and an aristocratic nose, both of which made her look intelligent and a little snooty.

Her mouth, though, was extremely lush. He could imagine that mouth sucking on a chocolate-covered strawberry. He stared at the lights of the Strip and reminded himself to focus on the mission—getting Bryce Landry out of town and Cynthia straightened out.

"It's mesmerizing, isn't it?" Giselle said.

"It can be. My dad used to love standing here and reveling in the fact that Harrison Cartwright was now denied this view."

"But Harrison built Illusions, which provides a mirror image from the north end of the Strip."

Something clicked when she said that. He looked over at her. "You've been on the top floor of Illusions, then?"

Her startled glance told him she hadn't meant to say that. "Uh, yeah. Briefly."

"It's a very exclusive casino and hotel. Booked up months ahead, I hear. Getting into Illusions is tougher than getting into Fort Knox."

"I've heard that." She returned her attention to the view.

"I didn't think to ask where you were staying while you're here. I'm guessing you're at Illusions."

She kept her gaze on the sparkling lights and the constant flow of traffic forty floors below them, but her cheeks had become rosy. "The Cartwrights are family friends."

He'd bet she hadn't intended for him to know that. Earlier he'd asked how she'd learned about his problems with Cynthia. Now he knew. "You and Vaughn Cartwright had a little conversation before you came over to the Moon to see me, didn't you?"

She turned to him, putting her back to the view. She looked beautiful standing there surrounded by the lights, and he wondered if he was dealing with a modern version of Mata Hari. If so, she wasn't a very good spy. They'd been together a couple of hours and she'd already revealed her connection to the enemy.

"Don't leap to the wrong conclusions, Luke."

"Like what? I—" His phone pinged. "Could be from Cynthia." Taking his phone from his pocket, he clicked on the message. He stared at the screen for a moment. "Busted."

"What do you mean?"

He turned the phone so she could see the picture embedded in the message. "They must have hidden a motion-activated camera in that room."

Giselle gazed at the image and sighed. "And now my brother knows I'm here and that I came unannounced. I'd better text him." Taking out her phone, she typed a brief message. "Maybe this is just as well. I told him I really wanted to talk with him and I hoped we could get together soon. If he's up for that, it might open the door for you and Cynthia to have a heart-to-heart, too."

"I'd like that." Except he didn't know what he planned to say yet. The more time he spent with Giselle, the more his perceptions seemed to shift. He was no longer exactly sure where he stood on the subject of Cynthia's future. Before he talked to her, he ought to figure that out.

Giselle tucked her phone away. "So where were we?"

He had to think about that. Surrounded by the gem-like colors of the casino lights, she was a vision. He'd been trying to ignore his attraction from the moment she'd walked into his office. Then he remembered they'd been talking about her connection to Vaughn Cartwright. Okay, that would help cool his libido.

He cleared his throat. "You were telling me about your friendship with the Cartwright family."

"I'm here to bring my brother home. That's my only agenda."

"I believe you." Partly because he wanted to. He plain liked her. She was smart, confident, and didn't pull her punches. Plus she'd come all the way to Vegas in an effort to talk some sense into her brother, and he certainly related to that.

"Whatever feud the Daltons and the Cartwrights have going on has nothing to do with me." She met his gaze. "I connected with Vaughn only because our families are acquainted, and so I e-mailed him to see if he had any idea what was going on with my brother."

"Is Vaughn a friend of his?"

"I don't think they've ever met. But I can tell you that Vaughn's not happy that my brother's hanging out with your sister. As I said, my family knows his family, and Bryce joining forces with a Dalton is seen as consorting with the enemy."

"So why are you here with me? Isn't that the same thing?"

"No. Vaughn understands that I need to do whatever it takes to get my brother back home. If Bryce had hooked up with any woman other than Cynthia, Vaughn would be helping me track them down. But he can't come to the rescue when a Dalton's involved."

Luke sighed. "I'll accept that. And speaking of Cynthia, I need to check the photo gallery and see if she's swiped any other pictures."

"Do you mind if I tag along?"

He'd assumed that she would go. "Why wouldn't you?"

"Because these are your family photos. It's personal."

"That's considerate of you." He was impressed with her respect for his privacy.

"If you're worried that I'm going to report everything to Vaughn when this is all over, I can tell you right now I wouldn't do that. I'm sorry the family lost Howlin' at the Moon. It means a lot to them, but—"

"It also means a lot to me."

"I can see that."

He was still waiting for the sense of jubilation he'd expected to feel. Maybe once this business with Cynthia was over, he'd be ready to celebrate. "Come on. Let's go see what my little sister has done to the family pictures." He gestured toward the hallway that branched off from the living area. "First doorway on your right."

He followed her into the gallery, which had been set up by a professional curator. A wooden bench ran down the center of the room, but that was the only furniture. The walls in the windowless room were covered with framed photographs of various sizes, some color and some black-and-white.

Each had a museum-style label underneath giving the date and occasion. He and Cynthia had their own walls, and the other two contained family groupings, pictures of his parents when they were kids, and pictures of them as a couple. Track lighting highlighted the photos without producing any reflection on the glass. His father had spent a fortune on this gallery.

Luke checked Cynthia's wall and swore softly to himself. He'd never counted how many pictures there'd been of her, but he guessed there had been at least fifty in various sizes. Close to a third of them were now only empty frames. "She took all her recital pictures."

Giselle walked over to Cynthia's wall. "She went through a lot of trouble. Why not take the whole thing, frame and all?"

"Too awkward. Whatever she plans to do with those pictures, she wants to be able to transport them easily. The frames would make that tough."

"Guess so." Giselle wandered around the room studying the display. "Sort of ruins the family photo album concept, doesn't it?"

"The albums still exist. They're in a vault. But the minute my dad saw this windowless room, he came up with the idea of turning it into a family gallery." He couldn't imagine how upset Cynthia must be to have done this. In a way, taking pictures from here was better than pulling them out of the somewhat fragile family albums in the vault. He suddenly realized he'd grossly underestimated her passion for dancing.

"I love this one of you wearing your Mickey Mouse ears."

He glanced over to where Giselle stood surveying all the pictures of him, a smile on that lush mouth. No wonder. He looked dorky in those ears. "Yeah, well, that was my Mickey phase. I wore that hat everywhere, including to church." She'd been right about the personal nature of this room.

"Well, now that I know what she's taken," he said, "we can go back out and enjoy the view, if you want."

"I'm enjoying this one." She pointed to a picture of him in a football uniform. "What position did you play?"

"Quarterback."

"Were you any good?"

He shrugged. "I guess. We took state my senior year."

"Then I'll bet you went to college on a football scholarship."

"You'd win that bet, but I'd rather not dwell on—"

"Just trying to get a bead on you, Dalton. Bachelor's? Master's?"

"MBA."

"I see. Football star and graduate student. Did your father dedicate another room for framed diplomas and trophies and such?"

Luke laughed and shook his head. The lady was certainly persistent. "Yes, but we're not going in there. It's plain embarrassing. Let's head back to the living room and wait for dinner to arrive."

"If you insist." She paused on the way out. "Is that your mom when she was still performing?" She gestured to a studio shot of his mother dressed in bright red sequins and feathers. Her headdress was nearly as tall as she was.

"That was a publicity shot she had taken right before she met my dad. She'd considered going to Hollywood and trying her luck out there."

"But instead she married your father."

"She did, and never regretted it. He was the love of her life."

"Cynthia looks a lot like her."

"I know, and people tell her that. I think it's part of the problem." He sighed. "Enough family history." He gestured toward the doorway. "After you."

With one more glance at his mother's picture, Giselle left the gallery and walked out to the living room. Once there, she turned to him. "What would you have done if the poker game had gone the other way and you'd lost this?" She spread her arms to encompass the elegant living space with its stunning view.

"I don't know." He'd played that scenario over in his head many times in the days leading up to the game. "I'd like to think I would have recovered and forgiven myself for being so reckless. But I don't know if I would have. I'm grateful that it didn't turn out that way."

"But you allowed yourself to take that risk, knowing that it could turn into a defeat for you."

He nodded. "No matter what happened, I wouldn't have to spend my days looking at a Cartwright-owned property and thinking about the feud that probably killed my dad. His doctors told him to stop obsessing over Harrison Cartwright because it was bad for his heart. But he'd been betrayed by his best friend, and he never got over it. Every time I looked at that bar, I was reminded of that. So I set up the poker game."

She gazed at the richly patterned carpet at her feet. Finally she looked up. "That's all Cynthia wants, Luke. To have that kind of control over her destiny."

He met her gaze and couldn't help smiling. "You're good, Giselle. I didn't even see that one coming. Nice try, but the two situations are completely different."

"I don't agree."

"Cynthia's a semester away from graduation. Her brain is fine-tuned right now, in the groove. She'll never be more ready to finish that degree than she is now. If she puts it off for a few years, I'm afraid she'll struggle like crazy to get back up to speed academically."

"Or she might come back more focused than ever and blow away the younger students."

"Dancing is like any other sport. It's great when you're young and athletic, but it's not a career for a lifetime."

"So what? I'm not very familiar with this field, but it seems to me she could teach, or choreograph productions, or—"

"Okay, sure." He gazed out at the kaleidoscope that was Vegas. "But I think she'd be bored to tears living the life my mother had."

Giselle stood there without saying anything for several seconds. Finally she spoke. "Okay, I get it."

He looked at her in surprise. "What do you get, exactly?"

"You see your sister trying to follow in your mom's footsteps without realizing she's nothing like your mom, even though she looks like her. You think she's liable to end up being miserable from the lack of mental stimulation."

"Yes, exactly! So how do I—" The doorbell chimed. "We can talk about it later. Dinner's here." But elation filled him. Giselle finally understood why he was so determined to get Cynthia back on track. Although he'd met her only a couple hours earlier, he no longer felt alone in his quest.

Chapter 6

A portly gentleman with all the bearing of an English butler rolled a double-tiered cart through the living area and over to the linen-covered dining table by the west window. Giselle breathed in the aroma of grilled steak, roasted veggies, and ... werewolf?

For one electric moment, her gaze met that of the formally dressed man in his sixties. No doubt about it—the butler was a werewolf. She was dying to know the story behind this bizarre situation but figured she wouldn't be getting it soon.

"Greetings, Mr. Thatcher!" Luke seemed really happy to see him. "I'd like you to meet Giselle Landry from San Francisco. Giselle, Mr. Thatcher has been serving our family for ... is it almost twenty years now?" He glanced at the butler.

"Almost, sir." He bowed in Giselle's direction. "Pleased to meet you, Ms. Landry."

"Same here, Mr. Thatcher." The butler hadn't reacted to her last name, and yet if he was Were, he would know the Landry pack was one of the most powerful in the

Bay Area. He'd probably spent twenty years learning to keep his expression neutral and his mouth shut. She wondered how he fit into the Cartwright/Dalton history. "Are you originally from London?"

"Hertfordshire, madam."

"You've brought us some heavenly smelling food."

"I daresay you'll enjoy it." He started unloading the contents of the cart onto the table. "Our chef is the best in the state."

"And he's not happy because I order pizza half the time," Luke said.

"He makes you a very good pizza, sir." Mr. Thatcher finished arranging everything on the table and took a lighter out of his pocket. "But he was pleased to get this order tonight." He lit the white tapers sitting in heavy silver candlesticks.

Luke winked at Giselle. "Guess I'll have to make him happy more often. I'd hate to lose the guy because he was sick of making pizza."

"After this meal, sir, you'll give up on pizza for good." With the kind of flourish that he'd probably perfected after years of service, Mr. Thatcher whisked the silver domes away, revealing two carefully arranged plates, each bearing a filet, grilled asparagus, and an artfully spooned serving of mashed root vegetables. A basket of bread, two pieces of chocolate mousse cake, and two glasses of ruby-colored wine completed the meal.

Giselle stifled a moan of pleasure. She hadn't realized how hungry she was. It was all she could do not to yank out a chair and sit down so they could get started.

"Will there be anything else, sir?" Mr. Thatcher stood poised beside the cart, prepared to roll it out the door.

Luke glanced at her. "Giselle? Anything more you need to go with the meal?"

"Not a thing." Except she'd love to know why a Were had served it to them, but she couldn't very well ask *that*. "This is a feast."

"Then I guess we're all set, Mr. Thatcher. Thank you."

"Have a great evening, sir. Just call when you're finished and want me to clear." With another slight bow, he rolled the cart into the foyer and let himself out.

"He's fabulous," Giselle said after he'd left. "So he's been with your family for almost twenty years?"

"Guess so. I've lost track of it, but I'm sure my dad knew. Twenty years ago he was finally doing well enough to start hiring live-in servants. According to my dad, Harrison Cartwright recommended Mr. Thatcher for the job."

"Now, that's fascinating." She had to say something to keep her jaw from dropping in amazement. Had Harrison Cartwright installed a spy in Angus Dalton's household?

That made no sense, because twenty years ago Harrison and Angus had been the best of friends. Yet she could think of no other explanation. Normally werewolf live-in servants preferred to work for Weres. Working for humans didn't give them enough privacy when they wanted to shift and get some wolf-style exercise.

She wondered if Mr. Thatcher had made do with trips to Howlin' at the Moon and its underground forest. Now that would be closed to him, too. "Does he have a first name?"

Luke laughed and moved over to the table. "It's Melvin. But I honestly didn't know that until I started signing his paychecks in January. He's always been Mr. Thatcher. Incredibly proper, but incredibly loyal. I was afraid my mother would ask him to go to France with her, but she didn't, thank God. Ready to eat?"

"You know it." Deciding to think about the werewolf/butler/spy thing later, she sat down and sighed in appreciation. "This really is terrific, Luke. I hope I won't embarrass myself by attacking this food."

"Please do." He picked up his wineglass. "But first let's toast."

"What are we toasting?"

"I haven't figured that out. My family is big into toasting, though, so it's a habit with me." His blue gaze warmed as he smiled at her. "I suppose a toast between the two of us could get complicated."

"It could. Your toast might be something I can't agree with."

"Then . . . here's to success."

She chuckled. "That's ambiguous enough, I guess. To success." She touched her glass to his and drank. The wine was pleasantly dry, the perfect complement to a steak dinner. "Nice."

"Glad it suits you. I just thought of another toast."

"Okay."

"To a cooperative effort as we work through our problems."

"I'll drink to that." She touched her glass to his again and then took another sip. She met his gaze and felt a tug of sexual awareness. Not good. "I keep thinking about that picture of you with the Mickey Mouse ears." She wasn't really, but maybe if she could, it would squash her growing interest in him.

He rolled his eyes. "Please don't."

"If you really hate it that much, you could take it down, couldn't you?"

"No."

"Why not?"

His expression softened. "Because my mom and dad loved that picture."

"Oh." And every time he looked at it, he remembered that. Her heart squeezed.

He cleared his throat. "Hey, let's not let this get cold. Dig in."

"You bet." With a quick smile, she picked up her fork and steak knife. But he'd touched her with that comment about the picture. She'd have to watch herself. She didn't believe in getting involved with any human male, and certainly not one whose name was anathema to Weres.

Luke had just made his first cut into his steak when his phone chimed.

Giselle kept eating, but she had a bad feeling about that chime and the future of her amazing meal.

Laying his knife and fork back on the plate, Luke took his phone out and checked the screen. "Text from Cynthia."

"And?"

"Looks like another damned riddle." He glanced from his phone to his plate.

"We can eat quickly while we figure it out." Giselle knew she wouldn't enjoy the meal as thoroughly because now they'd be focused on Cynthia's next step, but she was determined to eat it. She took a bite of steak, chewed quickly, and swallowed. It was incredible, as she'd expected it would be. "Lay the riddle on me, Dalton. Let's see what we've got."

"I'll read it to you in a minute. First let me look at this other text from Owen."

"I'm going to keep eating, and it's just a suggestion, but I would do the same if I were you."

"Yeah, you're right." He scooped up a forkful of mashed root vegetables. "I'll check his message in a minute. I'm praying he's located her and we can give up this wild-goose chase."

"What's he supposed to do if he finds her? I hope you didn't tell him to hold her prisoner."

"No." He looked up quickly from his plate. "Despite what you think, I realize this should be handled diplomatically. Owen's not supposed to let her know he's around. If he sees her, he reports that to me."

"Good. And then what?"

"I have to hope she'll stay in one place long enough for me to get there and talk with her."

She chewed and swallowed. "Do you know what you're going to say to her?"

"I'm working on it. Do you know what you plan to say to Bryce?" Luke tackled more of his food.

"Pretty much. First I'm going to find out if he truly doesn't want to take over from our dad. If he doesn't, then I have to hope he'll come back anyway. We miss him. That'll be my main message, that we all love him and miss him." She hoped Luke would start with telling Cynthia he loved her. But she wouldn't offer that advice unless he asked.

After swallowing another bite, Luke read Owen's text and groaned. "He's lost their trail. He's beginning to think they might have disguised themselves."

"I wonder if that has anything to do with the fact Bryce knows I'm with you."

"How would that change things?"

"I'm not sure. He hasn't texted me back yet, so I don't know how he's reacting." She took a quick gulp of her wine and went back to cutting into her steak. "At first I was afraid he wouldn't like that I flew down here without telling him."

"That would be my guess."

"But my brother is complicated. If he's tired of his rebellion routine, he might be grateful that I've come for him. That way he can say he came back because I was so pitiful." She popped a piece of steak into her mouth.

Luke smiled at that. "I'd love a demonstration of you looking pitiful. It's hard to imagine."

The steak was so tender that she could chew and swallow it in no time. "Watch this." She gave him her best sad, soulful look, the one where she looked like the big-eyed characters in a Japanese anime cartoon.

"Hey, that's pretty good. You should definitely use that on him. In fact, you should probably teach me. It might work on Cynthia." His grin had a boyish quality to it.

She was charmed by that grin. Too bad. She couldn't let herself be charmed. "I doubt it. She's not going to believe you're pitiful at this stage in the game."

"Probably not. But maybe if you talk your brother into going back to San Francisco, I'll have a better chance of convincing Cynthia to finish her degree."

"Maybe." She thought it would depend entirely on how much empathy he showed for his sister's dreams. Giselle also realized the more empathy he showed, the more appealing he would become to *her*.

She vowed to be on guard for that. "Of course, Bryce might not be getting tired of his Las Vegas adventure. He might be furious that I showed up and even more determined to help Cynthia run us ragged. That's the other possibility."

"Well, unless Owen figures out their disguise, I guess we keep solving the riddles and see where it takes us. Maybe if we solve all their riddles, they'll agree to a meeting."

She saw the frustration in his eyes. "I can tell you don't like this."

"No, but I'm willing to go along with the game. It seems as if she really needs me to do that."

"I think she does." Giselle hoped that Cynthia's campaign worked to change his mind. Maybe becoming a showgirl wasn't the best choice for his sister or maybe it was the perfect choice. All she knew for sure was that Cynthia should be the one to decide.

Giselle also thought that bringing about a truce between Cynthia and Luke might open the door to a conversation with Bryce. A part of her wanted to twist his ears off for being so contrary, but after seeing the way Cynthia was struggling with Luke's expectations, she had a lot more sympathy for Bryce's position.

Maybe he didn't want to be an alpha. If so, he shouldn't be forced into the role. She didn't want it, either, but maybe there was a decent alternative—although she couldn't think of one right off the bat. None of her cousins were alpha material.

She'd been so engrossed in her thoughts that she hadn't noticed that she'd finished her meal. She glanced over at Luke's plate, and his was nearly empty, too.

He glanced up. "What do you think about the riddle?"

"You haven't given it to me yet."

"I haven't? Oh, sorry." He put down his fork and picked up his phone. "I may even know what this one refers to, but let's see what you say. *Water has rhythm and so do I. Watch it dance and watch it fly. Love is reaching for the sky."* His voice roughened on the last sentence. He cleared his throat.

Giselle's chest tightened. This young woman positively ached with her desire to dance. And Luke knew it, too. Otherwise he wouldn't have choked up on that last sentence. She gazed at him and wondered if he'd relent, right there at the dinner table.

If he was considering that, he didn't let on. "It's the Bellagio, right? The fountains out front?"

"I think so."

He pushed his plate aside. "We might as well get going, then. There are other fountains in Vegas. Could she mean somewhere else?"

"I doubt it." She picked up her wineglass and then put it back down. "Guess I'd better not have any more wine if I'm driving."

"We could walk. It's not that far."

"Then let's walk. The exercise might do us good." It would do her good, at least. When he'd become emotional while reading the riddle, she'd wanted to put her arms around him, although that would have been dangerous and she wouldn't have risked it. But now she wanted to shake him until his teeth rattled, and that wouldn't solve anything, either.

They put on jackets and headed out. Luke wore leather instead of the blue denim, which he'd hung up because it was still damp. They took the private elevator down, but this time they walked out through the lobby. Coming in, they'd gone straight from the parking garage to the elevator, so Giselle had missed seeing how the hotel had changed since her first visit.

Apparently she was getting tired, because she spoke when she should have kept her mouth shut. "It's changed."

He glanced at her. "You were here? Oh, wait. Of course you were. Family friends of the Cartwrights would get rooms when no one else could."

"Yes." And the less she said about her previous visit, the better.

"My dad thought it was way too *blah*. All that soft lighting and greenery wasn't for him. Or maybe he just didn't like it because Harrison did."

Giselle had loved the way it used to look and feel. The lobby had been an oasis of tropical plants and waterfalls, thick carpets and soothing birdsong. She remembered walking in from the hubbub outside and sighing in relief.

Now the place was filled with glittering surfaces, marble floors, and crystal chandeliers with lights so bright they hurt her eyes. The sound of flowing water had been replaced with rock music that bounced off the mirrored walls and made her want to cover her ears. Conversation and laughter seemed twice as loud because nothing absorbed the noise.

"You don't like it."

She opened her mouth to say something diplomatic.

He put a hand on her arm and shook his head. "Don't bother. I didn't expect you to like it. You were the one who nearly fainted in a crowded elevator."

"What I think of the lobby shouldn't matter, anyway."

"That's true, but you got that look on your face as if you wanted to spare my feelings. You don't have to worry about that. I was younger when my dad remodeled the lobby, and I thought it was awesome. But lately it's been getting on my nerves. Too noisy and glaring."

She laughed. "Luke Dalton, you're turning into an old fogy."

"Could be, and that's not a good thing. The marketing people have conducted exit surveys, and most guests love the lobby. One woman said she felt as if she'd stepped inside a giant tiara."

"Perfect description. I've never wanted one, giant or otherwise."

"No? I thought most women loved tiaras."

"Not me." And she wasn't a woman, either, but that was beside the point. She knew female werewolves who liked those things, but she'd never yearned for one, not even when she was a little kid.

He studied her. "I guess that makes sense. You aren't wearing any jewelry, either. I hadn't noticed that before. Are you allergic?"

"No. I'm just not attracted to the idea of wearing it. One more thing to worry about."

"That must be frustrating for any guy who wants to buy you a gift."

She smiled at him. "Not if he has some imagination."

"Mmm. Interesting challenge." He gestured toward the revolving door that led to the sidewalk. "Shall we?" He followed her out.

As they started north toward the Bellagio, she was jostled by the crowd. Not much, but enough that she temporarily lost track of Luke. She figured he'd have no trouble finding her, considering her height and red hair, so she kept walking.

Besides, she didn't want to waste time looking for him when she'd caught the unmistakable scent of a Were nearby. With so many competing smells, she couldn't identify Bryce for certain, and he wouldn't be the only werewolf walking along the Strip.

Yet the breeze carried the scent back toward her, and she noticed a tall, broad-shouldered male ahead of her. His hair was black, not red, but if Owen was right and they'd disguised themselves, then it could be Bryce up there. She hurried, trying to catch up with him.

A strong hand closed around her upper arm. "I almost lost you," Luke said. "Maybe we'd better—"

"Just a sec." She kept her attention on the tall figure walking about twenty feet ahead of them. Definitely a werewolf. Besides the faint scent, she could tell by the way he moved.

With the breeze blowing in her direction, he wouldn't be able to scent her, which gave her the element of surprise. She slipped out of Luke's grip and grabbed his hand. "Come with me. I think I see Bryce."

Chapter 7

"Which one are we following?" Luke scanned the crowd and tried to ignore the warmth created by their interlaced fingers. Holding hands was a good idea in this mob, especially if they had to try to catch up with her brother. There shouldn't be anything personal about it, but holding hands with Giselle as they hurried down the sidewalk felt extremely personal. He liked holding hands with her way too much.

"It's that tall one up there with the longish black hair. See him?"

"Yeah, but what makes you think that's Bryce?"

"He's the same height, and Bryce has shoulders like that. If he's disguised, like Owen thinks, then the black hair could be a wig. Doesn't that look like a wig?"

"I don't know. Maybe. I'm no expert. Is there a woman with him?"

"I can't tell. Somebody's walking on his left, but from my vantage point, I can't see whether it's a woman or not. You're taller. What do you think?"

"Hard to say. I think it's a woman, but she has on a

bulky coat. I don't recognize it, by the way, so if that's Cynthia, she's wearing someone else's clothes."

"Or she bought some new things for her disguise."

"I guess that's possible, too." He wanted to believe that was her because he would love to end this ridiculous charade she had going. He gave Giselle's hand a squeeze. "Let's catch up with them. Stay behind me. I'll run interference."

"Go."

Years of playing high school and college football came in handy sometimes. He kept a tight grip on Giselle's hand, and she tucked in behind him as if she'd played the sport herself. When they reached the corner, he was close enough to tap the shoulder of the person walking on the tall guy's left. "Cynthia? Is that you?"

The person turned. He wasn't Cynthia and he obviously wasn't happy to be mistaken for a woman, either. He stopped and scowled at Luke. "You looking for a problem, buddy?"

"Sorry. Mistaken identity."

The guy puffed out his chest. "I'm thinking you need your eyes checked, mister."

"Forget it, Stanley." The tall guy, who didn't look anything like Bryce Landry, jerked his head toward the MGM Grand. "We're gonna miss the poker tournament if we don't get a move on."

"Yeah, okay." Glaring once more at Luke, the shorter man turned and followed his friend across the intersection.

Giselle sighed heavily. "I'm so sorry. I thought there was a good chance it was them."

"Hey, it was fun." He grinned at her.

"It was?"

"Absolutely." Tugging on her hand, he started across the street. Might as well go before they lost the WALK signal. "I got a little adrenaline rush thinking we might actually catch them. Didn't you?"

"Maybe."

He glanced over at her. "Just maybe?"

Her apologetic expression changed and she smiled. "Actually, yes. I was trying to decide what I was going to say to Bryce as we shoved our way through the crowd, and my heart was going a mile a minute."

"And what were you going to say to him?"

"Something simple, probably. Like, 'Let's talk.' I—whoops. That was a phone just now. Might have been mine."

"Then let's stop a minute and get over to the side so you can check."

Pulling her phone from her coat pocket, she clicked on her message. "It's a text from Bryce."

"And?"

"'Gotcha, Sis.'" She looked at Luke. "He was watching all that! I wasn't wrong that he was nearby. I just picked the wrong candidate out of the crowd!"

Luke turned and scanned the area. "Okay, if they're following us around, I need to get Owen involved."

"What good would that do if they're in disguise?"

He blew out a breath. "I don't know. I just . . ."

"Hey, you said you were having fun a minute ago."

"That was when I thought *we* were following *them*. It's not quite as much fun imagining them following us."

"Because you like to be in control of the situation?"

"Yes." He continued to search the people going by. Cynthia might be in disguise, but she was his sister. He'd know her if he saw her face, even if she was wearing a wig, different clothes, and wild makeup. But the sidewalk was crowded. They could be anywhere.

"Well, we're not in control," Giselle said, "but we can choose our next move. I suggest we continue on to the Bellagio, watch the fountain show, and see what happens."

"Might as well." He took her hand as they made their way to the front of the Bellagio and found a spot by the railing. At that point he couldn't come up with a good excuse for holding on to her, so he let go. He missed that connection instantly.

"Perfect spot." She smiled at him.

He was beginning to look for ways to make her smile because he enjoyed seeing her do it. That probably wasn't a good sign that he was ignoring his attraction to her. "At least I don't have to worry about getting wet this time," he said. "I doubt Cynthia could jimmy the fountain so it sprays on me."

"I doubt Cynthia would want to face vandalism charges for jimmying the fountain at the Bellagio."

"I wish I knew how long they intend to keep this up." Then something occurred to him. As long as they chased around after Cynthia, he had an excuse to be with Giselle. Once this exercise was over, Giselle would leave. He realized he wasn't looking forward to that.

"I suspect she's hoping to wear you down. I—" She abandoned whatever she'd been about to say as the music swelled. "Oh, look. It's starting."

He'd seen the current show dozens of times, both from this vantage point, where he could hear the music, and from the windows of the penthouse, where he could only watch the plumes of water arching into the air. From forty floors up, the effect wasn't as spectacular as it was standing here, surrounded by music from top-grade speakers.

Luke always enjoyed the experience, but never more than now, when he was able to watch Giselle's reaction to it. She held on to the railing as if needing to anchor herself to reality. Her expression was rapt, almost child-like, as she watched the dancing water.

The music vibrated around and through them, arousing Luke in a way it hadn't before. The bass seemed to resonate with greater force, and the violins sang along his nerve endings, teasing him with desires he had no business having. In his imagination, he and Giselle were the only two people here.

Inappropriate though it might be, he pictured them making love in time to the music and the cascading water. Eventually the crotch of his jeans pinched, reminding him that they were not alone, and he'd better imagine something else. He'd be wise to imagine Giselle getting on a plane in a few days, because she would definitely be doing that. She was the CFO of Landry Enterprises and her life was in San Francisco.

Then another thought hit him. The bad news was that Giselle would be going back to San Francisco. But maybe the good news was that Giselle would be going back to San Francisco. What happened in Vegas stayed in Vegas.

No, he was thinking crazy. Sure, he'd caught her looking at him during dinner in a way that might mean she was interested in him. But for all he knew, she had a steady guy back home.

If she was in a similar situation to his, and she was attracted to him at all . . . but he didn't know the answer to those things. Still, the idea had taken up residence in his brain and he doubted it would go away anytime soon.

He glanced over at her and let the idea simmer a bit. She had a hotel room at Illusions, but while they were dealing with her brother and his sister, they really ought to stick together. Close together. Then he could find out the answer to some of his burning questions about her.

The more he thought about inviting her to spend the rest of her stay at the penthouse, the more he saw it as the perfect solution. They needed a command central, and the penthouse made the most sense. Having him at one end of the Strip and her at the other would be impractical.

The music swelled to a crescendo and the water shot into the sky with breathtaking force. The drama of the final moment was reflected in Giselle's expression of awe. She'd been swept away. Luke longed to see that same dazzled look in her eyes in a far more intimate setting.

As if she felt his gaze on her, she looked at him. If he was any good at reading the message in a woman's eyes—and he was—then her thoughts might not be so different from his. But he would make no assumptions about that. He'd keep watching her and try to pick up on her cues.

He gestured toward the fountain. "Great show, huh?"

"Wonderful." Her breathing was quick and shallow, which meant that she'd been excited by the show, or excited by other thoughts that ran along the same lines as his. Maybe both.

"I think it was especially good tonight." Now *that* was a boneheaded comment. The show was computerized, and unless the program didn't work right, it would be the same exact presentation every time. He glanced up at the sky. "Perfect night for it."

"I agree." She had that cute little smile going on again,

the one that told him she thought he was goofy. But she didn't seem to mind goofy. But then she looked away, and the smile disappeared.

So maybe she did have someone else and had just reminded herself of that. He took a deep breath. "Well, nothing's happened in connection with Cynthia, so maybe we should think about—"

"Excuse me." A heavily tattooed woman with multiple earrings and a nose ring approached him. "Are you Luke Dalton?"

He wasn't sure whether to admit it or not. The woman seemed a little scary. And she wasn't Cynthia. His sister might be in disguise, but she'd never be able to make herself look like this without spending hours in the hands of a Hollywood makeup team. Cynthia hadn't had hours to devote to such a project.

"It's nothing bad," the woman said. "I'm not going to serve you with a subpoena or anything. But you fit the description I was given, and I was told you'd be here with a redhead, watching the Bellagio fountain do its thing." She pulled a manila envelope out of her large tote.

Luke recognized his sister's handwriting on the outside of the envelope. "When did you get that?"

"I'm not supposed to say. I'm just supposed to give it to you and leave." She smiled. "I wouldn't refuse a tip, though."

Luke dug out his wallet and located a hundred-dollar bill tucked behind the twenties. "If you'll tell me when and how you got the envelope, and what the woman was wearing at the time, you can have this."

Her eyes widened. "Uh . . . no. As much as I could use that, I promised her I wouldn't tell you. You should let her dance, though. It's not like she's going to strip. I can see why you'd object to that, but what she wants—to dance with the Moonbeams—that's classy."

Luke was very aware of Giselle standing next to him listening to every word. "She told you about that?" he asked.

"Sure. We shared a moment. My family didn't want me to get the tattoos and the piercings, but it's my life, you know?" She glanced at Giselle. "You get what I'm saying, right? Once you're an adult, you get to decide."

"I agree," Giselle said.

"I thought you would." The woman moved a little closer to Giselle. "You look like a take-charge kind of lady. We can't let other people push us around. Like present company, for example."

Luke sighed.

"I completely agree," Giselle said, suppressing her smile. She could see Luke was suffering through this conversation.

"Here." Luke shoved the hundred-dollar bill at the woman. "Take it with my blessings. Now give me the envelope."

"You bet." She handed it over.

"Thank you. Now, if you'll excuse us, we need to get—"

"Wait. I have something else for you." She reached into her tote, pulled out a pink squirt gun, and shot him in the face. "Bye, now!" She hurried away.

As water ran down Luke's face and into the open neck of his shirt, he didn't look at Giselle. "Don't you dare laugh."

"I won't." But her voice quavered as though she wanted to. "I have a tissue in my pocket, if that would help."

"Thanks. I'd appreciate it."

The white tissue fluttered in front of him like a flag of truce. "Can I hold the envelope for you?"

"Sure." He handed it over and accepted her tissue so he could mop his face. "I don't know where Cynthia found that squirt gun, but it packs a punch."

"Luke, I have a confession."

"Oh?" Balling the tissue in his fist, he glanced around for a trash can. One happened to be nearby, so he lobbed the wet tissue into it. Two points. "About what?"

"My brother. As a kid, he was fascinated with practical jokes. The bucket of water trick is something he spent hours getting right. And he knows his squirt guns, too. He considers the superpumper ones too obvious. So he'll take a normal-sized one and fool with it until it delivers a blast of water that'll drown you on the first shot."

Luke stared at her in disbelief. "And your brother is how old?"

"Thirty. And you know what? I never connected that significant birthday with him shucking his responsibilities and coming to Vegas. But that might be part of it. Maybe this is a last fling before he has to settle down."

"Bully for him." Luke was in no mood to hear about some guy's birthday angst. When he'd turned thirty, he'd been watching his dad's health deteriorate. He'd prayed that the hardworking man he idolized would live to enjoy a ripe old age. His prayers had gone unanswered.

"I honestly thought he'd outgrown the practical joke stage, and for the most part I think he has. But he seems to have appointed himself Cynthia's champion, so he's come out of retirement to help her harass you."

"Does he have any more tricks like this up his sleeve?"

"Probably. I'll have to think back to those days and

make a list. Some things he did were never blamed on him. Others he couldn't resist taking the credit for and was willing to accept being grounded in exchange for the glory of a prank well and truly executed. He was at his peak around twelve, and I was only ten and easily impressed."

"I'm thirty going on two hundred, and I'm not impressed at all." He heard the martyred tone of his voice and winced. He'd inherited a fortune, and he'd acquired the education to manage it. He was grateful for what he had.

But maybe he was wound a little too tight. He had a pretty good idea of how to unwind, but he also had a strong suspicion Giselle had a sweetheart back in 'Frisco. Even if she didn't, she couldn't think kindly of a man who'd made cutting remarks about her brother.

He took a deep breath and a mental step back. "Look, I apologize for that crack. I don't know Bryce at all, and it's possible I've made some unfair assumptions about him."

Her eyebrows lifted. "I'm glad to hear you say that, Luke."

"From his viewpoint, he might think he's helping solve the problem."

"I believe he does. I'll bet they've bonded over the fact their relatives are leaning on them in ways they don't like."

"I don't want them to bond permanently." Luke realized that didn't sound very complimentary, either. "Nothing against your brother, but—"

"I know. Believe me, I'm hoping they're just good friends." She glanced over at him. "Are you going to look at what's in the envelope?"

"I can guarantee it's another of her recital pictures. Maybe I should leave it in there for now, where it's protected. At this rate, I don't know where another blast of water might come from. Listen, would you be willing to head back to the penthouse so we could have a strategy session without me being in danger of water sabotage?"

She hesitated. "I'll walk back with you, but I was thinking I should fetch the Harley and go back to my hotel room. It's been a long day."

That clinched it for him. She wasn't interested in spending any more time with him than necessary. "Okay. I'm sure you're tired. How would you like to handle any more communication from them, assuming they stick together?"

"We can forward texts to each other. I'm willing to meet you if it looks as if we need to do that, but we probably should both get some sleep and continue this tomorrow."

"Fair enough. I'll walk you back to the Silver Crescent parking lot." This time, he didn't reach for her hand. She was making it pretty obvious that wouldn't be a welcome gesture from him. The depth of his disappointment took him by surprise. In a very short time, Giselle Landry had gotten under his skin.

Chapter 8

During the water show at the Bellagio, Giselle had found herself thinking about something she was strongly opposed to—having sex with a human. And not just any human, either. She needed to put some distance between herself and Luke ASAP.

They walked in silence back to the Silver Crescent. The music from the water show thrummed in her veins, and pictures of Luke flashed through her mind. She'd been aware of him watching her during the show, and his presence there had been exciting—way too exciting.

His comments afterward had tickled her, because they told her he'd been thinking similar thoughts, but he'd wanted to appear cool and composed. But when she'd looked into his eyes and felt that click of recognition, that moment when she could all too easily allow herself to get carried away, she'd pulled back.

Seeing the sadness in his expression hadn't made her feel very good, but she was doing the right thing for both of them. Giving in to the pull of their mutual attraction wouldn't be doing either of them any favors.

He stayed with her until she'd retrieved the Harley and was ready to leave. He scrubbed his fingers through his hair, which reminded her of the moment in the hotel room when he'd done the same thing. His gestures, his smiles, his laughter, were becoming important to her. That had to stop.

"So if anything happens," he said, "I'll text you, and vice versa."

"That works."

He smiled. "We didn't eat the cake, but I'm sure they have great desserts at Illusions, too."

"I'm sure they do." She started the engine. "We'll keep in touch."

"Right."

She started down the street and fought the odd sensation that she was leaving someone important behind. No, she was leaving *temptation* behind. Maybe Luke Dalton was a test of her resolve not to get sexually involved with a human male. If so, it had turned out to be tougher than she'd ever imagined it would be.

Traffic was heavy, and she was held up by a red light. Her cell phone chimed, but the light changed and she had to concentrate on her driving. Two lights later, she finally glanced at the message. *Another riddle. Want me to take this one?*

Damn, her heart started pounding as if she were seventeen and had been asked to a dance. That was bad. Pulling into the circular drive at Illusions, she balanced on her bike and looked at the riddle. *Romance in the air, voices raised in song, artistry in movement as they glide along.*

Had to be the gondola rides at the Venetian. She sat there telling herself to let it go. But doggone it, she wanted to know what Bryce and Cynthia had cooked up for the gondola ride at the Venetian. She could meet Luke there, satisfy her curiosity, and come straight back here.

But not on the Harley. It *had* been a long day, and an emotional one. Her reflexes might not be as quick as she needed them to be in Vegas traffic. She'd cab it this time. After quickly texting Luke that she'd meet him at the Venetian in about twenty minutes, she turned the Harley over to valet parking and hopped in one of the cabs parked at the curb.

Luke must have been watching for her, because when she got out of the cab in front of the Venetian, he was right there. "Thanks for coming. No Harley?"

"I was ready to let someone else drive."

Sympathy flashed in his eyes. "You really are pooped, aren't you?"

"I am, but my curiosity got the better of me."

"You understand it's a water ride, right?"

"Yep."

"And you're willing to risk it, knowing that Bryce has cooked up something special?"

She decided to be as honest as possible. "I tried to talk myself out of meeting you here, but I couldn't stand the idea of not knowing firsthand what they've come up with now."

His boyish grin flashed. "Let's go check out the gondola rides." And he took her hand.

She could have pulled away, but the simple fact was she didn't want to. Holding his hand earlier tonight had been a pleasure. She would go back to Illusions after this, so she told herself she could allow herself to hold his hand now.

As they started into the building, a young guy who looked to be around twenty stepped forward. "Are you Luke Dalton and Giselle Landry?"

Luke glanced at Giselle and she gave him a thumbs-up. They were here now, so they might as well see what happened next.

"Yes, we are," Luke said.

"Then come with me. Someone has paid an obscene amount of money for you to have a custom gondola ride."

"Wait a minute." Luke caught his arm. "How custom? Are we going to get wet?"

"How would you get wet?"

"Oh, I don't know," Luke said. "The boat capsizes, or sinks, something like that."

The guy shook his head and smiled. "Not gonna happen. I think the custom part is that you go to the head of the line, and the gondolier has agreed to sing something special for you." He looked at them with a twinkle in his eyes. "Special night for you two, maybe?"

"Yes," Giselle said. "Very special." She enjoyed the shock in Luke's expression. "He just popped the question."

"Excellent!" The kid beamed at them. "Congratulations! We love romance at the Venetian. Right this way. I'll take you to your gondola."

"What question?" Luke asked as they followed the guy at a brisk pace. "I didn't pop any question."

She lowered her voice. "Yes, you did. You asked if I was ready to risk a water ride with you."

"Yeah, but that was *a* question, not *the* question. You nearly gave me a heart attack."

"Relax. I have no interest in a trip down the aisle. But

that kid was expecting something, so I played along." Pretending to be his engaged girlfriend might not be the wisest thing she'd ever done, but again, it seemed like a harmless bit of silliness and it made the gondola folks happy.

A little voice in the back of her mind taunted her with the possibility that she was acting out a fantasy of her own by masquerading as Luke's one-and-only. So what if she was? It was just a water ride, over in a few minutes. It didn't matter.

Much as Luke chafed under the constraints of this game Cynthia was playing, it had its rewards. The lure of a riddle had brought Giselle to the Venetian, and even though she was playacting this gondola scene, he intended to enjoy himself, at least until he became drenched. He knew it would happen. He just didn't know when.

"This lucky couple is celebrating a very special night," said the guy who'd brought them to the gondola landing. "I know you'll take good care of them, Luigi."

"Luigi?" Luke looked at the gondolier. "Really?"

"While I'm giving gondola rides." The dark-haired, olive-skinned man in a shirt with vertical stripes flashed his white teeth. "Are we ready?"

"Absolutely." Giselle looked at Luke and lowered her voice. "You should put your arm around me."

"Oh." This experience continued to improve. He discovered that Giselle made a very good snuggling partner. She understood exactly how to nestle her curves against his angles so they fit like a couple of puzzle pieces.

"Perfect," Luigi said. "Don't forget the tradition."

Luke glanced at the gondolier. "What tradition?"

"Couples in love usually kiss going under the bridges."

"Oh." Luke felt Giselle stiffen.

"And we're off," Luigi said.

Luke put his mouth next to Giselle's ear. Breathing in her scent jacked up his pulse, but he made himself say what he figured she wanted to hear. "Don't worry. I won't honor that tradition."

"Okay." She relaxed against him in obvious relief.

So he wouldn't kiss her, but that didn't meant he couldn't enjoy the cuddling. He had an armful of very beautiful woman, and she felt warm and exceedingly willing. That wasn't real, of course, but he could dream.

The boat did, indeed, glide along, and he could understand why couples found this to be a stimulating experience. The phallic shape of the boat and the liquid canal . . . well, it was obvious, right?

The gondola ride drew spectators, a cheerful lot who waved at the passing boats. Luke kept a sharp eye out for Cynthia and Bryce, but even if they were in the crowd, they wouldn't be close enough to aim a squirt gun accurately.

All was well in his world until the gondolier began to sing. It wasn't his voice, which turned out to be a deep baritone and was probably one of the reasons he'd been hired. It was his choice of songs, or rather Cynthia's choice of songs. The song was "I Hope You Dance."

She was determined to break him. The lyrics of the song fit her campaign, but the song cut deeper than that. Every time he heard it he was transported back to a dark auditorium where he and his folks had watched his little sister perform her first solo, a ballet to this very number. She'd been fourteen, which was young to be dancing a solo number. But she'd begged her teacher for the chance and had knocked one out of the park.

He swore softly under his breath, which helped to block the relentless parade of sentimental images. Giselle obviously heard his muted but colorful language, because she began to shake with silent laughter.

Cynthia was playing dirty, but she was sure focused. That had been Giselle's evaluation, and boy, had she nailed it. Cynthia had decided that she wanted something and she was by damn going to get it, no matter how long she had to torture him.

He wondered if she'd find a way to work water into this gig after all. But the Venetian couldn't risk having guests end up in the canal, either accidentally or on purpose. No matter how much money Cynthia had thrown at them, they weren't going to dump his ass overboard.

Besides, that lacked finesse. He was in a boat, and shoving him into the water would be crude and obvious, in addition to lawsuit-worthy. Even though Giselle hadn't listed her brother's various pranks yet, Luke had already figured out that Landry went for the unexpected and the relatively harmless.

Bryce was, Luke grudgingly acknowledged, a good match for Cynthia. She had always been so pressured to use her intelligence to excel, and she probably admired Bryce for using his for smart-aleck tricks. Luke only hoped she wouldn't admire anything else about him. Being in league together against the uncooperative big brother was one thing. Being in love with each other was more serious.

The song continued endlessly as the gondolier gave it all he had. He'd probably been told this was *their* song. Ironically, it would become their song tonight. Now every time he heard it, he'd think of Cynthia's dance recital, but he'd also remember this gondola ride. He had a feeling memories of Giselle would haunt him long after she'd left town.

For the time being, though, she was very much here. As she sat next to him, she was quickly losing it. Her shaking had become more pronounced, and little snorts of laughter were escaping around the hand she'd clamped over her mouth.

The gondolier was really getting into it, and the crowd lining the canal loved the performance. They clapped and whistled their approval, which only encouraged Luigi to ham it up some more. As he flung his arm into the air and projected the single word *dance,* someone lobbed a baseball-sized object toward the boat.

Luke barely had time to shield Giselle before it landed on his head and broke. A water balloon! He should have guessed.

"Security!" Luigi bellowed as he abandoned his song. "Someone's throwing water balloons! Security!"

"No big deal," Luke said. He'd rather not have Cynthia and Landry arrested, although they were probably long gone by now, anyway.

Luigi turned and crouched next to Luke. "Sir, I'm so sorry. Are you okay? The Venetian will make this right. I've never had someone throw a water balloon at my boat before. I'm really sorry. And on your special night, too."

Luke ran a hand over his dripping face. "I'm fine, really. It's only water. Takes me back to my high school days."

Luigi still seemed concerned. "I wish I could promise that we'll find whoever threw that balloon, but with crowds like this, it's nearly impossible."

"I doubt you will find him," Giselle said. "I'm pretty sure it was my brother."

"Oh?" Luigi looked surprised, and then he grinned. "A little welcome-to-the-family prank on this guy, huh?" He glanced at Luke. "I suggest you keep your honeymoon plans to yourself, my friend."

"Luigi, those plans are so top secret even I don't know what they are."

"Ah." Luigi's smile widened. "So you're letting your future bride handle the details. Smart man. The happier she is, the happier you'll be."

Luke met Giselle's gaze. "My thoughts exactly." Her emerald eyes were filled with laughter, and he sure did enjoy when that happened. Maybe it was worth getting a little wet.

Representatives from the casino met them at the dock. One of them recognized Luke and insisted on giving them gambling tokens, coupons for free drinks, and a complimentary dinner for two. Luke could tell they all were relieved as hell that he wasn't going to make a problem for them over a water balloon.

Eventually they left and he turned to Giselle. "Want to drink and gamble?"

She smiled at him. "Not particularly. You handled that well, though."

"Apparently I'm getting used to dripping."

"You have to admit that song was hysterical."

He gazed at her sparkling eyes and flushed cheeks. Damn, but she was a pretty woman. Good company, too. "I could tell you thought so. I'm surprised the boat didn't start rocking, the way you were trying to keep from cracking up."

"He was so sincere that I didn't want him to know I was laughing."

"So tell me, does your brother repeat his tricks or does he tend to move on to new ones each time?"

"I'd be surprised if he repeated anything with you. He considers himself something of an artist in this regard."

"He's got a hell of a throwing arm. Accurate, too."

She nodded. "All-star pitcher for the high school baseball team."

"Huh." He had to admit the baseball information made a difference in how he perceived Bryce Landry. An all-star deserved some respect for all the work involved in getting to that level. A total screwup couldn't accomplish it. He should know.

"Under different circumstances, you two might have become friends."

"Tell you what. If he'll give up this campaign and convince Cynthia to go back to school, I'll be his friend for life. I'll name my first kid after him. I'll put him in my will. I'll—"

"So are you saying that after all this, you're still dead set against her plan to be a showgirl?"

He looked into her eyes. Sadly, the laughter wasn't there anymore. "That's what I'm saying. Somebody has to keep her from making bad choices. I'm the only one available to do that."

Chapter 9

Giselle was ready to whack Luke upside his incredibly thick skull. The odds against keeping a twenty-two-year-old from making bad choices were far worse than the odds against hitting a million-dollar jackpot on a one-armed bandit. But Luke, who was at least as focused as his sister, had decided that Cynthia had to finish her last semester and get that sheepskin, and apparently that was that as far as he was concerned.

There was a thin line, Giselle realized, between being focused and having tunnel vision. She suspected that Angus Dalton had been a very focused individual, as well, and he'd passed on that characteristic to both of his children. Now they were butting heads, each of them determined to outlast the other.

"At least there's no envelope this time," Luke said. "Maybe she gave up on that. I hope so, because I *think* we have duplicates of everything in the vault, but I've never made an inventory to be sure. Trusting any pictures to strangers is risky."

"Maybe she's willing to take chances if it can get her

what she wants." Giselle wished that he'd see how devoted Cynthia was to her art. If he allowed himself to see that, he might soften his position.

"The pictures aren't going to change my mind, so she might as well quit finding clever ways to give them to me. It's a waste of . . ." He stopped talking as a little blond girl about five years old walked toward them.

She wore a black leotard, white leggings, and pink sneakers. Her hair was pulled back into a bun, and a small tiara rested on her golden head. She was clutching a manila envelope.

Giselle scanned the crowd and saw a woman watching the proceedings very carefully. The woman held a black canvas tote with PAM RAU DANCE STUDIO lettered on it in neon pink. Everything about her alert stance signaled that she was this little tot's mother and that she wasn't about to let anything happen to her kid.

Once Giselle satisfied herself that the little girl was well chaperoned, she turned her attention to the drama unfolding in front of her. Luke had hunkered down so that he was on the same level as the child. The tenderness in his expression caught Giselle by surprise.

She hadn't seen this side of Luke Dalton. He might talk tough and act macho, but apparently he could also be a total pushover. This cherub had him completely in her power.

She held the envelope in two hands, as if carrying a tray. "Are you Mr. Dalton?"

"I am." He spoke with such gentleness that without her Were hearing, Giselle wouldn't have caught what he'd said. "And who might you be?"

"I'm Ella. My mommy's over there." She turned to point, let go of one side of the envelope, and had to make a quick grab for it. "Whoops. Almost dropped it. The lady said to be *very* careful." Her solemn blue gaze returned to Luke. "It's a picture. She showed us it."

"Tell me, Ella, is that lady still here?"

Ella shook her head, which made her tiara jiggle. She let go of the other side of the envelope to grab for it and would have dropped it entirely if Luke hadn't slid his hand underneath.

"Thank you for holding it for me." After adjusting her tiara with one hand, Ella clutched the side of the envelope again. "You can let go now."

"Are you supposed to give it to me?"

"Yes."

"Are you ready to do that?"

"No."

"Why not?"

"First I'm s'posed to tell you something." She took a deep breath and blew it out again. Then she looked up and began to recite. "Dancing is good for people. People . . ." Her smooth little forehead wrinkled. "People are . . . very happy when they dance! There. That's it. You can have the envelope now." She shoved it toward him.

"Thank you, Ella." Luke took it as if accepting a Nobel Prize. "And thank you for delivering the message." He stood.

"It's true!" Released from her responsibilities, Ella grew more animated. "Dancing is *great*!" She began hopping from one foot to the other. "My dance teacher, Miss Pam, she entered us in this dance contest, and we're all here in Las Vegas, and this is what I wore, except I had to take off my ballet shoes so they wouldn't get all dirty, and we're having so much fun!" She jumped up and down and would have lost her tiara if she hadn't clapped her hand to her head at the last minute.

"Time to go, Ella." Her mother came over. "You delivered your message, so let's leave this man and his friend in peace."

"Okay." Ella glanced up at Giselle as if noticing her for the first time. "Are you a dancer, too?"

"No, I'm afraid not."

"That's too bad. If you were a dancer, you could be in this contest. There's a whole *bunch* of us. Even *mommies* are in this contest." She swung her arms wide. "Wanna see me do something?" She placed one sneakered foot against her calf, balanced on her other foot, and put her hands together over her head. She wobbled only a little bit.

Giselle clapped enthusiastically. "Bravo!"

"That's lovely, Ella," her mother said. "Now we need to go. Everyone's ready to leave." She smiled at Luke and Giselle. "The woman who gave us the envelope showed us the picture. She said it was important that you get it back and that you'd understand what it was all about."

"I do," Luke said. "Your daughter is something else."

The woman laughed. "Oh, yes. She is definitely a dancer! I swear she was dancing before she was born. I could feel her twirling around in there. Well, have a nice night." Holding Ella's hand, she walked away.

Luke stared after them. "My mother used to say that about Cynthia. That she could feel her dancing before she was born."

Giselle chose to keep quiet. If that adorable little girl hadn't turned the tables for Cynthia, nothing would. Anything Giselle said now might dilute the Ella effect.

After watching mother and daughter join a group of other parents herding a large group of girls in black leotards, Luke turned to Giselle. His expression was unreadable. "That must have been the grand finale of that stunt."

"Guess so. Listen, I should find a cab and get back to Illusions."

"My driver's on his way. Let me drop you there."

Refusing seemed unnecessarily abrupt. "All right."

He hesitated. "If this is out of line, just say so, but when we're together I feel like we're a team. When you head off to your hotel, it's as if the team's broken up."

"But Illusions is where I'm staying."

"I understand that, but . . ." He glanced away in frustration, but when he looked into her eyes again, his gaze was completely open. "I'm going to level with you. I've had completely inappropriate thoughts about us, but that's over."

"I'm glad." And she was, wasn't she? If her heart started racing because he'd admitted he wanted her, she'd get over that inconvenient reaction. "This isn't the time or place."

"I realize that, so you have nothing to worry about from me. But the thing is, I'm more confident that Cynthia's deal will come to a reasonable conclusion—"

"I don't know what you mean by *a reasonable conclusion*."

"Hell, neither do I. And that's the point I'm trying to make. Talking it out with you, face-to-face, helps me sort out my thoughts. I didn't realize how much I depended on your insights until you went back to Illusions. Like I said, it was as if the team had broken up."

She took a calming breath. "What are you suggesting?"

"Check out of Illusions and stay in the penthouse."

"No." Her senses went on red alert. "That's not a good idea."

"The place is huge, even bigger than it looks. You'll have your own room. But the main thing is, when there's a new development, you'll be right there. We can discuss it together." His phone pinged and he glanced at it. "That's Jim with the car. He's pulling up now."

But Giselle was no longer paying attention. She'd caught the unmistakable scent of her brother, and he was close, very close. "Luke, wait here." Instinct kept her from mentioning that she thought her brother was mere feet away. She wouldn't be able to explain how she knew, and maybe Bryce only wanted to connect with her, not Luke. "I'll be right back."

His blue gaze sharpened. "What is it?"

"A feeling. Stay here, okay?"

"But—"

"Please."

"All right." His jaw flexed. "I'll text Jim and have him wait at the curb. He won't be able to stay there long."

"I won't be long." Turning, she searched the crowd going in and out of the Venetian. Then, following her nose, she headed toward a tall blond guy. Except he wasn't a guy. He was Bryce.

He walked away, and she followed. A quick glance over her shoulder confirmed that Luke was nowhere in sight. She'd asked for his cooperation and he'd given it. She appreciated the effort that must have taken for a guy who liked to be in charge.

Bryce drew her deeper into the crowd, but at last he turned around and stopped. The blond wig was a good one. He looked sort of like Brad Pitt when the actor was younger.

Although he seemed to be alone, Giselle glanced around, hoping to catch a glimpse of Cynthia.

"She's not here."

She looked into her brother's eyes, their green a shade lighter than hers. "Where is she?"

"Somewhere else. Listen, I don't know how long before Dalton comes looking for you, so I'll make this quick. He's right. You're a good influence on him. Cynthia loves the guy and wants him to be on board with her choices. The more time you spend with him, the better."

"You don't know what you're asking. He's . . . interested in me."

Bryce laughed. "Of course he is. You're a knockout. But he's barking up the wrong tree, poor guy. I'm not worried about you. You can handle him. Cynthia reminds me of you, which is why I want to help her. Anyway, that's all I wanted to say. I'd better go." He turned.

"Wait." She caught his arm. "Are you involved with her?"

He shook his head. "I wish I felt that way about her, because she's cool, but I don't. We've talked about it. No chemistry for either of us." He shot her a quick grin. "Feel better?"

"Yes. Infinitely."

"Then I'm off. Don't follow me." He slipped into the crowd. His scent lingered for a few seconds and then was swept away as several women wearing strong perfume walked past.

As Giselle made her way back to Luke, her thoughts were jumbled. She'd been face-to-face with her brother and had been so distracted by the issues with Luke and Cynthia that she hadn't asked him the question that had brought her here. She still didn't know if he wanted to be the Landry pack alpha or not.

But she was reassured that he hadn't fallen in love with Cynthia. That was something to hold on to. Now she had to decide what to do about Luke.

Luke paced while he waited, although pacing wasn't easy in an area of high pedestrian traffic. He felt certain she'd caught a glimpse of her brother and thought she had a better chance of talking to him if she went after him alone. She could be right, but he wished she'd trusted him enough to say that.

Yeah, that was what bothered him more than her taking off without him. *He* might think they operated as a team when they were together, but it looked as if she didn't feel the same way.

It struck him that his life had been spread out in front of her, literally in the case of the photo gallery, but he knew very little about hers. Maybe she didn't trust him enough to tell him that, either. And that bothered him.

Before he had time to examine why that was, she appeared, walking toward him with that graceful stride he admired. Yeah, he still wanted her. He couldn't turn off his natural reaction, although he wished he could.

She held his gaze as she approached. "Thanks for waiting."

"You saw your brother, didn't you?"

"I talked to him, but—"

"What about Cynthia? Did you—"

"She wasn't there."

"What did he say?"

She hesitated, as if deciding what to tell him. "I asked if they were involved, and he said no. There's no chemistry."

Luke's tension eased a fraction. "That's good, but did you ask him if we could sit down and discuss this?"

"No. He didn't want to stay long. They must not feel the timing is right."

"Yet it seems he deliberately created an opportunity to talk with you. Why?"

"He thinks I'm a good influence on you."

"Which he obviously thinks I need." At first he was indignant, but that began to fade as he recalled that he'd basically told Giselle the same thing. He just didn't like Landry saying it. He sighed. "Well, he's right."

"I've decided to accept your invitation to stay in the penthouse in one of your guest rooms."

"You have?" Relief flooded through him. Until he'd resolved this issue with Cynthia, he needed Giselle nearby.

"I'll need my things."

He forced himself not to appear overly eager. "No problem. Jim will drive us down there so you can pick up your suitcase and check out." He wondered what Vaughn Cartwright would think of Giselle leaving his hotel.

She spoke as if reading his mind. "Vaughn will hear about it. Because I'm a family friend, his staff will report that I've checked out."

"Do you care?"

"Only to the extent that I don't want to be rude. He's been nice to me."

"So send him a text and explain that we're on the trail of your brother and my sister, and we need to be together for efficiency's sake."

Giselle pulled out her phone. "Would you repeat that? I liked the wording."

Luke went through the logical explanation again. "And thank him for his hospitality."

"Right." Her thumbs moved rhythmically as she completed the text. "Done."

"The town car is right over here." He gestured toward it. When Jim saw them coming, he got out and opened the back passenger door.

"Jim, this is Giselle Landry, a guest from San Francisco. Giselle, this is Jim Hicks. He drove my dad for about fifteen years, right, Jim?"

"About that." The burly chauffeur smiled at Giselle. "Nice to meet you, Ms. Landry."

Luke knew Jim had to be curious. Giselle was the first woman Luke had been seen with, other than his sister, since his dad died. But Jim was a professional and would never let his curiosity show. "We need to go to Illusions," Luke said, "to pick up Giselle's suitcase."

"Very good." Jim's gaze didn't flicker. He waited until they were both seated in the backseat and then he closed the door.

Luke settled back against the leather seat. "How did you know Bryce was close by, anyway?"

"Just a hunch."

He glanced over at her. "Pretty good hunch. Do you two have a mental telepathy hookup?"

"Sometimes."

"When Cynthia and I were younger, I used to think we had one. When she was two, she managed to sneak out to the pool and fell in when nobody was around to see her. But I got this panicky feeling and raced out there. She was already at the bottom."

Giselle's eyes widened in horror. "How awful!"

"It was awful." Luke would never forget that moment.

"I don't remember screaming for help or diving in. But I must have, because I do remember working on her once I got her out. I was only ten, but thank God we'd studied CPR in school. And help came, so I must have screamed pretty loud."

"Wow. Scary."

"It was. I watched her like a hawk for the rest of that summer, and the next summer she learned to swim, so I relaxed a little." And here he was, once again, revealing details of his life when he knew so little of hers. "Sorry. Ancient history."

"Vivid history, though, I'll bet. Were there other times you sensed she was in trouble?"

"A few." Actually, more than a few, but he wanted an exchange of information this time. "How about you? Did you and Bryce come to each other's rescue?"

"All the time when we were little. But as we got older, not so much."

He didn't know if she would have expanded on that or not because just then they arrived at Illusions. Jim parked under the portico.

Leaning forward, Luke spoke to Jim. "No need to get out, Jim. Giselle has to check out, but we shouldn't be long." He'd never walked into Illusions, and he was damned curious.

"Luke." Giselle laid a hand on his arm. "You can't come in with me."

"Why not? Can't a guest bring someone in?"

"No. Only registered guests are allowed through the front door. You're not registered."

"Not even into the lobby? I've never heard of something so ridiculous. Who stays here, the president of Iran?"

"No."

"I don't get it. We've hosted Tom Hanks and Lady Gaga, and neither of them required that level of security."

"It's the way the Cartwrights want it, I guess. But come up to the door with me and we'll see if you can step inside for a few minutes and then come right back out."

Luke thought about not going because he was ticked off, but in the end, curiosity won out. "Okay." He helped her out of the car and walked beside her to the double doors of the lobby.

Impressively muscled doormen in gray uniforms stood on either side of the entrance. They both smiled at Giselle. "Good evening, madam."

"Good evening. I was wondering if—"

"Your companion is not staying at the hotel, correct?" The doorman on the right eyed Luke with suspicion.

Luke wondered how in the hell the guy knew that. Was it written on his forehead?

"No, he's not," Giselle said. "But he's with me. I was wondering if he could step inside for a minute. I wanted him to see the lobby decor."

"I'm afraid not, madam." The doorman gazed at her stoically. "You know the rules."

"I know, but I thought a few minutes wouldn't be a problem."

"Sorry."

That was enough for Luke. He didn't go where he wasn't wanted. "That's okay, Giselle. I'll wait in the car."

She looked embarrassed. "But—"

"Seriously. It doesn't matter."

"Okay. I'll be very fast. I didn't bother to unpack, so I'll be out in no time."

"I'll be waiting." He walked back to the car and climbed in.

"Wouldn't let you go in, would they?" Jim said.

"Nope."

"I didn't think they would. I've seen plenty of folks get turned away from that door. Must be some really famous people staying there."

"I can't imagine who. Really famous people stay in hotels all along the Strip, and they don't keep you from walking into their lobbies."

Luke was just as glad to get Giselle out of there. The Cartwrights were paranoid about security, and paranoia was never a good thing to be around. She'd be better off at his place.

Then again, the restriction could be a marketing tool. Only those who paid the high price of a room were allowed to walk through the front door. Judging from the way Harrison Cartwright had decorated the Silver Crescent, this lobby would be similar in tone. Waterfalls and green plants, no doubt. The kind of atmosphere that Giselle preferred.

He thought about the penthouse, which had fresh flowers in vases, but not too many potted plants. None, actually. Now he wished that he had some, and maybe a water feature. But at least he didn't have to worry about whether his bedroom was too white. She'd never set foot in it.

Chapter 10

Giselle literally didn't have to do anything besides walk into her hotel room, quickly maneuver through video checkout, grab the handle of her rolling bag, and head for the elevator. After leaving Vaughn's office that afternoon, she'd been too intent on getting over to Howlin' at the Moon to take the time to unpack.

She was on the way down to the lobby when Vaughn called. The elevator was empty, so she answered.

"Giselle, are you sure you know what you're doing?"

"Not exactly, but I talked briefly with my brother a little while ago, and he would like to see this situation resolved between Luke and Cynthia. Bryce thinks my presence helps."

"Is Bryce serious about her?"

"Fortunately not. We can relax on that score."

"Then it seems as if the rest isn't your fight."

"True." Then she thought of something. "But while I'm there, maybe I'll think of some strategy that will help you get back the Moon and the playground."

"Good luck with that. I didn't find any give to Luke on that subject."

"But everyone has the ability to change." She believed Luke *was* changing, and after hearing the story of Cynthia's near drowning, Giselle sympathized more with his overprotectiveness.

"Just be careful. He's a Dalton."

Giselle couldn't help smiling at Vaughn's ominous tone when he said the name *Dalton*. "I know he is. I'll be careful. And I'll let you know what happens." The elevator slid to a stop. "I have to go. Oh, by the way, I met Mr. Thatcher tonight."

"Mr. Thatcher? Should I know who that is?"

"He's the Daltons' butler. Very English." She started to say more and changed her mind. She wasn't sure what was going on, and she certainly didn't want to cause a problem for Mr. Thatcher.

"Oh, yeah. Now I remember him. I always thought it was strange that he wanted to work for a human family. Benedict was fascinated by the idea, though. He used to like getting Mr. Thatcher's insights into human behavior, partly because of the accent, I think."

"His accent is cool. I felt a little like I was in some period drama."

"Just remember you're in enemy territory."

"I'll remember. Talk to you later, Vaughn." She disconnected the call and stepped into the lobby. Too bad Luke couldn't come in and see this.

The forest effect really was spectacular. Earlier today the woodsy atmosphere had been enhanced with chattering birds and dappled sunlight, but now moonlight filtered through the branches. The hoot of an owl blended with the sound of wind through the tops of the trees.

After their discussion about the lobby of the Silver Crescent, Luke might not appreciate having her gush over this one, especially when he wasn't allowed to see it. She'd always accepted the restrictions when it came to Weres and humans, but she couldn't imagine what could be wrong with letting him step inside the lobby of Illusions for five minutes. It wasn't as if guests would be shifting in the middle of the lobby or strolling through it in werewolf form.

But she supposed having a Were hotel and casino in the middle of Las Vegas was an unusual security challenge. The resorts in Washington State and Denver were far less accessible. This hotel had a front door that was steps away from a bustling street full of humans. Obviously the Cartwrights thought limiting access was the only way to maintain secrecy.

A valet took her suitcase and rolled it out the door.

"I'm in that town car." She gestured to it as she pulled tip money out of her jeans pocket. Whenever she rode a motorcycle, which was often, she liked to use her pockets so she didn't have to carry a purse.

The valet opened the back door of the car and accepted her tip before putting her suitcase in the trunk. As she scooted in, she noticed that Luke had opened the envelope the little girl had given him and was looking at the picture inside. The light in the Illusions portico was bright enough to read a book.

She scooted onto the seat. "Can I see?"

He turned the picture toward her as the car pulled into traffic. "This is one of my favorites. She was a water sprite, and the costume was made of this flowing blue-green stuff. She was six."

"The costume's beautiful." But what Giselle noticed

most was the brilliant, gap-toothed smile. "She looks really happy."

"I'm sure she was. She loved getting dressed up and dancing for an audience. She was never scared."

"A born performer."

"She is. But this was a sideline, something she did after going to school. It wasn't her whole life. I can't believe she'd be happy if she had nothing else."

She thought Cynthia needed to find that out for herself. The longer Luke stood in her way, the more she'd be convinced that dancing was exactly what she wanted.

"You don't agree with me."

"Actually, I don't disagree. You could be right that she's glamorized this life and has no realistic idea of how she'd feel if she lived it."

Luke turned to her. "Then help me get her to see that!"

She gazed into his eyes as the lights from the Strip flowed past, painting their faces in every color of the rainbow. "I don't think that's possible right now. I think she can only find that out if she tries it."

"Sure it is. She won't listen to me because I'm her overbearing big brother and she thinks I don't understand. But you don't have a vested interest like I do."

"Not specifically, but in a general sense, I'm invested in how this turns out for her. She's an adult woman who deserves to make her own choices, wrong-headed though they might be."

"So I'm supposed to stand by and let that happen?"

"Yes, you are." She turned to him. "In reality, she shouldn't have to coax you into agreeing with her, although that's what she's attempting to do with these riddles and tricks. She should just do it. But she loves you and doesn't want to cause a rift."

He groaned. "I don't want a rift, either."

Hearing the pain in his voice caused her to speak more gently. "Did you open the envelope you got at the Bellagio?"

"Not yet. Left it in the suite. There's only so much of this I can take at one time. The pictures are bringing up all kinds of memories, times when the family was all together. Her recital nights were special times. I — " His cell phone chimed. "I'd better get that."

"Yes, you'd better." While he was checking his phone, she took hers out and sent a text to Bryce. *Stop the pranks. We all need to sit down and talk this out.* She sent it off with no expectations, but a little hope.

Luke put away his phone, too. "That was Mr. Thatcher. He says we have a little issue in the kitchen I need to handle, but while I do that, he'll escort you up to the suite."

"Perfect." She could use this chance to get better acquainted with the mysterious Mr. Thatcher.

Jim pulled the town car smoothly into an underground garage and parked near an elevator. No sooner had Jim taken Giselle's suitcase out of the trunk than Mr. Thatcher stepped out of the elevator.

"I'll take that, my good man." Mr. Thatcher snapped the handle into place and gestured Giselle toward the elevator.

Luke thanked his chauffeur and came over to join them. "So what's going on in the kitchen?"

"Some dispute over hours, I believe." Mr. Thatcher frowned in obvious disapproval as he followed them into the elevator and pulled the bag in after him. "Apparently they were ready to start brawling in the midst of hot kettles and sharp knives. Dangerous, not to mention unseemly."

Luke sighed as he punched the button for the first floor. "My dad used to settle these things by telling everyone a joke."

"I hope you don't feel you have to do that, sir."

"I would if I could, but that's not my style."

"Then you should handle it in your own way."

"Thanks, Mr. Thatcher." Luke handed the envelope with the picture to Giselle as the elevator stopped on the first floor. "If you wouldn't mind taking that upstairs, I'd appreciate it."

"Of course."

"I shouldn't be long." He stepped out, turning back with a smile. "Mr. Thatcher will get you settled into your room."

"That I will."

The doors closed again, and Giselle was alone with Mr. Thatcher as the elevator traveled forty floors upward. She was trying to decide how to broach the subject of his being a werewolf when he saved her the trouble.

"This is fortuitous, Miss Landry. I was hoping I'd have a chance to talk with you."

"Likewise, Mr. Thatcher. Your circumstances are intriguing."

He nodded. "Just so. I knew the moment I walked into the penthouse and found you there that you'd wonder what was going on."

"I've never heard of a Were working as a household servant for humans. How did that happen?"

"A combination of things. I'm devoted to the Thatcher

pack in Hertfordshire. I go there for a month every year."

"I'm sure that's a nice break for you."

"It is, but this is home now. I've been drawn to humans ever since I can remember. They fascinate me, and the best way to satisfy my curiosity is to work intimately with them, but I couldn't do that in England. My pack wouldn't have understood. They'd have considered it inappropriate."

"So you put an ocean between you and them so that you could live as you wanted to."

"Precisely." He cleared his throat. "I had to begin by using my werewolf connections, and I met Harrison Cartwright when he was touring England. We talked, and he turned out to be an open-minded alpha who was willing to help set me up with a human family. At the time, he was friends with the Daltons and knew they'd suit me perfectly. Which they have."

"But then Harrison gambled away the Silver Crescent."

"Yes, and what a sad day that was for all of us. I worried that Mr. Cartwright would consider me disloyal for staying with the Dalton family, but by then they were *my* family. I talked with him about it, and he understood completely. He told me not to worry about it."

The elevator reached the fortieth floor and the doors opened again.

"Ah, here we are." Mr. Thatcher swept his arm toward the double doors of the entry. "After you, madam."

She preceded him out of the elevator, yet he still managed to hurry around and open the door for her. Once they were both inside the suite, she turned back to him. "So then you moved into the Silver Crescent with the

Daltons, a human family in a former werewolf hotel. That must have seemed strange."

"Very strange at first, but I adjusted. And I was closer to the Moon, which was nice. But I missed those days when everyone got along. I especially missed chatting with Benedict Cartwright."

"Vaughn told me that you and Benedict were friends. What did you think when Luke set up the match with him?"

Mr. Thatcher shook his head. "I was horrified, of course. I did what I could to discourage Luke from following that course of action, but I'm the butler. I'm not his father, although sometimes it feels that way, especially now that his actual father is gone."

"And the werewolf playground is unavailable to you and everyone else."

"Yes. What a tragedy. But fortunately, Benedict came to me about that. Luke had the locks changed at the Moon, which one would expect, but I have a key, just as I have keys to everything else around here."

"But I thought the workers blocked off the entrance to the playground?"

"They modified it so that all anyone sees is a solid wall at the end of the hallway where there used to be a door. In actuality, it's a panel controlled by a remote device. I have the key to the establishment, and Benedict has the device. He plans for us to check on the playground at various intervals."

Giselle gazed at him and thought of the courage he was showing by agreeing to such an arrangement. "You can't ever get caught doing that."

"I'm well aware of the risks to us all. And although I

wrestle with my disloyalty to Luke, I can't allow the playground to fall into ruin." He brightened. "In effect, I'm protecting Luke's property by watching over that installation. If problems occurred down there, the Moon would be in jeopardy."

"Don't get me wrong. I'm glad you and Benedict are planning to check on the playground." She thought about the thoroughness with which the butler did his job. "I have no doubt you'll be extremely careful."

"More than you can imagine, madam. May I show you to your room?"

"That would be lovely." She followed him down the same hallway where Luke had taken her to view the photo gallery, but he continued past that door on the right and wheeled her suitcase into a room on the left. "I trust this will do."

She stepped into a spacious bedroom. Although the window looked out on Vegas, the atmosphere was that of a seaside resort. White furniture set against warm beige walls gave a crisp feel to the room. Blues and greens dominated the color scheme for the bed linens, the curtains, and the upholstered reading chair in one corner. Framed beach scenes decorated the walls.

She turned to him with a smile. "It's very nice, Mr. Thatcher."

"There's an attached bath through that door. I believe you'll find everything you need, but if not, this will summon me in no time." He pointed to an intercom on the wall beside the door.

"Excellent. Thank you so much."

"Then I'll take my leave." He started out the door, but turned back. "This is an impertinent question, and you certainly don't have to answer, but are you and your brother aligned with the faction that encourages Weres mating with humans?"

"I can't speak for my brother, but I'm not."

Mr. Thatcher cleared his throat. "I only mention this because Luke and Cynthia are like my own offspring, and I want the best for them. I'd always assumed they'd end up with human mates. But now Cynthia has run off with your brother and you're here with Luke."

"Let me set your mind at ease, Mr. Thatcher. I have no intention of getting involved with Luke. I'm here as an intermediary between him and his sister. As for my brother, I spoke with him today. He and Cynthia are good friends, but that's it. He's the one who asked me if I'd continue to advocate for Cynthia's dancing ambitions, so here I am." She spread her arms. "The resident advocate."

Amusement glinted in his eyes. "I'm grateful to you for that. I'm most distressed when Luke and Cynthia are at odds."

"No one likes to see their children fight."

"Precisely."

"I can't guarantee results on that score, but you can stop worrying that either of them will end up mating with a Were."

"I'm not sure that *worry* is the correct word," he said. "I've come to respect many things about humans."

That's when she realized she might have jumped to conclusions about him. "How do you stand on the Were-human issue, Mr. Thatcher?"

"That discussion would take far too long, madam. It's time I left you to get settled in."

"But we'll talk again?"

"I'm counting on it."

"Friends?"

"More than that. Allies."

"Thank you, Mr. Thatcher." She didn't know how this drama would play out, but having Mr. Thatcher as an ally was a bonus she hadn't expected.

Chapter 11

Luke had convinced himself that he didn't mind straightening out personnel issues when he was handy. Dalton Industries had a personnel manager with regular office hours, but the staff at the Silver Crescent had become used to his dad being available for any unexpected after-hours problems. Luke had done his best to uphold that tradition.

As he stood in the hotel kitchen, where tempers steamed along with the giant kettles of food, he wondered if he should follow his instincts and delegate late-night staff disagreements to someone else. Just because his father had been something of a micromanager didn't mean he had to keep that up. He'd copied Angus's style because it had seemed like the easiest way to make the transition, and maybe it was time for some things to change.

His father hadn't been dealing with Cynthia in full rebellion mode. She'd been a daddy's girl who'd gone along with his wishes. And his father had been lucky enough to have a wife who'd adored him and smoothed his path whenever possible.

Luke wasn't in that position. Beginning tomorrow,

he'd make some alterations to the chain of command. Someone else would be called in for disputes like this instead of him. For now, though, he was it.

A simple mistake had turned into World War III, with two waiters squaring off in the kitchen, fists raised and insults flying. Luke had moved between them. Fortunately, they both decided not to hit the CEO.

Luke hadn't been positive they would come to that conclusion, and he was relieved when they backed off, muttering about the unfairness of it all. He'd rather not go upstairs with a shiner. Sorting through the problem took more time than he wanted to give it and only solidified his decision to put someone else in charge of after-hours staff issues.

He'd find a person with conflict-management skills because he couldn't afford to have his waiters brawling in the kitchen. They could make a hell of a mess in there.

After sending both waiters home, he walked to the elevator and used his card key to access the button for the penthouse. As the wood-paneled elevator rose, so did his spirits. He took off his jacket and hooked it over his shoulder.

He was grateful to Giselle for agreeing to hang out with him in the penthouse while he waited for Cynthia's next move. He'd hate to think of the squirrel cage his mind would become without her steadying influence. Yes, she called him on his behavior sometimes, and he didn't always appreciate that, but she was helping him see Cynthia in a different light. Apparently he needed to.

He found Giselle in the kitchen looking through cupboards.

She turned, obviously hearing him come in. "Do you suppose there's any tea here?"

"I'm sure there is." He walked over to the drawer where his mother had kept her stash and opened it. Colorful tins of loose tea and boxes of tea bags filled the drawer. "Take your pick."

"Awesome. Thanks."

"There's one of those electric kettles in a cupboard, too." He opened a few cabinets and located it. "My mother loves tea. Or she used to. I can't say if she still does."

"Well, I do, so this is great." She glanced at him. "Want a cup?"

"No, thanks. I'm strictly a coffee guy. Think I'll make some." As they moved around the kitchen together, he had the oddest feeling of domesticity. It seemed perfectly natural for them to be fixing their respective beverages together, as if they'd done it hundreds of times before.

"How did the issue in the kitchen turn out?"

He almost laughed. The question sounded a lot like, "How was your day?" But he decided not to make a point of their cozy little setup. He kind of liked this feeling and didn't want to ruin it.

"It's handled for now," he said. "I need to hire somebody to take care of these after-hours problems. My dad used to say he was right here so he might as well deal with it, but he enjoyed wading into those issues. I don't."

"Don't blame you." While the water heated in the electric teakettle, she contemplated the drawerful of tea choices. "I like tea, but even I don't have a supply like this."

"My dad was always coming home with something new for her to try. He got a kick out of surprising her with some exotic new blend. After he died, she stopped drinking it. I hope she's started again. I hate to think she's given up everything that reminds her of him."

"Maybe I'll try this." She picked up a tin of loose tea. Then she paused. "Am I stirring up sad memories for you?"

He turned on the coffeemaker and looked at her standing beside the tea drawer. His mother used to stand there debating just like that. "Nope. I'm happy that someone appreciates the selection the way she used to." He snapped his fingers as he remembered what else was in the cupboard. "You'll need a teapot and a tea strainer of some kind."

"I will, but are you *sure* I'm not trampling in your memory garden by doing this?"

"If anything, you're pulling up the weeds. This stuff needs to be used." He opened a cupboard above the counter, where several teapots were lined up. Most had elaborately painted designs of flowers or landscapes.

But he took down his mother's favorite, a bright yellow one that held about two cups' worth. "This might not be the prettiest of the bunch, but she loved it because of the strainer inside." He handed it to Giselle.

She took it from him carefully, almost reverently. "Thank you."

"The cupboard next to that has all kinds of mugs and teacups. Help yourself." If anyone had told him he'd be having a great time helping a woman make tea in what used to be his mother's kitchen, he would have laughed. Sharing a bottle of champagne in the bedroom was more his style.

But at the moment, he wouldn't change a thing. In spite of his worry about Cynthia, he felt relaxed and happy for the first time in . . . well, since December twenty-fifth, to be exact.

"Did Mr. Thatcher put you in the beach room?"

"He did." She finished measuring the tea into the pot, snapped the lid back on the tin, and returned it to the drawer. "It's very pretty."

"It used to be Cynthia's, but when she moved out, my mom redecorated."

Giselle poured hot water into the pot. "What did it look like before? Or do I even have to ask?"

"Probably not."

"Dance themed?" She glanced at the clock on the stove, no doubt to time her tea.

"Yep. Posters of famous dancers, collages of programs and ticket stubs from shows she'd seen. The color scheme was dramatic—red, black, and silver." He smiled, remembering how she'd had to fight for those colors. No wonder she'd thought his white bedroom was boring.

Giselle leaned against the counter. "Meanwhile, what were you up to?"

He shrugged. "The usual. I got a degree in business, came home, and started helping my dad. Not very interesting."

"No missteps? No rebellious behavior?"

"I wouldn't say that. I had my share of wild nights with my buddies. Made some insensitive mistakes with the women I dated." He lobbed a question in her direction to see if she'd give him a decent answer. "How about you?"

"Not very fascinating, I'm afraid. I majored in finance so I could eventually become the CFO of the family business." She smiled. "I've had a few wild nights with my buddies, too."

"And then you found Mr. Right?"

She blinked. "What makes you say that?"

"Maybe I was imagining it, but a few times I thought

you looked at me as if you might be sort of interested. Then you seemed to catch yourself, as if you couldn't go there. I assumed there's someone back home."

"Oh." She met his gaze, but she didn't confirm or deny.

He couldn't push for the information, either. She'd agreed to this arrangement with the understanding there would be none of that. "Never mind," he said. "Shouldn't have brought it up."

"No, you shouldn't have."

"I'm sorry." He let out a breath. They needed a change of venue, and the small kitchen table and chairs seemed too cozy. "Let's take our tea and coffee into the living room and talk about something else. I like having you here, and I don't want to mess that up."

"Neither do I," she said gently. "I'm enjoying being here."

"You are? Really? You're not just tolerating the situation, and me, for your brother's sake?"

"No, I'm not. Now that I know you a little better, I understand why you feel so protective toward your sister. I'm not condoning the overprotective part, but I really do see how this whole situation developed." She checked the time again and picked up the teapot.

"Thanks, I think."

"Besides that, you've shown remarkable good humor with the water tricks. I've seen firsthand how ticked off someone can get over those pranks, and you're letting it roll off your back. That's great." She finished pouring her tea.

"That sounded like an actual compliment."

"It was."

"On that positive note, I'll pour myself a cup of coffee and we can toast our developing friendship."

She laughed. "Sure, we can do that. Let's move to the living room. I'm hoping you'll open that other envelope. If Cynthia went to that much trouble, we need to look at what's inside."

"You're right." And he would open it, now that she was here. The psychic punch would be easier to handle with Giselle around.

As they went into the living room, Giselle thought Luke seemed to be buying her apparent lack of interest in him, and she was grateful for that. He thought she had somebody back home, and she was willing to let him make that assumption, too. Just so he didn't guess the truth, that she was more drawn to him with every second that passed.

Sure, he was a gorgeous man. She'd noticed that right off the bat. But she'd thought his overprotective behavior toward his sister would keep her from being the least bit attracted to this off-limits human male. Now, however, she had a clearer picture of why he was that way.

He hadn't said that his parents had been so absorbed in each other that they hadn't always known what their kids were up to. Yet she had the strong feeling that might have been the case. Even if it hadn't been, a psychic connection with his sister made him superconscious of when she might be in danger. Maybe the link wasn't as strong now that they were both adults, but he'd maintained the habit of watchfulness.

He did that not because he was a controlling jerk, which she'd first supposed, but because he'd considered it his job ever since he'd fished her out of the swimming pool and saved her life. He might doubt that anyone else cared as much as he did. That was touching, although he had to realize that she now cared about herself, which meant he could ease up on his constant watchfulness.

She thought he might be getting there. His struggle to evolve had captured her, too. He was beginning to see that if he didn't, he'd lose his relationship with his sister, and she was the most important person in the world to him. Judging from her concerted effort to make him accept her new plan, the feeling was mutual.

So now, as Giselle lowered herself to the plump cushions of the sectional, being careful not to spill her mug of tea, she looked across at the guy sitting a few feet away and saw a loving, caring man. When he'd walked into the kitchen earlier, her heart had leaped with pleasure to see him. He'd looked a little mussed, a little tired. She fought the urge to go over and wrap her arms around him.

He set his mug on the coffee table and picked up the envelope lying there. "So you want to see what's in here?"

"I do."

He nudged open the flap. "Considering what song the gondolier sang to us, I have a good idea which picture this is. She probably intended for me to see it before we went on that ride. A preview of what was to come." He pulled it out. "Yep."

"What is it?"

He handed her the eight-by-ten. "That's what she wore for her 'I Hope You Dance' solo when she was a freshman in high school."

Giselle gazed at the golden-haired young woman who was almost too beautiful to be real. She was dressed in a knee-length ballet gown that complemented her slender, just-beginning-to-bloom figure.

"There's something else in here." He pulled out what looked like a program. "Oh, man. She took this out of her collection of souvenirs. I can't believe she risked giving it to some stranger." He unfolded the program.

Giselle gazed at him and wondered if he even remembered she was in the room. He seemed transported to another place, another time.

"She had everyone in her dance class autograph this, and the teacher, of course," he said. "And then . . ." He paused and took a shaky breath. "She asked my parents and me to sign it. She said she couldn't have danced the solo without our support." He stared at the program for a moment longer, and then laid it on the coffee table. His hand trembled slightly when he did that. "Excuse me. I'll be back in a minute."

Giselle sat cradling her tea mug and wondering what to do. Obviously, he was overcome by emotion and didn't want her to see that. If she were smart, she'd stay right where she was until he composed himself and returned to the living room.

Obviously, she wasn't all that smart. She set down her tea and stood. She'd been the one who'd urged him to open that envelope. He shouldn't have to deal with the consequences by himself.

He'd gone through a door that she assumed led to his bedroom. The room was dim, but she saw him, his hands braced against a low dresser. Although he made no sound, his shoulders quivered.

Walking over to him, she placed her hand on his back.

He jerked as if she'd laid a hot iron there. His choked response was definite. "No."

"Luke."

"Go."

"I want to help."

He turned, and the glow from the lights of Vegas revealed the tears glistening on his cheeks. "They told me I needed to cry," he said in a thick voice. "I couldn't. Until now."

"Then go ahead." She held out her arms. "Go ahead and cry."

With a groan, he gathered her close. His big body shook, and he held her so tight that she had trouble breathing. But that was okay. Crooning words of comfort, she stroked his silky hair. No one should be alone when they mourned the loss of all they'd held dear. She was here, and there was nowhere else in the world she wanted to be.

Chapter 12

Luke knew he should be embarrassed for losing control, but holding Giselle felt so damned good that he was willing to deal with the embarrassment. And as his grief eased, he felt cleansed, as if he'd stepped out of a clear mountain waterfall into a bright ray of sunshine. What a gift she'd given him.

He relaxed against her, loving her combination of strength and softness. "Thank you."

"You're welcome." She continued to comb her fingers through his hair. "I think you needed that."

"Guess so." He drew in a breath. "I'm okay now."

"You're sure?" She eased back to gaze up at him.

The light wasn't great, but he could see the shine of her glorious eyes and the outline of her lush mouth. "Yeah." He should release her and step back, but he kept looking at her mouth.

Then the most amazing thing happened. She braced her hands on his shoulders, stood on tiptoe, and pressed that velvet mouth against his.

For a moment he stood there in shock, unable to register that *she* had kissed *him*. What's more, she wasn't being very quick about it, either. She stayed right there and increased the pressure.

What he'd thought would be a fast, over-before-it-started brush of lips was turning into something quite different. The tip of her tongue slid over his mouth. His pulse went crazy.

Still, he didn't believe it. He lifted his mouth a fraction away from hers. "Giselle?"

"Don't say anything. Just kiss me back."

"What about Mr. Right?"

"He doesn't exist."

That was all he needed to know. He settled his mouth over hers. He'd suspected that he'd like kissing her. He hadn't known that he'd love it. He could devote hours to kissing Giselle. Her lips fit against his with the kind of perfection he'd only dreamed of.

He shifted his angle to see if it would lessen the pleasure. Nope, perfect that way, too. And this way, and oh, God, when she began to heat up, and their tongues were involved, he lost all sense of time and place. Kissing was supposed to be a prelude to more intimate activities, wasn't it? Yet he couldn't imagine what could be more intimate than this—breath linked with breath, mouths seeking and finding, soft moans so alike that he was no longer sure which of them had created the sound. He was so absorbed by the wonder of her kiss that he didn't realize she'd unbuttoned his shirt until her palms flattened against his bare chest.

Ah, that felt good. She stroked him and toyed with his nipples as she continued to devastate him with her hot mouth. Pressure built in his groin, and her breathing grew as erratic as his.

Things became a little crazy after that. She seemed as eager as he was to get rid of their clothes. He couldn't remember ever finding himself naked and rolling around on top of his bed that fast, but there they were, and she seemed to want him as desperately as he wanted her.

But he wasn't so far gone that he forgot about condoms. Leaning over her, he reached for the handle on the bedside table drawer.

"You don't need those."

"Yes, I do."

"You don't. I can't get pregnant, and there's zero chance of disease."

Bracing himself on his forearm, he gazed down at her. "That's the kind of speech an irresponsible guy makes because he doesn't want to use a condom."

"Use one if it makes you feel better, but I'm telling you, you don't need it."

He quickly calculated why she'd say that. If she couldn't have children, that was the obvious answer to the pregnancy issue. And if she claimed to be healthy, he was inclined to believe her.

Who was he to argue when he had a warm, moist, and exceedingly willing woman in his bed? And he intended to enjoy every second of this experience. "Thank you for being here," he murmured as he lowered his mouth to hers.

Her soft moan of pleasure and the arch of her body against his filled him with wonder. She felt so damned *right* in his arms. He knew exactly what to do, how to touch her, how to stroke her.

When he pressed his mouth to her soft skin, she gasped out his name. He loved hearing her say it, loved having her acknowledge who was caressing her and making her pant and beg for more.

"Please, Luke . . . please!"

"Yes. God, yes." With a groan of ecstasy, he sank deep and thanked whatever twist of fate had brought him Giselle Landry in his hour of need.

She rose to meet him and gave him as good as she got. This wasn't going to be long and languorous. She urged him to be wild, and he didn't need much urging. He'd been sweeping emotions under the rug for months, and now they came pouring out.

They rocked that king-sized bed. As they did, he took a moment to celebrate the wonders of making love to a woman without wearing a condom. Being a responsible man in an enlightened age, he'd never done that before. And he'd had no idea. No. Idea.

They were so in tune with each other that they even came at the same time. He'd tried to orchestrate that with other women and had failed to do so. But with Giselle, it happened naturally, as if that was the way things were meant to be.

They lay in the semidarkness holding each other, and he wondered if that would be it. This might have been a gimme on her part because she'd felt sorry for him. If so, he'd take it and be glad. She'd started them in this new direction, and he'd take his cues from her.

She rubbed his back and arched against him. "That was terrific."

"Yes, and you deserve the credit. I would never have—"

"I know. I was dead set against this, but . . . you're worth it, Luke."

That comment sounded slightly ominous, but he chuckled, as if she'd cracked a joke. "I hope you're not about to get in trouble. Will someone come after us?"

"No. It's a personal thing. Don't worry about it."

"As mellow as I feel right now, I'm not sure I could worry about anything."

Well, she'd done it, and the world had not come to an end. Giselle had expected to feel guilty afterward, but, like Luke, she was too mellow to work up a decent case of guilt. If she wanted to drum up excuses for herself, she could always blame Luke's obvious grief.

But that wouldn't be fair. She'd been edging toward this ever since she'd met him. Something about him—his quick grin, his blue eyes, his devotion to his sister, his willingness to take a joke—had told her that Luke Dalton was her Waterloo.

Ha. That was funny, in view of the water-related pranks going on. Bryce would get a kick out of that if she ever told him, which she wouldn't. She'd done this thing—had sex with a human male—but that didn't mean she'd take any more steps down that dangerous path.

Well, she needed to modify that statement. Luke would be her one-and-only adventure in human sexuality. But as long as she'd gone this far, she couldn't see wasting the chance to explore the issue for as long as they had time to do that. Maybe she could consider it research. How could she counsel female Weres to avoid sex with humans if she had no knowledge of the temptations involved?

With those thoughts in mind, she lifted her head and murmured in Luke's ear, "Can we do that again?"

He lifted his head and gazed down at her. "Oh, thank God. I thought maybe you felt sorry for me, and you'd think one time was enough to express your sympathy."

She started to laugh and couldn't seem to stop. "Sorry." She tried to catch her breath. "But that's hysterical. FYI, that's not normally how I express my sympathy for someone's loss. Ordinarily I send a card."

He snorted. Then he laughed. Before long they had to break apart because they were both laughing so hard they needed extra room to roll around.

Finally, gasping, they lay on their backs on his bed.

"The answer to your question," he said, "is yes, we most definitely can do this again. But I'm warning you, once we turn on the lights, you'll see that this is a very white bedroom."

"So?"

"No, I mean *everything* is white. The walls, the curtains, the sheets, the comforter—everything."

"Why?"

"Because it was the easiest way to match everything."

"Oh." She was silent for a minute. "You have a ton of money, right?"

"I suppose."

"So why didn't you hire an interior decorator to fix up your bedroom so it wasn't all white?"

He sighed. "You're not the first person to ask me that, but you're the first person I'll answer honestly."

"Oh, good. I love secrets."

"Was that sarcasm?"

"No! I do really like them! Please tell me, Luke. I promise I won't laugh."

"Oh, that's reassuring. You're expecting you might want to laugh, aren't you?"

"Sort of."

"All right. I didn't hire an interior decorator because this is my bedroom, the most intimate place in the house, and I figured that the person who chose the color scheme should be me."

"A decorator would let you choose."

"Yeah, but they'd be putting in their two cents' worth. I wanted it to be all my idea."

"So it could reflect your personality?"

"In a way."

"So your personality is plain vanilla?"

"I *knew* I shouldn't tell you."

She rolled to face him. "Yes, you should, because I won't breathe a word of that to anyone. Trust me. I know how to keep a secret."

He reached over and touched her cheek. "I'll bet you do. I'll bet you plan to keep what happened here a secret."

"I do, and I'd appreciate it if you would, too."

"I will, Giselle. But that answers another question I had running around in my brain. Looks like what happens in Vegas stays in Vegas."

"It's for the best, Luke."

"And you swear that you don't have some guy waiting for you back in 'Frisco? You can tell me if you do. I won't judge."

"I don't." She held his hand against her cheek. "You don't know me well enough yet if you'd even ask that."

"I'm sure I don't. And once you leave, I probably still won't. But whatever happens, I will be forever grateful that you're here with me tonight."

"You're welcome." She caught his hand and placed a kiss in his palm. "So you never really grieved for your father?"

"Stupid, isn't it? We're given so many opportunities. At the deathbed, at the viewing, at the funeral, at the graveside, after the funeral. But all those occasions were so public. I'm a macho guy. I'm not supposed to start bawling in front of all my friends and family."

"I'm honored that you trusted me enough, then."

"You didn't give me much choice. I tried to escape, but you came after me. I'm so glad you did."

"So I could deliver my sympathy card."

"Exactly."

He tried to remember if he'd ever lain in the dark talking to a woman this way. He couldn't remember a single instance. He'd heard people rave on about soul mates and had never believed in the idea. But he'd never met someone like Giselle, either, a woman he'd felt at home with from the beginning, despite some of the prickly comments she'd made to him. She was so easy to get along with that he was considering turning on the light and letting her see his white bedroom, even though she'd already made fun of it.

But lying in the dark and talking was fun, too. They had their own private world right now, where no one besides them knew that a special connection had taken place. He gave her hand a squeeze. "Tell me what you were like as a little girl."

"Bossy."

"I can believe that."

She kicked him, but her bare feet tickled more than hurt.

"Tell me more." He admitted to being fascinated by the subject of Giselle, maybe because she hadn't given him much to go on. "Did you have pigtails? Did you play with dolls?"

"Yes on the pigtails, no on the dolls. I had a brother

just two years older, and I thought he and his friends were so cool that I tagged after them. We built forts and ran races and staged elaborate battles."

"Sounds like fun. Cynthia was eight years younger, so we never really played together. She was like . . . a little doll." As he said that, he realized how it sounded. "Don't jump on that, Giselle. Don't read too much into it."

"How can I help it? That statement illustrates the problem perfectly. You have to stop thinking of her as your doll-like little sister and think of her as an adult who is capable of taking care of herself."

"I'm trying."

"I know." She reached out and brushed his hair back from his forehead. "I see that you are, and that's fantastic."

He lay there quietly and let her comb her fingers through his hair again. He couldn't believe how much he loved having her do that. "So you were a rough-and-tumble kind of kid who liked to build forts and stage battles, right?"

"That's right."

"Did you ever play in the mud?"

"All the time. San Francisco has a moist climate. There's always some mud around somewhere."

"So you like the concept, then?"

She stopped combing his hair. "I did, when I was a kid. I can't say I go out and roll around in it now that I'm an adult. Is there a point to this conversation?"

"There is." The more he thought about it, the more he liked it. "It's time to turn on the lights and let you see what sort of all-white environment you've stumbled into."

"If you insist."

"I do. Cover your eyes." Reaching over her, he turned

on the bedside table lamp nearest to him. One thing he hadn't counted on with his all-white color scheme—white reflected light like crazy. There was a reason they used it in operating rooms. It made everything so much brighter.

In a bedroom, though, where he wouldn't be doing surgery, it could be a mistake. He was beginning to realize that, but as long as he had the white going on, he might as well find a way to exploit it.

Giselle continued to hold her hand over her eyes. "Can I look now?"

"You can, but try not to be blinded."

She uncovered her eyes slowly and gazed around the room. "You weren't kidding, Luke. This is *white*."

"Technically, it's called linen, but I won't quibble. It's very white. Too white. I realize that now. Everything has to go."

"No, it doesn't! Keep the white comforter and put on different sheets. Leave those gorgeous pictures on the walls, but paint the walls a different color. White's a perfectly fine choice in moderation."

"Maybe, but are we agreed that the white sheets are history?"

"That would be the least expensive change to make."

"Then, before they go, I want to give those white sheets a walk on the wild side. And since you once used to love playing in the mud, I'm hoping you'll play along."

"I hope you're not planning to bring a vat of mud into the penthouse, Luke."

"No. Mud is for kids. Grown-ups play with chocolate mousse."

Chapter 13

Giselle was semihorrified when Luke announced his plan. But sure enough, he mounted an expedition into the kitchen and retrieved the two pieces of cake from the refrigerator, where Mr. Thatcher had tucked them away.

Once Luke had their cake, each on a serving plate, he announced his intention to eat the cake in bed. He suggested they'd have more fun if they used their bodies as serving platters.

"No way!" She tried to take the plates away from him. "If you're hungry for cake, we'll eat it in the living room."

"Nope." He held the plates over his head. "It's my bed and my sheets. If I want to eat chocolate cake in here, I will."

"And you accused my brother of not acting his age! Seriously, even if you try to be careful, you'll ruin these sheets."

"I have no intention of being careful." He started toward the bedroom with the plates. "But I have every intention of licking chocolate off your—"

"Luke, don't do this. You're about to make a huge mess."

"No, *we* are. Unless you're not coming. Oh, but I think you will come. Many times. Chocolate is an aphrodisiac. Did you know that?" He continued walking toward his bedroom. "Not that I need an aphrodisiac with you around. I'm getting hard again. That's good, though, because then you'll have an easier time putting chocolate on it."

"You're incorrigible." But she followed him, despite her misgivings. She was also laughing, which wasn't helpful. And when she pictured him smearing chocolate over her body and licking it off, her resolve slipped another notch.

He stood in the bedroom on his white carpet, holding the plates and gazing at her. "You look good naked, but you'll look even better in chocolate."

"I have an idea. Let's keep the plan but move the venue into the bathroom. We can lie in your Jacuzzi tub without any water, do this chocolate body paint thing, and shower off afterward."

"Sounds sensible."

"Good. Then let's do that." She started toward the double doors into his large bathroom.

"I don't want to be sensible. The white sheets are history, anyway. Let's mess them up." There was a stubborn light in his blue eyes.

She began to understand what was behind his insistence. Like her brother, he was expected to shoulder a huge amount of responsibility. Unlike her brother, he didn't have the luxury of running away. His father had died, and he was the only one who could step in and take over.

Perhaps ruining a set of high-thread-count sheets was exactly what Luke needed to blow off a little steam. As rebellions went, it wasn't particularly destructive. And as he'd pointed out, he was going to get rid of the sheets anyway.

She also liked thinking that she'd help create a once-in-a-lifetime experience for him. Chances were slim he'd ever buy white sheets again, let alone defy common sense by playing chocolate games on them. This night would be one for the record books. Although reason told her they had no future, her feelings for him were strong enough that she didn't want him to forget her.

"Okay, I'm in," she said.

"Excellent." His grin was triumphant. "Then I can put these down without worrying that you'll snatch them away." He walked over and set the plates on a low dresser.

"But can we at least take the white comforter off first?"

"I dunno." Arms folded, he surveyed the bed, which looked like a giant marshmallow. "I doubt that I'll keep that, either, so why save it from its fate?"

"Let's say you decided to buy black satin sheets. A white comforter on top of that would be very sexy and sophisticated."

"Hm."

"Come on, Luke. Don't ruin that beautiful goose-down comforter."

"How'd you know it was goose down?"

"I can sm—" She caught herself. "Anybody could tell it is. It's obvious."

"That's not what you started to say." He uncrossed his arms and walked over to her, his expression curious.

"You started to say you could smell it. But it's supposed to be supersanitized goose down. It shouldn't smell any different from the polyester filling in other comforters."

Well, damn. This was what she got for jumping into an intimate relationship with a human. She couldn't say the first thing that popped into her head the way she might with a werewolf lover. The werewolf lover wouldn't have asked the question, though. He would have been able to smell the difference, too.

"You've already told me you have better-than-average hearing," Luke said. "Do you have a better-than-average nose, too?"

"Apparently." She had to see this through. "But I tend to freak people out if they know that, so I try not to let on."

Luke smiled. "But you let down your guard with me." He reached for her and drew her into his arms. "I'm flattered. But now I wonder if I should shower before we take this evening any further."

"No!" Whoops, that was a little too emphatic. "I mean, please don't. I like the way you smell." She more than liked it. She was drawn to it in a way that shocked her.

Technically, she shouldn't be so turned on by a human's scent, but something about Luke's natural aroma hit all her olfactory pleasure centers. And when he was aroused, like now, her response was off the charts. She had to stifle the urge to bury her nose in the curve of his neck and inhale.

"Are you sure?" He looked at her as if he thought she might be making that up. "Most women I know like the scrubbed version of me, complete with aftershave."

"I like this version." Giving in to her primitive needs,

she stood on tiptoe and sniffed the hollow of his throat. "Mmm." Then she licked him there.

He chuckled. "I believe you, and you're turning me on with that routine. If you don't watch out, we'll be doing it doggie style next."

No, they wouldn't, she thought with some sadness. That position was reserved for the werewolf tradition of binding, when a male and a female mated for life. She would never experience that with Luke.

Stepping back, he surveyed her from head to toe. "You're wonderful," he said softly. "And you are going to look so good covered in chocolate."

That propelled her into action. "Not until I take off that comforter!" She hurried over to the bed.

"I don't give a damn about the comforter." He grabbed her from behind, wrapped his arms around her midriff, and hauled her against him. "Leave it." His mouth found the curve of her neck, and he nipped her there.

She quivered with lust. Without realizing it, he was behaving in a very wolflike manner by grabbing her from behind and nipping at her throat. He couldn't know that was the very thing that would drive her wild, and yet somehow he'd instinctively done it.

"You smell good, too. And you taste good." He nuzzled her shoulder as he cupped her breast with one hand and slipped the other unerringly through the triangle of red curls to his ultimate destination. His voice roughened. "And you feel good. Especially here."

She gasped as he probed deep with his fingers. Her desire had been no secret before, and it was no secret now, either. She was drenched and he knew it.

"The chocolate might have to wait," he murmured as he moved his fingers rhythmically back and forth.

She couldn't speak. Having him hold her like this, imprisoned by his arms and her own desperate needs, was incredibly erotic. She couldn't move and didn't want to.

He pressed her close, so the long, hard length of his cock was wedged in the cleft of her backside, pinning her to him. And all the while he massaged her slick heat and gently squeezed her breast.

His warm breath feathered across her sensitive earlobe. "Come for me, Giselle."

She would have laughed if she had the breath to do it, but she was too busy gasping and moaning.

"That's it." Murmuring soft words of encouragement, he pushed in deeper and curved his fingers, seeking her G-spot.

When he found it, she knew the game was over.

"There." His voice tickled her ear. "Right there. I can feel you tightening around my fingers. That's the magic place, and you're going down, lady."

Helpless beneath his practiced touch, she surrendered. Bathing his questing fingers with her climax, she pressed her head against his broad shoulder and cried out with the joy of it.

As she slumped against him, she admitted that humans knew a thing or two about sexual pleasure. At least this particular human did. And the night was young.

So many possibilities. Luke wanted it all, but he had to take his delights one at a time. They had all night, or what remained of it. He might want to plan how best to use these special hours.

Much as he longed to sink into Giselle's supple body again, he had a feeling that if he went for full-body sex a second time, he might not have the creative energy to handle chocolate mousse cake the way it should be handled. So it was chocolate time, and he agreed maybe they should stow the white comforter before they began.

She quickly stripped off both the comforter and the top sheet, leaving only the bottom sheet and the pillows. "We didn't discuss the top sheet," he said. "We might need that."

Her gaze swept over him, lingering for a few gratifying seconds on his cock, which stood proud and free. "Think about it, Luke. If we're decorating each other with chocolate mousse cake, why would you need or want to cover that situation with a top sheet?"

"We might when we're done." He'd never tried this maneuver before, so he wasn't sure how it would work out.

"Ick. Speak for yourself, but once we've played with our cake and eaten it, too, I'm not going to settle into that sticky mess for a cuddle and a snooze. I'm hitting the showers."

"That could be fun. I have a pretty awesome shower."

Her eyebrows arched. "Sounds promising."

And to think he'd almost missed being with her like this. He vowed not to spoil what time they had together by obsessing about how quickly it would end. But did it have to?

He understood that she was a key player in her family's business, and so was he. But telecommuting was all the rage these days. Geography and competing jobs didn't have to be a deal breaker the way they'd been once upon a time.

They weren't even close to having that kind of discussion, though. Even so, he might suggest at some point that they stop putting a time limit on their relationship. Given the way they reacted to each other, that seemed too rigid. Compromises might be possible if they gave themselves permission to think creatively.

He planned to start by thinking creatively about chocolate mousse cake and where it might do the most good on his sweet lady. She'd been resistant to this idea, but he expected her to loosen up once he got rolling.

"We need to take turns." He picked up one of the plates. "It was my idea, so I get to do you first."

She laughed. "I thought you were reforming, but here you are acting bossy again."

"Hey, in case you haven't heard, I am the CEO of the Dalton Corporation, which is only slightly less important than being a leader of the free world." He couldn't remember ever joking about his responsibilities before. With Giselle, he could, and that felt great.

"Oh, *excuse me,* your CEO-ness. I suppose I should be treating you with more deference, since you're so important and all."

"Obedience will do. Lie down."

"Sunny-side up or over easy?"

He considered the options. He'd love to have both, but once he started, she'd probably refuse to turn over and get even more chocolate on the sheet. Coaxing her to do this at all was a victory. "Sunny-side up. I want to be able to kiss your mouth and watch your expression while I play."

"The neat freak in me is already screaming for you to reconsider this plan. I forgot about the mattress pad and the mattress underneath."

"Don't worry about it." He savored the graceful way

she stretched out on the soon-to-be-ruined sheet. "We've reached the point of no return." And he upended the plate on her stomach.

"Yikes!" She stiffened but didn't move, because if she did, the cake could slide off. "You might have given me a little advance warning!"

"And have you tell me no? Now it's done. There's no turning back. You'll need to lie very still, though, or it might start to shift."

She raised her head to look at the slice of chocolate cake resting midway between her breasts and the red curls covering her sex. "You need to do something, Luke."

"I intend to." He dropped to his knees beside the bed.

She rolled her head to one side and gazed at him. "This isn't at all how I imagined you doing this. I thought you'd leave the cake on the plate and dip into it with your fingers."

"You can do that when it's your turn, if you want. I like this method." Now that the cake was resting on her stomach, he debated his next move. He hadn't planned this out in advance, which was half the fun. He'd spent too much of his life calculating his actions several moves in advance.

"You should be very glad I have good abs so I can balance this piece of cake."

"I see that you're controlling it beautifully. I'm impressed. You look great with that piece of cake on you. It's like performance art."

"Luke. Do something!"

"Okay." Reaching out with his right hand, he pressed it down into the cake. It squished up through his outstretched fingers as Giselle gasped in surprise. He loved the sloppy feel of it, like mud, only better because he could eat it.

She lifted her head and stared at him. "What are you doing?"

"Enjoying myself."

She let her head fall back to the pillow. "Oh, dear God. You really did love playing in the mud when you were a kid, didn't you?"

"Yes, ma'am, I did." He began to slowly smear chocolate mousse over her breasts. The sensation of creamy mousse mixed with nubby pieces of cake rubbed over her breasts was outstanding. His body pulsed with excitement. "Why are your eyes closed?"

"I'm afraid to look."

"You should see this. I've turned your breasts into truffles."

Her lashes fluttered up and she raised her head again. "You are making an unholy mess."

"Look me in the eye and tell me you're not turned on by it."

She met his gaze, and heat flashed in her eyes. "I'm not turned on by it."

"Your eyes say different." He massaged the chocolate into her breasts with slow, erotic strokes and watched the flame leap in those emerald depths. "Your nipples are all tight and happy."

"Of course they are. You're rubbing them."

"And you like it."

"I would like it without the chocolate."

"So would I, but this is more fun." Sliding his hand between her breasts, he returned to the remaining cake and began spreading that over her stomach and down the tops of her thighs.

"You're insane."

"Right at this moment, yes, I am. And getting more so by the second." He covered her knees and her shins and finally reached her toes. "Now, *this* is what I've been waiting for." He had enough mousse on his hand to work it between her toes with their sexy apricot toenail polish. "Remember walking through the mud in your bare feet?"

She braced herself on her elbows. "Luke, do you have a foot fetish?"

"Not yet." Now that he'd distributed the chocolate mousse cake fairly evenly over her body, he was ready to work his way back up. "But I might before this is over. You have extremely sexy toes."

"You've put chocolate all over them."

"The better to suck them clean, my dear." Scooting to the end of the bed, he wiped his chocolate-covered hand on the sheet. So it was done. He'd officially christened the sheet. If she thought he'd made a mess before, wait until he really got into it.

Now that he'd spread the chocolate all over her, he knew exactly how to proceed. Cradling one foot in both hands, he carefully sucked and cleaned each of her toes.

He found it arousing as hell, but he couldn't tell if she felt that way. Not at first. Then he heard little noises coming from the other end of the bed. As he turned his attention to her other foot and began licking between her toes, he realized she was whimpering.

He paused. "Are you all right?"

Her reply was slightly breathless. "Uh-huh."

"You're sure?"

"Okay, I'm admitting it. That feels amazing. I had no

idea my feet were so sensitive. You're ... Luke, you're getting me really hot."

"Good to know." He continued to lick and suck her toes.

"I mean *really* hot."

"I'm glad." He started working his way up her leg.

"Luke ..." She was breathing pretty fast. "I can't wait."

"I still have a lot of chocolate to go."

"Um, slippery and sticky might be fun."

That jacked up his heart rate considerably. "Is that you talking? The neat freak?"

"Yeah." She moaned softly. "I need you. All of you, sliding over my chocolate-covered body."

Lust surged, hot and heavy. "Alrighty, then." He'd planned to lick most of the chocolate off before moving to the next phase, but then again, why do that? Why not see how it felt to make love to a woman covered in chocolate?

With a groan of surrender, he changed position. His knees picked up some chocolate as he moved between her thighs. Holding her gaze, he thrust deep ... and nearly came. She felt good, too good.

She raised her hips and wrapped her legs around his. He could feel the slippery chocolate against his thighs, and once again, he almost lost it. He tried to speak, to tell her to take it easy, but the words stuck in his throat.

He didn't want to take it easy, anyway. He wanted to abandon himself to this chocolate-covered experience and hope that he didn't embarrass himself by coming immediately. Lowering himself to his elbows, he drew back, and as he slid forward, he rubbed his chest against hers.

The sensation of slippery mousse and the friction of cake combined into an erotic banquet. He swore softly and clenched the muscles of his jaw. It would be so easy to—

"I'm going to come." Her breathy announcement was followed by a high, keening cry as she arched her back.

Luke absorbed her contractions and fought to keep his own at bay. Something this mind-bending was meant to last, and he would last, by God. They were going to enjoy this together, every chocolate-smeared minute of it.

Chapter 14

Giselle sank back to the mattress and gazed in wonder at the man braced above her. One easy stroke had touched off a climax that left her limp and gasping. She struggled for air. "How . . . did you do that?"

"I think you did that. And you damned near took me with you."

"But you held back." She raised unsteady hands to his chest, where wide streaks of chocolate marked him like war paint and bits of cake clung to his dark blond chest hair.

"After debating the ruined sheet issue for so long, I didn't want the fun to be over too quick." He sounded as if the effort had cost him, though. The fight for control had left him short of breath, which made the mousse and the cake on his chest quiver.

She ran a finger over a smear of chocolate. "Is it good?"

"The sex is great. And the chocolate's not bad, either."

Smiling up at him, she licked her finger. "The chocolate *is* good. And I don't care about the sheets anymore."

"Glad to hear it, because we're changing positions. Hang on." With that, he quickly rolled over, bringing her with him. Somehow he managed to keep them connected.

She yelped in surprise. Then she wiggled, trying to settle herself more securely in her new position.

His arms tightened around her. "Don't move for a second." Beneath her, his chest heaved. "Let me get my mojo back."

"Luke, if you want to come, it's—"

"Oh, I want to, honeybunch. I want to desperately. But I also want to lick all that chocolate off your beautiful breasts, and I need to do that before I come or the shower will get the thrill of it. That would be a crying shame."

Imagining him licking and sucking had a predictable effect on her. She accidentally gave his cock a little squeeze with her muscles, and he inhaled sharply. Deep inside her, she felt him twitch.

"Stay still," he murmured. Then he let out his breath. "Okay. I'm good."

"You sure are." She was impressed. Most males she'd known would have given up the fight long ago, but obviously when Luke wanted something, he focused on it until he got it.

His chuckle was part groan. "I didn't mean it like that. I don't go around bragging on my bedroom skills."

"Maybe you should. Wait—I take that back. You probably already have females chasing after you. You don't need more."

"At the moment, I need only one." He stroked both hands down her back and cupped her backside. "I'm going to hold you still right here. No moving in that area just yet. But I want you to lift those truffles so I can taste them."

"You really are bossy."

"I told you. This is my turn. There's another whole piece of cake left."

"I wonder if you'll be up for it, pun intended."

"You let me worry about that. Now, lift up."

"Nag, nag, nag." Bracing her hands on either side of his shoulders, she started to push herself up and met resistance. "We're stuck together."

"Are we, now? Let's see what I can do." Drawing in a breath, he slipped his hand between her stomach and his. Then he gently worked his hand up between them, pausing to caress her along the way.

She became so turned on by his touch that she forgot his instructions. Instinctively, her hips rocked.

"Nope." He pulled his hand out and clamped it over her fanny again. "Not yet, my sexy woman." Then he squeezed and rubbed her there. "Now you have chocolate spread over your cheeks, too. I might have to find a way to lick that off."

"Sounds good to me." She was ready for anything with this guy.

"Ah, Giselle, you do turn me on, lady. Now, see if you can lift up."

"Okay." Moisture from their bodies had mingled with the chocolate so they were now more slippery than sticky. She braced herself with her hands on either side of his shoulders and glanced down at him. "How's that?"

Heat glowed in his blue eyes. "Almost perfect. Can you put another pillow behind my head?"

"Sure. Lean forward." As she balanced one-handed

and grabbed a pillow, his warm mouth closed over her nipple. She gasped. "You'll make me fall!"

He sucked once and released her with a soft laugh. "I couldn't resist. I mean, you were right there."

"I think that was the idea." Reaction to his liquid caress hummed through her. She shoved the pillow behind his head and flattened her palm against the mattress again. She ignored the streaks of chocolate that now appeared everywhere on the snowy linen.

Then she looked at Luke and noticed he had chocolate on his mouth. "I can't resist this, either." She dipped her head and kissed those wicked lips. He tasted of chocolate and passion, a passion greater than she'd found with anyone.

He moaned and thrust his tongue deep as he pressed his fingertips hard against her backside. If he hadn't, she would have moved against him. Her body ached for the chance to do that. Even without moving, she felt her climax build just from the sensuality of their kiss.

Pulling back, she looked into his eyes.

He looked right back, his gaze almost fierce in its intensity. "I feel . . ." He paused and cleared his throat. "I feel like I've been struck by lightning."

She nodded. "I know."

"We said this was temporary, but—"

"Shh." She pressed her mouth to his and drew back. "Not now."

"But I—"

"Enjoy your truffles." Leaning forward, she offered herself shamelessly. This she could give him. The other, what she was very afraid he was about to ask, she could not.

*   *   *

As a distraction, Giselle's chocolate-covered breasts worked like a charm. Luke abandoned his long-term goal of talking about their future for short-term pleasure, insanely good short-term pleasure. He would love sucking on her breasts no matter what, but having chocolate all over them gave him an excuse to be extremely thorough.

He loved knowing that he was making her crazy, too. She began her whimpering routine, which he knew was a prelude to getting serious about a climax. And so was he. Dear God, but he was proud of himself for holding off so long.

"I need to move." She tried to free herself from his grip on her firm backside. "*You* need to have me move." She sucked in a breath. "You must be ready to explode. I am."

She had that right. With one last tug on her sweet nipple, he leaned back. "Done. You're all clean."

She glanced down and then looked at him, eyebrows raised.

"Mostly clean."

"Good enough." Her voice was husky. "Going to turn me loose now?"

"Yeah. Be gentle."

"Gentle? Really?"

"Just kidding. Ride me, lady. It shouldn't be a very long ride, but make it good."

"You've got it." She flattened her palms against his chest. "You're still very sticky."

"You can work on that later. For now . . ." He loosened his hold on her fanny. "Work that." He groaned as she eased slowly upward. "Work it hard."

"Don't worry. I plan to." She came down on him much faster than she'd gone up.

Everything after that was a blur of Giselle pumping him for all she was worth. Her breasts shook with every downward slap of her body on his. They both made noise, lots of it, as they surged toward the finish line.

He figured he might cross it first. The pressure felt like a bomb was about to detonate. "Can't hold on," he whispered as he felt his control slipping.

"Go for it." She pumped harder and threw back her head. "I'm right there. Right *there*."

"Ah . . . Giselle . . . *Giselle* . . ." He drove upward once more and came so hard it took his breath away. Blind and deaf to anything but the pounding in his groin, he couldn't even yell. But inside he was shouting his amazement and wonder. Good, so good, so damn good!

Her spasms rippled over his pulsing cock and seemed to gently squeeze out every last drop, as if she wanted all he could give her. She'd completely spoiled him. Sex without a condom was awesome.

Her breathing slowed, and she eased down onto his sticky chest. "Excellent." She said it with such a deep sigh.

He smiled and stroked her back. "You were excellent. You were great. You were—"

"An unexpected surprise." She lifted her head and propped her chin on her fist so she could look him in the eye. "I never planned for this to happen."

"I know you didn't, and I'm grateful." He rubbed circles in the small of her back. He was still fairly hard, and he didn't want to move and break the connection. Lying here with her was nice. Sticky, but nice.

"It was pretty wonderful."

"And although I won't harp on the subject, you gave me a gift by letting me in without one of those little raincoats. I was told from the time I hit puberty that I had to wear one until I had a steady girlfriend."

"Did you ever?"

"No." He ran his hand over the delicious curve of her backside. "But I was the heir to the Dalton fortune, and that made me an extremely eligible bachelor, or maybe just a baby-daddy candidate with money to shower on a pregnant girlfriend. So I played it safe and wore condoms rather than risk accidentally fathering a kid."

"You're a very responsible man, Luke Dalton."

"Raised that way."

"I apologize for carrying on about the sheets. I should have figured it out. My brother was raised to shoulder the responsibility in my family, and so he blew off steam playing practical jokes."

"And taking off for Vegas." Knowing that he and Giselle's brother had much in common made him curious. "You said it was a bunch of things piling up that made him bolt, but usually there's one straw that breaks the camel's back."

"I'm sure that's true, and I think I know the straw, but he didn't confide in me before he left."

"What do you think it was?"

"He'd chosen a mate . . . I mean, a marriage partner."

"Mate isn't such a bad word to use." He brushed a lock of hair away from her cheek. "Sort of old-fashioned, but I like it. It implies more permanence. Like the term *soul mate*." And when he said that, the most amazing thing happened. Her green eyes became almost luminescent, as if he'd touched a chord in her. "Do you believe in soul mates?" he asked softly. Until this very moment, he hadn't given the matter much thought.

"I . . . suppose I do."

"How do you think it works, this soul mate thing? Do you just meet someone and know right away?"

"Maybe." Her gaze searched his. "Or maybe it takes time to figure it out."

"Since you're single, I have to assume you haven't met yours." He was more interested in her answer than he wanted to admit.

"No, I haven't."

The certainty in her voice bothered him. Now that the subject had come up, he had to wonder if their instant attraction was a sign that they were meant for each other. He was willing to entertain the possibility. But apparently she wasn't thinking that way. That was kind of depressing.

Maybe he'd better get back to discussing her brother and stop imagining that she viewed their attraction with the same starstruck wonder that he did. "Has your brother found his? Because if he has, I hope he didn't run out on her."

Giselle sighed. "That's why I'm a little confused on the soul mate issue. I thought he and Miranda were soul mates. He acted as if they were. But then it became all about the ceremony, and the two mothers started pushing for dates and details. I think that's why Bryce took off. It turned into this whole big thing—the joining of the two families, the expectation of children, what house they would buy—and he just blew."

The expectation of children. Was that why she couldn't take over as CEO? Did her family have some traditional idea that the head of the business had to procreate, and she was unable to have kids? If so, that was bullshit. He longed to ask her more about that, but now wasn't the time.

His dad had expected him to marry and have kids, preferably a son who could be trained to take over from Luke the way Luke had been raised to take over from Angus. Angus Dalton hadn't been very evolved in that respect. If Giselle thought Luke was a throwback, she should have met his dad.

"So your brother dumped Miranda, who may or may not have been his soul mate." Luke was relieved that Cynthia hadn't decided Bryce was her soul mate. He wanted her to have more time to explore all sorts of possibilities before committing herself to one man.

"He dumped her," Giselle said. "And she's done with him."

"Don't blame her."

"Me, either." She grimaced, and he could tell the conversation had broken the mood for her. "We should probably each check our phones and see if they've texted us."

"And what if they have? What if Cynthia's sent me another riddle? Are we going to get dressed and tear around Vegas in the wee small hours of the morning so that your brother can find another way to douse me with water?"

"I see your point. That is getting old."

"Personally, I'd rather choose my own method of getting wet."

She smiled. "I checked out your shower before you came back up here."

"Then you're aware that I have multiple jets in there."

Her smile widened. "I am."

"Do you like the idea of multiple jets?"

"I love it."

"Then what are we waiting for?" He climbed out of their chocolate-smeared bed and held out his hand to help her.

Giselle was one hell of a playmate. The more he thought about taking her into that shower, the more he liked the concept. He'd fantasized about having shower sex with a woman, but other than doing it orally, he'd never been able to because of the need for the damned condoms.

But now, for as long as she was willing to hang around, he had Giselle, a woman who didn't need no stinkin' condoms. He would be a fool if he didn't find all sorts of creative ways to enjoy that freedom. Once she was gone, and it sounded as if she would go, he'd be back to the little raincoats.

He needed to honestly evaluate if that bareback option, which had given him considerable pleasure, had fooled him into thinking that Giselle was the one for him. After all, he hadn't known her very long, and a guy could be convinced of many things that weren't true when his cock was happy.

Giselle started to put her foot on the white carpet but drew back with a squeal.

"What? A bug? A mouse?"

"No, silly. I'm not that kind of girly girl. But I almost stepped on the white carpet, and I'll bet you didn't get all the chocolate off my toes. I was willing to mess up the sheet and the pillowcases, but once you get chocolate on this carpet, you'll have a real problem."

"Then I have the perfect solution." Leaning down, he slipped one arm under her knees and the other under her shoulder blades. "Put your arms around my neck."

"Oh, wow. I haven't been carried anywhere for ages."

"Well, you have good abs for holding cake, and I have good biceps for holding you." He lifted her and blessed all the hours he'd spent in the gym. Although she wasn't a small woman, he didn't even groan when he picked her up, and he didn't stagger when he walked toward the bathroom with her in his arms.

"This is cool, Luke. Thanks. But we're here, so you can put me down now."

"Where should I put you?" He glanced around as he reminded himself that creativity was the watchword tonight. The marble counter wrapped around two sides of the bathroom. And so did the mirror. "I think I'll put you on the counter."

"On the counter? I thought we were going into the shower."

"We will." He settled her naked tush into the corner section of the broad expanse of marble and checked for sight lines. Very nice. "We'll get to the shower. Eventually."

Chapter 15

Human males, Giselle concluded, or at least this particular human male, seemed to enjoy the element of surprise when it came to sex. She'd never been plopped down on a counter and told to watch in the mirror while her partner did her. She had to admit it added quite a bit to the experience.

It became especially erotic when he hooked his arms under her knees to lift and spread her thighs. Arms braced behind her, she could glance to the side for a full view of his cock sliding back and forth in long, measured strokes. She could admire the way his tight buns flexed with each thrust.

He watched, too, and met her gaze in the mirror. "Beautiful," he murmured. "I love how smoothly we come together. No rush. Just an easy rhythm."

"But my heart's going like a bongo."

"Mine, too. But let's see how long we can keep it slow, build up to it."

She swallowed. "All right." But she didn't think she'd last much longer. Every time he pushed home, she felt a zing. It got stronger with every forward motion of his hips. "But I should warn you that I'm . . ." She moaned as he rocked into her and made direct contact with her clit.

"Ah, hell. Forget slow. I want it too much." He pumped faster. "That's good. Open a little more. Like that. Oh, yeah. Come for me, Giselle. I want to watch you come."

She gasped as the first wave hit. Abandoning the mirror, she arched forward as he pounded into her and took her up, up, and even higher. With a cry, she came apart.

He rode her climax to his own, his body shuddering as he drove home. His breathing ragged, he lowered her legs to the counter and placed a soft kiss on her mouth. Then he closed his eyes and bowed his head. "Thank you. Thank you for indulging me."

She smiled at the sweetness of that comment. He really was a nice guy. Sexy, too. "Oh, you're welcome. Anytime."

His head came up, and his blue eyes shone with an emotion that struck fear into her heart. "Careful. I might take you up on that."

She considered explaining that it was only an expression, an offhand remark that didn't mean quite what it sounded like. But then she'd spoil the moment, and she couldn't bear to do that. He couldn't be blamed for thinking what they'd found together could go on.

No, she was the one with all the info on that, and she felt guilty as hell. What if he fell in love with her? Or thought he had? She'd have to leave him, and without a decent explanation, too. What if she broke his heart?

She cupped his face in both hands. His chin was slightly prickly where his beard had started to grow. "I really have to go back to San Francisco when this is over."

"I understand. You're an important part of the Landry operation. I'm an important part of the Dalton operation. But this is the twenty-first century. We have such things as telecommuting and direct flights from here to there. Geography isn't the barrier it used to be. And for what it's worth, I don't give a damn if you can have kids or not."

Her heart wept. Sure enough, he'd been building castles in the air. She searched for an argument that would make sense, because she certainly couldn't tell him the truth.

Learning that he'd been having cozy sex with a werewolf would likely send him screaming in the other direction. Although that would accomplish what she needed, he'd be a pack security risk. He'd be monitored twenty-four-seven, no matter how fervently he promised not to expose their secret. Life as he knew it would be forever altered.

This was why she'd stayed away from having sex with a human male. The potential problems weren't worth the risk. She took a deep breath. "Luke, I—"

"You know what? Forget all that. Don't mind me. I'm letting good sex convince me we've found this grand passion. I'm overreacting."

She hoped he was right about that. It would make the rest of her time with him much easier. "Even so, maybe we shouldn't keep having sex. I didn't realize it would be such an unusual treat for you." And that was another mistake she'd made. She should have let him wear a condom. She'd assumed he'd experienced that before in a long-term relationship and hadn't realized it would be such a big deal.

In the heat of the moment, she'd spoken without

thinking, rejecting the use of something that was so foreign to her concept of sex. But hindsight told her that had been a tactical error.

"No, please. Don't let my idiotic thoughts louse up a good thing. Just forget what I said."

She gazed into his beautiful blue eyes. Maybe she'd break her own heart in the process of breaking his. "I don't know if I can forget it."

"Bet I can make you." He gave her a crooked grin. "Come into my shower, little girl. By the time I'm through with you, you won't even remember your own name."

"That's tempting, but I still think—"

"I need you to help me figure out what's going on with Cynthia. And you need me, because once we get Cynthia to the bargaining table, you can have a heart-to-heart with your brother."

"That's true."

"So we're going to be hanging out with each other anyway, and after the incredible sex we've had so far, I don't think we can dial it back to platonic, do you?"

"Maybe not." Much as she thought that would be for the best, she couldn't picture it. They'd crossed the line, and there was no going back.

"We agreed to a temporary situation, and I'm the one who screwed up by suggesting something different. So erase that from your mind. I'm all about temporary. I promise."

She was caught in a trap of her own making. He might be able to keep his heart out of it now that he'd declared their relationship strictly sexual. She wouldn't bet on it. She wouldn't bet on her ability to do that, either.

But if she rejected the olive branch and insisted on keeping him at arm's length until this episode was over, that would be torture of a different kind. She wasn't convinced either of them could maintain their distance from each other.

"What do you say, Landry? Ready to hit the showers?"

She leaned forward and kissed him. "Yeah," she murmured. "Show me your jets."

He'd damn near blown it, but maybe he'd managed a last-minute save. Painful though it was to think about, she might not be into him the way he was into her.

After lifting her off the counter, he took her hand and led her toward the large walk-in shower. "Wait here. Let me get the temperature right. How do you like your jets?"

She laughed. "Rhythmic."

"I'll set it for that, but I meant the temp."

"Warm, not hot. Don't want to scald anything important."

"Right." He was encouraged by the way she'd entered into the spirit of the shower experience. Maybe he hadn't ruined everything, after all. Yeah, he wished she'd responded differently to his suggestion they could take this to the next level.

But she hadn't. He needed to accept that and move on. He'd been granted a reprieve, because she could just as easily have decided to sleep in the guest bedroom and let him go hang. She obviously didn't want a pushy guy with hopes for the future.

So he wouldn't be that guy. As he stuck his hand under the closest jet to test the temperature, he mapped out his game plan. He would enjoy the gift of Giselle to the fullest. And he would give as good as he got.

She probably wouldn't change her mind about him, and he wouldn't expect that. He wasn't campaigning to win her hand, for God's sake. He had some pride. But if, at the end of their time together, she had weakened on her stated position, he'd be there.

Because he didn't think it was the bareback sex or the unusual nature of their meeting that had created this spark between them. Whether she acknowledged it or not, he believed they had something special going on here. He wouldn't mention it again—God, no—but he would watch, and wait, and hope that eventually she'd see that they were meant to be.

In the meantime, though, he had a killer shower and she was going to leave it totally wrung out, or his name wasn't Luke Dalton. The counter sex had sidelined him for a while, but the jets could fill in for him until he was ready to rock and roll.

Females were amazing creatures, and he envied them their multiorgasmic capabilities. He had to pace himself, but they didn't. Oh, sooner or later they'd call a halt, but their staying capacity was way beyond his. When he was looking at a limited time with a hot woman, he regretted his longer recovery time.

"It's ready." He glanced over at her. "Are you?"

She laughed. "I don't know. I've never had the multi-jet experience before. Will I overload on pleasure?"

"I hope so." He held out his hand. "That's my goal."

"Mmm." She gazed at him with those emerald-green eyes. "And you're a goal-oriented person, just like your sister, so I'd better watch out. You make this shower sound like the setting for an orgy."

"A two-person orgy would be a good description."

"You've done this before?"

He shook his head. "I told you that I haven't brought a woman up here until tonight."

"So how do you know so much about the shower? Have you been having a little solo fun in there?"

He didn't usually admit such things to a sexual partner, but Giselle invited honesty. "Maybe a time or two. But my equipment is decidedly different from yours. What I have in mind for you is a product of my imagination."

Heat blazed in her green eyes. "You've certainly fired up mine."

He gestured toward the walk-in marble enclosure, complete with a built-in marble bench. The water beat a steady tattoo against the creamy walls. "After you."

She stepped into the spray, raised her arms, closed her eyes, and turned in a slow circle. "Ah. Wonderful. No more sticky chocolate." Arching her neck, she let the pelting water sluice through her hair until it hung in a slick curtain down her back.

Luke swallowed a moan of longing. He'd heard of mythical water nymphs, and now he knew what they must look like. The high-intensity lights in the ceiling created rainbows in the mist and turned the rivulets of water sliding over her body to ribbons of silver. He'd never seen anything so beautiful in his life. He ached to have her, and sex was only part of it. He'd always wondered if he'd know when the right one came along. Well, fate hadn't been kind to him. The right one didn't want him for the long haul. That wasn't fair, but he'd have to suck it up and deal.

In the meantime, she was here, standing in his shower, and he had pleasure to provide. "Keep your eyes closed. Let me give you a tactile tour of the place."

She laughed. "Okay."

"Hold out your hand."

She stretched out her right hand. So graceful, that hand. She had apricot polish on her toes, but her fingernails were bare. No rings, either. She was unfettered and seemed to like it that way.

He grasped her right hand with his, like a handshake, and slipped his other arm around her slick shoulders. "This way." He guided her gently toward a spot where the jet was about crotch high—hers, not his. Water spattered on them from all sides as they moved across the marble floor, which was subtly ridged for safety.

"This feels like one of those trust games, where you're blindfolded and let your partner lead you around."

"Mmm, blindfolds. Kinky." His balls tightened. "Want to try that after we dry off?"

"After the way you described this shower experience, I might need a nap afterward."

"It's possible." He rebelled at that idea, and then his conscience pricked him. Just because he didn't want to sleep while they had a chance to be alone didn't mean she felt the same. "Okay, stop here, and turn this way." He edged her around until she faced the jet from about two feet away.

"Oh." She trembled as the water beat firmly against the tops of her thighs. "I think I get this idea already."

"Move up a little and spread your feet apart." He lifted her hand to the moist wall. "Brace yourself with your hands on the wall."

"Oh, Luke. If you let this secret out . . ." She groaned and stepped a little closer.

That's when he realized that two side jets were also stimulating her nipples. He hadn't figured out that would happen. Bonus. He really didn't have to do a thing. He could stand back and watch the jets do their work.

But that was no fun. Dropping to his knees behind her, he nuzzled her firm backside.

She gasped. "Luke, no."

"Easy." With her enthusiasm for sex, he was surprised she seemed to be resistant to doggie style. "Just let me touch you. You're so pretty back here." Kissing her smooth cheek, he felt her quivering response.

Maybe she only needed a little coaxing, and since she was breathing quickly, nearing her first climax, now would be the time. As he slipped two fingers into her moist channel, her spasms began. She surrendered to her climax with a wail as he used quick strokes to heighten the sensation of the jets. Her cries echoed against the walls of the shower.

Her contractions subsided for a brief moment, and then he felt her tighten around him again. She moaned and pushed against the motion of his fingers. Her hips lifted, inviting him deeper. She wanted this, wanted more than this.

His cock swelled in response. Standing, he grasped her hips. With one firm thrust, he sank deep. When he was buried up to the hilt, primitive instinct took over and he went a little crazy.

The rapid slap of his thighs against hers beat in rhythm to the staccato sounds of their breathing, their groans, and finally, a climax that found them both at the same moment. She was loud, but he was louder, yelling at the top of his lungs, wild with the glory of it.

They stayed coupled together as the jets beat all around them. Luke had thought he'd experienced sex with Giselle before, but he hadn't touched the very core of her until now.

She dragged in a breath and uttered one soft word. "Enough."

He understood. Sliding his hand around her body, he cupped her mound, shielding it from the jet. Then he wrapped his other arm under her breasts as he slowly eased his cock free.

Although he was a little shaky, he called on his iron will. Turning her limp body around, he lifted her and carried her out of the shower. She would hate it if he put her back in that sticky bed, but the comforter was lying in a heap at the foot of it.

When he laid her down on it, she made a sound of protest.

"It's fine." Walking back into the bathroom, he grabbed up several large towels, also white. He'd been thorough in his color-coordination efforts.

She lay curled on her side when he returned, but when he began drying her, she rolled to her back and opened her eyes. He didn't know what he'd expected to find there, but it hadn't been fear. She looked terrified.

A million thoughts ran through his head. "What is it? What's wrong?"

"I can't tell you."

"If you don't tell me, how can I fix it?"

"You can't fix this. Nobody can. But . . . we shouldn't have sex anymore."

Her statement hit him like a medicine ball to the gut. "Look, I'm sorry. But you acted as if you wanted—"

"I did. I wanted you to do exactly what you did, and that's why we have to stop having sex."

He frowned. "Giselle, there's nothing wrong with that position. People have sex like that all the time."

"I know."

"Did someone tell you it was wrong? Were you taught that?"

"No. I was taught that anything that brings pleasure to both partners is fine, but . . ."

"But what? Did I hurt you?"

"No." Some of the fear left her eyes. "I loved it. And that's why we can't have sex anymore."

He stared at her. "You're not making any sense. I can't speak for you, although you said you loved what just happened. As for me, it was the best sexual experience of my life, bar none. I've never felt so deeply connected to a woman as I did while I was making love to you in that shower."

"Oh, God." She buried her face in her hands. "I know! I know! That's the problem!"

Frustration made him get agitated. "How can it be a problem? Are you engaged? Married? You're not wearing any rings, and you sure have acted like you were single, but if there's another guy, then damn it, tell me!"

She looked up and her expression was bleak. "There's no one else. But there is a reason why we can't ever be together, and I can't tell you what it is. I thought we could have a little sexual fun together and be done, but that's not how it's turning out."

"Hm." Some of his indignation leaked away as he saw how truly miserable she was. "Well, I can't imagine what this big secret is that you can't reveal." Then he had a terrible thought. "Please don't tell me you have a horrible disease. No, wait. Please *do* tell me, so that I can help."

"You are so sweet." She seemed on the verge of tears. "I'm not dying, and I'm not sick. Not at all. But thanks for the sympathy you would have given me if I were."

Luke blew out a breath, hugely relieved. "Thank God. But that leaves . . ." He racked his brain for a logical explanation. "I know. You have psychotic episodes. Maybe you even killed someone and your family covered it up.

You're afraid it could happen again, so you can't get deeply involved with anyone. And you had your tubes tied to make sure the trait wasn't passed on." He glanced at her. "Is that it?"

She shook her head. "I'm not psychotic. Stupid, yes. Psychotic, no." She gazed up at him. "Can't you just accept that we have no future and let it go at that?"

"Absolutely! I thought we'd covered the subject and we'd have lots of no-strings sex until you left for 'Frisco. I was on board with that. Then you announce we can't have sex, after all."

"I'm afraid we're going to fall in love."

Once again, he was sucker-punched. Yeah, it could happen. Probably had begun already, but he wasn't a poker player for nothing. "Hell, no, we're not! This is about sex, lady, not love. Do you see me writing you little notes? Bringing you flowers? Finding out your birthday?"

"No." For the first time since they'd left the bathroom, she managed a tiny smile.

"That's what I do when I'm falling in love, and if you don't notice those behaviors, you can safely assume I'm only here for the S-E-X and nothing else."

"But you looked really upset when you thought I might be sick."

"Hey, I tear up at sad movies. I hate hearing about tragedies thousands of miles away. You could be a total stranger and I'd still be upset if you said you were really sick."

She cocked her head to study him.

He stared right back. Her hair was a disaster, soggy strands that desperately needed to be combed out. All her makeup had been washed away, which meant he could see the pale freckles sprinkled across her nose. She was a knockout.

"How about if I crack jokes while we're having sex?" he said. "Will that convince you this is strictly a physical attraction?"

"Do you know a lot of jokes?"

Hope bloomed where before had stretched a Giselle-less desert. "Will I need a lot of jokes?"

She grinned at him. "You might."

"Aha!" Moving over her, he urged her back onto the quilt and settled himself between her thighs. All this depressing talk had taken the lead out of his pencil, but in this position he'd be good to go in no time. "These three monkeys walked into a bar, and the first monkey said—"

"You're wonderful."

"No, he didn't say that. He said—"

"I mean *you* are wonderful, Luke Dalton. Now kiss me and quit talking about monkeys."

So he kissed her and silently congratulated himself on dodging a bullet. He also hoped he still had a joke book tucked away somewhere.

Chapter 16

Giselle had more sex that night than she'd known was possible. Once they'd agreed a bed would be more comfortable than the floor, Luke had suggested moving to a different bedroom. Apparently, the penthouse had several. But Giselle had become fond of this bedroom and this particular bed, so she'd asked to stay.

Consequently, they'd stripped off the chocolate-covered bottom sheet and put on the top sheet. Only one pillowcase was smeared, which left three others for them to use. When they'd added the comforter, dry side down, they'd been in business.

Eventually exhaustion had claimed them in the early-morning hours, and they'd slept. Giselle woke up first, as pale light filtered in from the window. She was disoriented until she glanced over and saw Luke sleeping peacefully beside her.

He was quite an Adonis, this human male she'd chosen as her one-and-only non-Were sexual partner. His dark blond hair was tousled from wild sex and deep sleep. He had a tiny spot of blood on his jaw where he'd nicked himself shaving in the middle of the night.

She'd tried to talk him out of that scheme, but he'd insisted that good oral sex required a clean shave, and he wasn't forgoing it because he was too lazy to get out his razor. She'd been the beneficiary of that resolve, and thinking about it made her flush with pleasure all over again.

He'd followed that with some good old-fashioned missionary sex that had curled her toes. And, boy, did he have staying power. She'd heard rumors that human males didn't possess the stamina of a Were when it came to the duration of each episode and frequency of said episodes. If Luke Dalton was typical, then the rumors were dead wrong.

She didn't think he was typical, though. True, having sex without a condom seemed to inspire him. Yet even taking that factor into account, his performance was nothing short of amazing. She, who'd always prided herself on being sexually fit, had begun to wonder if she'd be able to ride her rented motorcycle the next day.

If not, it was her own fault. After the shower incident, she'd made the decision to pull away from this unwise attraction. She could have stuck to her guns and not allowed him to charm her right back into his arms. But her willpower, something she'd always been so proud of, seemed to be AWOL when it came to Luke.

She melted every time he smiled at her. Then warning bells would clang in her head because she shouldn't be melting at the sight of a human male's smile. A loud siren screeched when she remembered that fateful moment in the shower when she'd allowed him to take her from behind.

Luckily, it hadn't been a binding. They would have

had to be on all fours for that, but still . . . they'd skated dangerously close to having Were-style sex. Worse yet, she'd wanted to have that kind of sex with him.

She'd even fantasized breaking her self-imposed rule against Were-human mating. Others had done it. The Wallace brothers from New York, Aidan and Roarke, both had human mates and seemed very happy. More recently Jake Hunter, the Alaskan Were who'd been so opposed to mating with humans, had done an about-face and chosen human Rachel Miller.

But she knew of only one female Were who'd taken a human mate. Penny Stillman from the Stillman pack in Denver had abandoned her Were family so that she could live as a human and marry in the human way. She hadn't told her husband, Tom, she was Were and had insisted on adopting children to guarantee she wouldn't end up with werewolf offspring.

Now that Giselle was involved with Luke, she could understand Penny's decision to live a lie. The truth might have driven away the love of her life. But whether he had stayed or not, he would have become the guardian of a dangerous secret, one he'd have to keep from every human he knew, including those he loved. It was a burden that some had agreed to carry, including the three human female mates Giselle knew of. But a Were always had to consider whether it was fair to ask such a thing of the human they loved.

Ultimately, Giselle couldn't imagine choosing Penny's solution, but expecting Luke to deal with the secrecy seemed presumptuous. Neither choice was a good one, which meant she had to let him go, and he would never know why. She should be filled with regret for allowing this relationship to happen.

Whatever it said about her, she didn't regret any of it. She didn't think Luke did, either. He'd made it clear that he'd take what was offered and be grateful. If they dealt with heartache when all was said and done, it was the price they'd both pay. Speaking for herself, she would willingly pay that price for the memories she'd have of loving Luke.

His nose twitched and he reached up to scratch it. Then, slowly, those dark lashes, surprising for his fair coloring, lifted, revealing his blue-eyed gaze. He ran a tongue over his lips. "Did you hear the one about the fireman and the pole dancer?"

She chuckled. "If that's an invitation for another round of mattress bingo, I should probably pass. I need to be able to function today, and I'm not sure I can walk."

"Really?" He pushed himself to a sitting position. "Did I hurt you? I didn't meant to—"

"It's okay, you sweet man. I could have stopped you at anytime, but I was having too much fun."

His frown turned to a grin. "So it's a good kind of sore?"

"Uh-huh. Every little twinge today will remind me of you."

"Good." He looked quite pleased with himself.

"You'll be on my mind constantly."

"And vice versa. Manly men don't usually reveal such things, but I'm a little sensitive this morning, too."

"So what was the deal with starting off with a joke? It sounded like a signal that you wanted to get it on."

He pushed the comforter away and stroked her breast. "I do. I'd put up with a little discomfort for the ultimate reward."

Delicious tension coiled tighter with every movement of his hand. "Keep that up and I'll agree with you."

"Nope. If you're sore, then we need to back off for a

little while." Leaning down, he kissed the swell of her breast before hopping nimbly out of bed. "I'll go get your suitcase out of the guest room and then I'll start a bath for you." He grabbed his phone from the top of the low dresser. "Mr. Thatcher can bring up Epsom salts." His thumbs typed in a message. "You can soak your tender parts while we wait for breakfast."

Epsom salts and a bath. She felt cherished in a way that she hadn't felt with her Were lovers. Then she realized why. Werewolves healed their injuries by shifting. If she shifted into wolf form and back again, her soreness would disappear.

Her Were lovers had known this. They hadn't needed to worry about any issues, from love bites to overworked muscles. She could take care of herself.

But Luke was a considerate human male who wanted to coddle her. She was touched by his impulse to do that. But it wasn't love notes and flowers, she reminded herself. He'd promised to stay away from that kind of gesture, and she was glad they'd established those ground rules.

After he'd wheeled her suitcase into the bedroom, he walked into the bathroom. Soon she heard water thundering into the large Jacuzzi tub. His caring gestures settled over her like a warm blanket, and she admitted that there were many ways to show affection besides love notes and flowers. Ordering up Epsom salts and running a warm bath were two of them.

With a sigh, she climbed out of bed. They were falling for each other, but maybe if they never acknowledged it, they could pretend it wasn't happening. The final separation would still hurt like hell, but at least they would have saved face.

Walking over to her suitcase, she unzipped it and rummaged around until she came up with a bag of elastic hair bands. She drew her tangled hair into a high pony-tail and fastened it with a bright green one. About that time, she heard the front door open. Mr. Thatcher must be here with her Epsom salts.

She put on the short terry-cloth robe she'd packed and belted it securely around her waist. When she walked into the bathroom, Luke glanced at her with ten-derness. "In that ponytail, you look about fifteen."

"Good thing I'm not, huh?"

"A very good thing. What's with the robe? Turning shy on me?"

"No. Mr. Thatcher just came in the front door."

"He did?" Luke grabbed a towel and knotted it around his hips. "I didn't hear him."

"The running water probably drowned it out."

"And anyway, you have that extra-keen hearing." He said it as if he'd accepted the fact in the same way he accepted that she had red hair and green eyes.

That was good, she decided. Now she could admit to hearing things that might prove useful to them without causing him to be suspicious. He didn't have to know how much better her hearing was than his.

He glanced over at the tub. "It takes a while to fill, but it's worth the wait. Don't get in yet. I'll go get the Epsom salts. We might as well give him our order for breakfast before he heads back down. What would you like?"

"Anything is fine."

"Aw, come on, Giselle. Test the system. Eggs Bene-dict? French toast stuffed with cream cheese and blue-berries? You name it, and the chef will fix it."

No love notes or flowers, but anything she wanted for

breakfast, no matter how exotic. Yep, he was falling for her. And when he gazed at her with that expectant expression on his handsome face, she couldn't stop herself from falling for him, either.

She thought of her favorite breakfast in the world. "A strawberry waffle with fresh strawberries and whipped cream, please."

"You've got it. Anything else?"

"Coffee and orange juice."

"I'll order that. And I'll be right back with your Epsom salts." He started out of the bathroom.

"Luke?"

He turned back. "What?"

"Do you think Mr. Thatcher will know why you wanted Epsom salts?"

"Maybe." He smiled. "But I'll tell him you turned your ankle getting out of the gondola at the Venetian."

"Thanks." She assumed Mr. Thatcher would figure out pretty soon that the relationship was no longer platonic, but she'd rather not advertise that they'd had enough sex for her to need a warm soak in Epsom salts. With luck, a maid would change the sheets and Mr. Thatcher wouldn't be privy to the chocolate smear-fest that had taken place.

She remembered the conversation about Were-human pairing and wondered if Mr. Thatcher would start worrying about Luke now. She'd thought of him as a Were ally, but he was also devoted to Luke and Cynthia. He wouldn't like knowing that she was going to make someone he loved suffer.

Luke came back in with the bag of Epsom salts. "He says to rest your ankle today. He asked if you needed an ACE bandage, and I said you didn't. I think he was prepared to disagree with me."

"Maybe I should have sprained my wrist instead."

"We'll figure it out. Look at that; he even opened the seal on the bag for me. Now, that's service." Luke sprinkled a generous amount of the granules into the water.

"He's very thorough."

"He's an amazing guy." Luke set the bag on the bathroom counter and turned off the water. "I don't know what I'd do without Mr. Thatcher. He's been like a spare parent. Now that my dad's gone and my mom's in France, I depend on him even more."

"I'm glad he's here for you."

"Me, too. He's as loyal as the day is long. Completely trustworthy. Well, the bath is ready. Want a hand in?"

She took off her robe. "I think I can manage."

"That's probably a good thing." He backed away from her. "Because watching you move around while you're naked is getting me hot. You realize there are jets in the tub, right?"

"There usually are in a tub like this."

"Want them turned on?"

She smiled. "No, thanks. I want a nice, peaceful soak. No jets involved."

He let out a shaky breath. "I'm glad. Because if you wanted the jets on, then I'd wonder what you were doing in there with those jets, and I'd have a really tough time keeping myself from climbing in with you."

"Maybe you need to be in here with me. You said you were sensitive after our two-person orgy."

"I couldn't handle it. You, me, and a big Jacuzzi would have a predictable outcome. Before long, I'd forget that the whole point was giving you a rest from me and my insatiable demands."

She laughed as she stepped into the warm, soothing

water. "Don't beat yourself up about that, Luke. Like I said, I was a willing partner in all of it."

"I know, but . . . Listen, would you mind sitting down in the tub? And sliding under the water so I can't see anything but your head?"

Glancing back at him, she noticed the towel he'd wrapped around his hips now jutted out at right angles to his body. "I see the problem." She lowered herself into the tub and scooted down until her chin touched the water. "How's that?"

"Better. But you know what? I'm going to check the messages on my phone. That should shut down my libido. I probably have about ten riddles piled up from my little sister." With that, he walked out of the bathroom and took his impressive erection with him.

She hadn't thought much about Cynthia and Bryce in the past few hours, but she needed to concentrate on that problem. She'd tried a direct approach to Bryce last night, but that had gone nowhere. Although he hadn't said so yesterday, he might be irritated that she'd come to town without telling him, even if he thought she was a good influence on Luke.

Well, he'd left San Francisco without telling her, either. She'd deserved some kind of explanation for his behavior. He had to know it'd impacted her.

Now that she'd had this experience with Luke, though, she'd be less hard on Bryce if he'd gone over to the side of those who believed Weres and humans should be allowed to mate without censure. His comment yesterday, that he wished he had been attracted to Cynthia, might mean he was, in fact, open to such relationships and wouldn't judge her too harshly.

Perhaps now he agreed with Duncan MacDowell, a

werewolf who championed integration of Weres and humans. Duncan had founded WOOF, Werewolves Optimizing Our Future, and his popular blog argued in favor of blending the two species. Many in the Were community strongly opposed that idea, but every time a human and Were mated, the hole in the dike widened. Bryce would have heard about Jake Hunter's recent decision to take a human mate. Although Bryce wasn't romantically interested in Cynthia, he might welcome some other human female into his life. Giselle hoped not. Such a move wouldn't go over well in the Landry household.

More than that, she had a feeling that Bryce and Miranda should be together. Whether Miranda would ever forgive him for cutting out on her was a whole other matter, but Giselle hoped that she might. They seemed right for each other, despite this current glitch in their relationship.

But if her brother had decided that a human female like Cynthia Dalton would suit him better, Giselle and her pack had big problems. A Were-human mating caused ripples throughout the Were community, and that was for starters. Either Bryce would abandon his pack, which left Giselle holding the bag, or he'd ask his human mate to become part of the Were world, which would create a set of problems for whoever that woman might be.

At least that woman wouldn't be Cynthia. Giselle's thoughts drifted to Luke's sister. Had Luke ever considered bringing Cynthia into the business? Maybe not. He was in so many ways the throwback she had imagined him to be when they first met.

Cynthia might not want to be an officer in the corporation, but if Luke had never asked her, that wasn't good.

Giselle had much to talk to the man about, but she had to choose her words carefully. These were touchy subjects.

Phone in hand, the subject of her thoughts walked back into the bathroom. He'd replaced the towel with a pair of gray sweats and a black T-shirt with *Silver Crescent* in metallic letters highlighting his impressive pecs. The T-shirt fit tight across his shoulders and hugged his biceps. She could stare at him all day and not get bored.

"Owen reports that Bryce and Cynthia picked up the Corvette, drove into the mountains, and rented a cabin up there. He has the cabin staked out and says they're still in there."

Giselle scrambled to her knees. "Let's go! We can grab a piece of fruit for breakfast and head on up the mountain."

His gaze swept over her half-submerged body and lingered on her breasts. "You need to slide back into the water. Now you look like a mermaid, and you know how tempting they are to us humans."

Even though he was talking about mermaids, having him refer to himself as a human while suggesting that she was not sent a chill down her spine. "But if they're staying put, maybe they're ready to talk. A mountain cabin would make more sense as neutral territory than some noisy restaurant or casino."

"I'm not convinced they're ready to talk to us face-to-face. I also have a rhyming message from Cynthia. I wouldn't call it a riddle, though. Back in the water, please." He lowered his hand as if pushing her there. "Down, down. That's good. Stay right there."

"I don't see the point in this. The water's clear as a bell."

"Yes, but from over here, I can't see much more than your head sticking up over the rim of the tub."

"Come on, Luke. Surely the sight of my naked body doesn't—"

"It does. And don't make fun. I'm seriously in lust with you, sweet peach, and after last night's boinkathon, I'm having trouble concentrating. All the research says that a man's sexual trigger is visual stimulation, so I'd appreciate your cooperation in the matter."

"Okay." She pressed her lips together to keep from laughing. No lover had ever said that kind of thing to her before, probably because Weres were stimulated by scent more than sight. A werewolf would be less interested in her sexually right now because the water and the Epsom salts muted her aroma. "So what's the message?"

"*Forest cabin, empty soon. Message waiting, happy tune.*"

"So they're leaving something for us in the cabin."

"Right. And sure as the world, something in there will be designed to get me wet." He glanced at her. "Maybe you can figure out in advance what that might be, given your knowledge of your brother's pranking skills."

"I'll try. Let me think about it."

Luke's phone chimed. "She sent a PS. *Don't send Owen in instead. I know he's watching the cabin.*" Luke glanced up. "She's really enjoying this."

"Of course she is. She's got your attention." Now, if he'd only listen, really listen and understand, they might get somewhere.

"I'll bet she's also got the DVD of all her recitals. That was in the vault."

"She has a right to them, after all. She's your sister, a part of the family." Giselle hesitated. Might as well give it a try. "Have you ever considered making her an officer in the corporation?"

His stunned expression was all the answer she needed, but he confirmed it verbally. "No. She's only twenty-two."

"What does that have to do with it? She must be really smart if she was on track to graduate magna cum laude from Yale."

"Yeah, but . . ." His gaze reflected his struggle with a concept that obviously had never occurred to him.

"Luke, what did you expect her to do with her degree?"

He shrugged. "My dad was the one who encouraged her to go. I don't know whether he had something in mind."

"Sounds as if the whole idea of college for her was based on some vague concept. If she is goal-oriented, there's nothing vague about becoming a showgirl. It's tangible and she has a role model—her mother."

"I know. I've thought of that."

"Her other two role models, her father and you, are in the business world, but apparently you've never invited her to be part of that world and neither did your dad. You were expected to take over because you're the son. She's the daughter, who's expected to do something brilliant . . . somewhere else. What's the appeal?"

"She wouldn't want to be part of the Dalton Corporation." He gazed at her. "Would she?"

"You'll never know if you don't ask her."

Luke massaged the back of his neck. "I have to think about this."

"I'm sure you do." She heard the penthouse front door open. "Our breakfast is here."

He blinked. "Your hearing is scary good." He paused to listen. "Okay, now I hear him moving around in there, clinking dishes and stuff. But you heard him come in the door, didn't you?"

"Yeah. It's genetic. Both my parents have the same excellent hearing."

"And Bryce?"

She nodded. "Bryce, too."

"That seems like an unusual genetic trait. I'll bet medical science would be interested in it."

"I suppose." Not to mention her canine DNA. But she'd never set foot in a traditional doctor's office. Her pack supported a clinic staffed by Were physicians trained at a top secret Were medical school.

"But you probably wouldn't want to go through a bunch of tests and stuff," he added.

"You're right. I wouldn't."

"Don't blame you. Nothing worse than being treated like some lab rat. Well, let me go see how breakfast is coming along and make sure that your waffle is fixed the way you ordered it. Once I'm gone, feel free to climb out of the tub."

"I will." She smiled at him.

"And put on something really ugly, okay?"

"I'll do my best."

"Bet it won't help. You're just too damned beautiful for your own good." With a chuckle, he left the bathroom.

She was really starting to like this guy ... a lot. And that made keeping such a big secret from him even tougher. She pictured the scene if she told him.

At first he wouldn't believe her. She'd have to shift to prove it. And he might be absolutely horrified. She shuddered. Good thing that was never going to happen.

Chapter 17

Luke found Mr. Thatcher putting the final touches to the breakfast table. He placed a small bouquet of roses in the center and stood back to admire the effect.

"Very nice, Mr. Thatcher. Giselle will love those."

"I daresay she will. She seems to appreciate small kindnesses."

"She . . . ah . . . didn't stay in the guest room last night. I don't want you to be surprised when she comes out of my bedroom."

Only a slight flicker in Mr. Thatcher's eyes registered his response to that. His demeanor remained calm. "That's between you and the lady, sir."

"True."

The butler cleared his throat. "But I would like to say one thing, if I may be permitted to do so."

"Sure. Go ahead."

"I would caution you not to get attached. I doubt that she'll be around very long."

Luke remembered that the butler and Giselle had talked the night before while Luke had been embroiled in the scheduling conflict down in the kitchen. "Did she say anything specific about that to you?"

"Not exactly. Call it intuition, but I don't see her as a long-term solution to your loneliness."

Luke caught his breath. Mr. Thatcher was always so proper and formal. He rarely made such a personal comment. "Who said I was lonely?"

"Pardon me, sir." His naturally ruddy cheeks turned a shade darker. "I forgot myself for a moment."

"No offense taken, but I am curious. Why would you assume that I'm lonely?" The word resonated within him, and it sounded far more valid than he'd like to admit.

"Well, I've . . . been thinking about loneliness recently. I may have erroneously thought I recognized behaviors in you that are similar to mine. My mistake. I do apologize."

"You're lonely?" Luke had never considered that possibility.

"I believe so, sir. Things have changed, as they always do, of course. I'm not caring for a young family any longer. And, no reflection on you, but I did enjoy the elegant parties your parents used to have in this penthouse. They kept me busy."

Luke nodded. "Makes sense. It's been a lot quieter around here since my dad died and my mom left."

"Of course. And you haven't been in a celebratory mood, which is perfectly understandable."

"Listen, Mr. Thatcher, if you want to take time off and visit your family in Hertfordshire, I can manage without you for a couple of weeks. I know you usually go in July, and you can still do that, but maybe you need a visit now." And in the meantime, Luke could figure out ways to liven up the place. Weekly poker nights in the penthouse, maybe.

What the butler really needed was for Luke to find a wife and produce some kids. If Luke had a wife, she might want to invite friends over for dinner. Mr. Thatcher would have a busy life again. But Luke couldn't just snap his fingers and make that happen.

"I appreciate the offer, sir. I may take you up on it, but not at the moment."

"Why not?"

"I want to make certain that your sister is, shall we say, settled before I leave the country for any extended period of time."

Luke was touched by that. He'd always thought of Mr. Thatcher as a second father to him and Cynthia, but he'd never known for certain that the feelings went both ways, and whether they were like a son and daughter to the butler. He was not a demonstrative man. But if he couldn't leave until Cynthia was "settled," as he'd put it, then he obviously cared for both of them in a fatherly sort of way.

"Thank you, Mr. Thatcher," Luke said. "I'll take all the moral support I can get right now." He glanced at the table, where the plates were covered with silver domes, as usual. "Mind if I check out Giselle's waffle?"

"Be my guest." The butler stepped forward and lifted the lid on the prettiest waffle concoction Luke had ever seen. An arrangement of blueberries, raspberries, and mint leaves ringed the waffle, which was mounded with whipped cream and topped with dark red strawberries. In the center of the arrangement sat a giant strawberry carved in the shape of a rose.

"Oh, how pretty!" Giselle exclaimed as she walked

into the room. She exchanged a glance with Mr. Thatcher, one Luke couldn't interpret. Then she clapped her hands together. "Let me get my phone and take a picture. That's a work of art." She ran back to the bedroom.

Mr. Thatcher gazed after her, a bemused smile on his face.

"She does appreciate small kindnesses," Luke said. "Give my thanks to Stefan."

"Of course." Mr. Thatcher removed the dome from Luke's meal, which looked about as nice as an omelet could, but it was obvious the chef had enjoyed decorating the waffle a lot more.

And the butler had loved bringing up the cart loaded with this special breakfast for two. He would have been even happier, Luke now realized, if he'd been serving brunch for ten. Something had to be done about that, although Luke wasn't good at planning parties. He immediately thought of Cynthia as the logical one to do that and realized that was sexist of him. She was a woman, so he assumed she could plan parties, but he'd never thought to ask if she wanted to be a corporate officer. He'd recently had thoughts that his dad hadn't been evolved, but Luke might as well put himself in the same category. How embarrassing that he'd never thought to ask Cynthia if she wanted to have a role in the corporation.

Giselle returned with her phone and moved around the table snapping pictures of the waffle from all angles. Luke wondered why her outfit looked so familiar, and he finally placed it. She'd found an old pair of his boxer shorts and a T-shirt that had seen better days.

It hung on her, effectively disguising her shape. He'd requested ugly, and she'd had to raid his dresser drawers to fill that request. Of course she looked cute as hell, and he wanted to do her as much as ever.

"My folks have a chef," she said, "but Isabella has never risen to these heights. I want to inspire her. My mom loves strawberry waffles, too. She should have one like this for her next birthday breakfast."

Luke was ridiculously pleased by Giselle's enthusiasm. "I told Mr. Thatcher to give our compliments to Stefan, our chef."

"Oh, my goodness, yes! In fact, later I'll go down and tell him myself." Then she glanced at Luke's plate, which was loaded up with his omelet and a big pile of hash browns. "Good golly, Miss Molly. Are you really going to eat all that?"

"I am if you'll stop taking pictures and sit down. Thank you, Mr. Thatcher, for bringing us such a great breakfast."

The butler inclined his head in acknowledgment. "Allow me to pour your coffee."

"Sure. That would be great." Watching the butler serve at the table was a treat Luke had enjoyed since he was a kid. A drop was never spilled, a dish never broken.

Mr. Thatcher finished pouring the coffee and stepped back from the table. "Will there be anything else?"

"Not for me," Giselle said. "Luke may need another omelet, though."

"Smart aleck." Luke glanced at the butler and caught his brief smile. "That should do it, then. Thank you."

"You are most welcome. Let me know when you're ready for me to clear everything away. Bon appétit." With a brief bow, the butler left.

Unable to keep his distance from Giselle, Luke walked around the table and helped her into her chair.

She laughed. "Thank you. How sweet. No one's done that for a while." She settled into her seat with her usual grace. "This waffle is so beautiful I almost hate to take a bite out of it."

"I could say the same about you. But I'll do it anyway." He leaned down and gently nipped the side of her neck.

"Hey!" She turned to glance up at him. "What're you do–"

He kissed her, stopping her protest. He shouldn't be kissing her, seeing as how they wouldn't be having sex. Mouth-to-mouth stimulation was nearly as potent as visual stimulation, especially when she kissed him back, which she was currently doing.

Swiveling in her seat, she took hold of his head and held him there while she angled her mouth and French-kissed the heck out of him. He grabbed the back of her chair for support and used his other hand to find out if she was wearing a bra under that gigantic T-shirt. She wasn't, which allowed him to play with her breasts until she began to squirm in her seat and whimper into his mouth.

He knew where this was leading, and he wasn't going there. She'd admitted to being sore, and one little soak in Epsom salts wouldn't be enough. She needed time. He wasn't sure how much, but more than a few hours.

With more restraint than he'd thought himself capable of, he stopped caressing her plump breasts and stepped back. He was breathing like a long-distance runner, and his johnson poked against the soft jersey of his sweats.

She was quite flushed herself. If she hadn't bothered with panties, then his boxers might be damp. He liked the thought of that. He might not throw them in the laundry for a while.

"My fault," he said once he got his breathing under control. "I started it. But we're not having sex again until you promise me that you're recovered."

Her gaze lifted to his. "We could take it slow and easy."

He groaned. "Don't do that! God, you're a seductress. Maybe we could start out slow and easy, but you know as well as I do that we wouldn't end up that way. We'd both get carried away, and before you know it, we'd be slamming into each other. That's how it is with us."

"Yeah." She smiled at him. "You're right."

"Stop smiling like that."

"Okay." She pressed her mouth into a thin line, but laughter danced in her green eyes.

He'd never get tired of the many moods of Giselle Landry. Whether she was laughing, or dreamy-eyed, or talking earnestly, or moaning with passion, she fascinated him. But somehow he had to keep himself from having sex with her right now, and probably this afternoon, and maybe even tonight. How depressing was that?

He walked around to his chair and pulled it out. "I'm going to sit right here and eat this huge omelet and all these potatoes. After that, I'll be too full to have sex."

"I would imagine that's true. After you've eaten everything, I would expect you to explode like an overloaded Hefty bag."

"I'm a man of action, a man who lives large. I need fuel for my many activities." He put his napkin in his lap and picked up his fork. About that time, he heard Giselle moan with pleasure. He didn't have to look to know why.

She'd taken a bite of her strawberry waffle loaded with whipped cream.

He kept his eyes on his plate and cut into his omelet. He didn't need to watch her eating that thing. Bad enough that he had to listen to her over there sighing in orgasmic delight.

Under different circumstances, he might not have thought that waffle presentation was especially erotic, but after his night with Giselle, everything seemed erotic. The baked waffle smelled like good sex, and the raspberries reminded him of her aroused nipples. He wanted to set that strawberry rose in her navel, or maybe lower than that, and nibble for a while. Then there was the whipped cream.... He could do a whole riff on the erotic possibilities of whipped cream.

"You said you wanted to know about some of my brother's practical jokes."

He risked looking at her, and sure enough, she had whipped cream on her upper lip. "You have some whipped cream on your mouth." He pointed to his own upper lip to show her where.

"Thanks." Her tongue darted out, and she licked it away.

He stared at her full mouth and remembered all the ways she'd used it to drive him insane.

"Do you still?"

"Still what?" Want her? With the heat of a thousand suns. Somehow he didn't think that's what she'd asked, but he'd lost track of the conversation.

"Want me to tell you about my brother's tricks?"

"Oh. Yeah, sure. That's a good idea. He'll probably booby-trap the cabin somehow." He dug into his omelet again. "Something to do with water."

"Once he set up an elaborate scheme with a bouquet of flowers and a sensor that would cause water to shoot out of the vase if someone leaned down to smell them. But that's not targeted to a specific person, so I don't think he'd bother to set that up in the cabin. He's not going to repeat his bucket over the front door, so I honestly don't know what to expect. He was never really into explosives."

Luke stared at her. "What do you mean by 'never really into'? Did he ever blow anything up?"

"Not much. Mostly baked goods. When he blew up a triple-layer Black Forest cake, he had to pay for the cleaning crew out of his allowance. I think that ended the explosion phase. After that, it was mostly water pranks."

Luke chewed and swallowed. "Then I guess we'll just have to drive up there and find out what sort of surprise he's concocted. I got directions from Owen."

"Want to take my motorcycle?"

"We'd better go in my car. We've had some snow in the mountains, and we might hit an icy patch of road. Plus it will be chilly up there."

She shrugged. "Okay. The car it is. Probably a better idea until I recover anyway. Is your omelet good?"

He'd barely tasted it. All he cared about was getting through the meal and out of the penthouse without grabbing her. "Yep. Delicious."

"Do you normally eat with such concentration?"

He put down his fork and looked at her. "No, but normally I'm not fighting the urge to have my dining companion stretched out under me in the middle of the table."

Her breath caught. "Do you have any idea how exciting it is to hear something like that?"

"Do you have any idea how close I am to becoming an inconsiderate jerk who takes you regardless of whether I'll hurt you in the process?"

Her lips parted and her cheeks grew pink. "I wouldn't care."

"I would." Shoving back his chair, he tossed his napkin on the table. "I'll move your suitcase back into the guest room. You can get ready in there."

"You're throwing me out of your bedroom?"

"Yes. For my sanity and your protection."

"You're very gallant, Luke."

"Don't say that yet. Wait until we're both heading down in the elevator. No, not even then. I could stop the elevator and take you before we get to the bottom. Congratulate me when we're in the car headed up into the mountains. I can't very well do you and drive a mountain road at the same time."

"I suppose not. In any case, thank you for making me feel so desired."

"If you were any more desired, I'd be in flames." He stalked into the bedroom and grabbed her suitcase. He had to carry it open because that was the way she'd left it and he didn't want to take the extra time to zip it up. That meant he had to breathe in the light but exotic scent of Giselle. She didn't wear perfume, so it had to be her natural scent. He loved it.

"Thank you!" she called out to him as he deposited the open suitcase in the guest bedroom and made a beeline for the master.

"I'll be ready in twenty minutes." He shut and locked the door.

"Me, too!" she shouted from her seat at the table.

He stood on the other side of his bedroom door, literally panting from the effort of separating himself from temptation. She'd become such a vital part of his existence so quickly that it scared the shit out of him. If this wasn't soul mate territory, what was?

She liked knowing that she affected him this way. He could see it in her eyes. And she craved their lovemaking as much as he did. That hot kiss at the table had told him so. If he hadn't called a halt, they would have been doing it—in the chair, up against the table, on the floor. And whipped cream would have ended up all over everything.

But he wouldn't have liked himself very much afterward. The woman had announced that she was sore, and unless he had become some sort of brutish cad, that should matter to him. Hell, he was sore, too. Anyone would be who'd had the sex marathon they'd been through.

Sadly, he didn't care about that. He would take a little twinge for the reward of having her again. He wasn't about to make that decision for her, though. When they made love again, and he hoped it would be fairly soon, he needed to know that he was giving her pleasure and not pain.

Therefore, he'd lock himself in the bedroom, take his shower, and get dressed while she performed the same chores in the guest bathroom. He would not think of her stepping into the shower and letting the water slide over her lithe body. He would not think of her lathering up, which would require touching all those intimate places he craved.

Right. He wouldn't think of it at all. Except every damn minute. Stripping down, he walked into the master bath and turned on the jets in the shower they'd shared only hours before. He could do this.

As he stepped into the spray, he was swamped by the erotic memories of Giselle turning to wash all the chocolate from her creamy skin, and of him leading her, with her eyes closed, to the jet that was perfectly positioned to give her a climax. After that ... He groaned as the potent image of Giselle offering herself turned his cock into an unforgiving steel rod.

Surrendering, he faced the nearest jet, took hold of his problem, and solved it.

Chapter 18

Giselle hadn't expected to have alone time, but she planned to make excellent use of it. The minute she'd heard the lock click on Luke's bedroom door, she'd made a dash for the guest room, abandoning the last of her strawberry waffle. That was a crying shame, but she had her priorities.

Once she left Vegas, she never expected to see Luke Dalton again, so while she was here, she wanted to soak up as much of his wonderfulness as possible. But they'd pushed the envelope the night before, and she needed to heal before she could partake again without wincing. That's where being a werewolf came in handy.

She made certain the guest room door was locked. Discovery would mean disaster. Then she pulled off the boxer shorts and T-shirt she'd borrowed from Luke and stretched out on the soft carpet. She hadn't shifted in at least a month because she'd been so busy covering for her brother. As she readied herself, she realized she wasn't as angry with Bryce about his disappearing act as she had been.

Although she still didn't appreciate the way he'd taken off without a word, his defection had brought her to Luke and a whole new appreciation for the sexual act. She also now had a template for what she was looking for in a mate. Unfortunately, Luke might be one of a kind, which would leave her settling for second best, but she couldn't help that. Luke was human.

Closing her eyes, she eased into her shift. Muscles expanded, bones realigned, and in a few short minutes a wolf with green eyes and dark red fur lay on the carpet. Giselle's flanks heaved. She'd like to walk around a little and work out the kinks, but there wasn't time.

A second shift following on the heels of a first one took extra energy, but she didn't mind. Luke was worth it. Her wolf eyes closed as she focused on reversing the process. The air around her seemed charged with electricity. Fur dissolved, facial features changed, and she was in human form again.

She couldn't resist reaching between her legs to test the shift's healing capacity. Her vulva was petal soft and moist with no sign of chafing. She smiled. Luke might not believe that she'd recovered so quickly, but she'd praise the value of Epsom salts. And when he realized he could love her again without restraint, he wouldn't care how or why. He'd simply enjoy.

The time she'd devoted to shifting meant she had to hurry through her shower and hair-washing routine. Luke would be ready before she was, but she knew human males were used to waiting for females to groom themselves. Giselle normally wasn't like that. She didn't believe in taking more time than necessary to dress for any event, whether it was a walk in the woods or a gala ball.

After blow-drying her hair, she dressed in jeans, boots, and a soft white sweater. She found Luke sitting on the leather sofa looking at the picture and the program that had affected him so much last night. He glanced up, and she glimpsed something soft and vulnerable in his expression before he chased it away with a brilliant smile.

"You look great."

The frank admiration in his blue eyes warmed her in a way that no male gaze had ever done before. Although she'd been complimented on her looks in the past, the praise hadn't meant so much. But one simple comment from Luke made her glow.

She walked over and sat beside him. "That's such a beautiful picture of Cynthia."

"It is. But the program is what really got to me. I was sitting here wondering why, and I think it was remembering that moment when she dashed up to us and insisted all three of us had to sign it. She must have felt so loved and supported by all of us, and now . . ."

She put her hand on his knee. "You still love her, Luke."

"Yeah, but what about the support? I thought that's what I was doing, but you've made me rethink everything."

"I have?" She looked into his eyes, excitement humming through her. "You're going to support her dream?"

"Even better. I'm going to offer her a vice presidency in the corporation."

Giselle groaned.

"What's wrong with that? You said I should ask her if she wants to be part of the business."

"I know. But asking her if she wants to do that is a whole other thing from offering her a top job without any prior discussion. It will come out sounding like a bribe."

"So I shouldn't offer her a job?"

"Maybe eventually, but first you need to let her know you understand her yearning to be a dancer. You can show you understand by hiring her at the Silver Crescent. Then, sometime after that, you can offer her—"

"Can't risk it. Once I give her a job dancing, she's liable to love it so much that she won't want to quit for some desk job."

If she'd been close to a wall, she would have banged her head against it. Or, better yet, banged his head against it. "Luke, can you hear yourself? If she does love it that much, then that's what she should do! Life's too short not to love your work."

His jaw tightened. "She might also love being a doctor, or a lawyer, or hell, an astrophysicist. But she'll never know if she goes into dancing instead."

"There's nothing wrong with that reasoning, except that—"

"Aha! You admit it's valid."

"I admit it's logical. But that doesn't give you the right to impose your logic on her and try to control her life. If she chooses to throw away a potential career as an astrophysicist so she can shake her booty on the stage of the Silver Crescent, that's her prerogative."

Folding his arms, he gazed at her with those incredible blue eyes. He didn't even seem particularly angry. In fact, he looked a little smug. "I'll remind you of that speech when you're trying to convince your brother to come home and accept his responsibilities."

"That's different."

"Not much. Why come chasing down here after him? Why not let him live his life the way he chooses?"

She hated to admit he had a point. But he didn't know the stakes in this game. He saw a wayward older brother who should be allowed to choose his own path. But she saw a werewolf who could create a political nightmare for the Landry pack if he refused to take over as alpha. That was different . . . wasn't it?

She tried to tell herself he was rebelling against the manipulation of his parents and future in-laws, not the concept of becoming the pack's leader. He'd be excellent in that role.

She handed Luke the photograph of Cynthia. "I realize it looks as if I'm trying to direct Bryce's future."

Luke nodded as he put the picture back in the envelope. "It does."

"But there are deeper issues at work." Most of which she couldn't talk about. "The family dynamic is—"

He laid the envelope on the coffee table. "You want to talk about family dynamics? Try this on for size. Your dying father puts you in charge of his beloved daughter's welfare. I can guarantee that if he hadn't died, she'd be about to graduate from Yale in a few weeks. He would have expected that of her, and she wouldn't have defied him the way she's defying me."

Giselle believed that. Fathers could have tremendous influence over daughters. Her dad hadn't specifically asked her to come down to Vegas and talk Bryce into accepting his place in the pack hierarchy, but she'd known that's what he and her mother hoped Giselle would accomplish. She was here to please her parents in much the same way Luke was trying to honor his father's wishes.

Taking a deep breath, she drew in a fair amount of humility along with the oxygen. "I owe you an apology. I have no business passing judgment on your behavior. Mine isn't all that different, as you so correctly point out."

His expression softened. "Thanks for that, Giselle." He came closer and rested his hands on her shoulders. "I owe you an apology, too, though." His gaze searched hers. "I was eager for you to help me figure out the situation with Cynthia. You seem to really get her. It's not fair if I turn around and reject your advice." He kneaded her shoulders with a gentle touch. "Bottom line, I'm glad you're here."

"Me, too." She saw the kiss shimmering in his eyes. Letting that happen would be so natural, but they had places to go and booby traps to deal with. One kiss would lead to two, and twenty, and . . . wild monkey sex. "We should go, or we'll never get to that cabin."

"When you're right, you're right." With a final squeeze, he stepped back. "Besides, I don't want to hurt you."

She decided giving him some hints would be okay. "Actually, the Epsom salts did wonders."

"Oh?" The glint returned to his eyes. "Care to elaborate?"

"No." She grabbed her leather jacket, which still lay over the back of the sofa. "That's for future reference. Right now we need to drive up to a mountain cabin and see if Cynthia and Bryce have found a way to soak you."

"And after that?"

She smiled. "Epsom salts work miracles. That's all I'm sayin'."

Luke dropped his Lexus into third gear as he navigated the winding roads leading to the pine-covered slopes of the mountains. As the desert vegetation gave way to evergreens, he found himself thinking more about Giselle's miraculous recovery than his little sister's rebellious behavior. That wasn't good.

His revved-up libido could take a hike. He needed to concentrate on the problem with his sister, and besides, Giselle might not be as recovered as she claimed. They were driving up here to check out Cynthia's latest message, not to find a suitable spot to get naked.

Giselle put her window down a couple of inches and inhaled. "Smells great out there. I love pines." Then she shivered and closed the window. "Chilly, though."

"That's the beauty of living in Vegas. You can go from the warm desert to the cool mountains in no time. Lake Mead's in the other direction, so Vegas has it all." He sounded like the damned Chamber of Commerce, and he knew exactly why. He wanted to gauge her reaction to the city, in case . . . well, just in case. He was a fool to keep hoping, but every time he looked at her, he was more convinced than ever that she was the one.

And it wasn't all about sex, either. Silly as it sounded, he liked the way they argued without getting nasty about it. She stood up to him, but she fought fair. She had the qualities he looked for in a friend.

"Obviously you're happy living here," she said.

"I am. It's where I grew up, so that's part of the reason. But I've seen other parts of the country, and Vegas suits me. I like the energy of the city, the mild winters, and the chance to head for the mountains or the lake for a quick change of scenery."

She nodded. "That's good."

Although he would have preferred a more enthusiastic response, at least she hadn't disagreed with him about the city's appeal. "Are you happy living in San Francisco?"

"Oh, yeah. The cool air, the fog, sailboats on the bay—love it."

So it wasn't only her job holding her there. That was discouraging. "Ever considered another part of the country?"

"Nope. Besides the fact that I love the area, my family's there. I'm very family oriented."

"I used to be." Whoa, that sounded pathetic. "The plain fact is, most guys would love to be in my shoes. I have plenty of money and the freedom to do what I want if I keep the corporation on an even keel."

"Sounds like a nice life."

"Exactly. Of course, Mr. Thatcher is hoping I'll get married and have a bunch of kids so he'll have something to do. I found out this morning he's bored out of his skull."

"So that's Mr. Thatcher's dream. What do you want?"

You. But he couldn't say that. "A better relationship with my sister." He hadn't meant to say that, either, but it was the truth. Now that his mother was in France, Cynthia was the only family he had close by. Fighting with her felt terrible and he wanted it to stop.

"You know the way to get that, right?"

"Yeah, give in."

"It's not giving in, Luke. It's letting go of your role as the father figure and becoming a brother and a friend."

The idea beckoned to him like an oasis in the desert. "As I've mentioned before, my dad would roll over in his grave at the thought of her dancing with the Moonbeams instead of finishing her education."

"Yes, but he's not here," she said gently. "Expecting

you to run the corporation is one thing. Putting you in charge of your sister's future is unfair. Of course she's not going to give you the same respect she gave your dad. If my brother tried to tell me what to do, I'd spit in his eye."

That made him grin. "I bet you would." Spotting a street sign ahead, he slowed the car. "There's the turn-off." The road was gravel, which made him doubly glad he'd brought his car instead of Giselle's rented motorcycle. Patches of snow lay in the shadows created by the tall pines.

No one else was on the road, so he braked the car and pulled out his cell phone. "I'm sure they've left and Owen followed, but let me double-check." He glanced at his text messages. "They took off about an hour ago. Owen tailed them to . . . the Silver Crescent? Damn it! They're running us around in circles."

"She's trying to prove a point."

Luke glared at the text. "Well, she's pissing me off." His phone chimed. "I'll bet that's her, gloating." He read the text. *"Game is over. Time to talk. Meet us here at eight o'clock."*

"Eight o'clock tonight? That's ten hours from now."

"I know. But Cynthia loves the number eight. We used to play Crazy Eights when she was little, and then in junior high she found out that turning an eight on its side was the sign for infinity."

"And it's the difference in your ages."

He nodded. "That too. I wonder if they're in the penthouse yet."

"Oh, dear."

He looked over at her. "Yeah. She could have a field day. Mr. Thatcher would have waited for my signal before he brought in housekeeping."

"Smart man, but if nothing's been done in the penthouse . . ."

He met her gaze. "Then the bedroom is as we left it—sheets covered with chocolate, pillows on the floor, bed a tumbled mess. There won't be much doubt what went on there last night. She'll figure that out right quick."

"So will Bryce." She took a deep breath. "Okay, so they find out we had sex."

He lifted his eyebrows.

"Well, so it was over-the-top sex, with chocolate mousse cake spread everywhere and our clothes strewn on the floor."

Luke speed-dialed Mr. Thatcher. "Maybe they're not in the penthouse. Maybe they went to Cynthia's apartment. That's logical. I don't have a key to her place, so they could hide out—hello, Mr. Thatcher? Please send a cleaning crew up to the penthouse ASAP. Thanks." He disconnected. "Call me old-fashioned, but I'd rather not have my little sister creating mental images of what went on in that bedroom."

"I agree. I'm not wild about having Bryce check out the aftermath, either. He knows I'm not a vestal virgin, but I'm not in the habit of advertising my sexual adventures."

"Me, either." Luke tucked his phone in his jacket pocket and let up on the brake. "Let's keep our fingers crossed that Mr. Thatcher beats them up there and clears away the evidence."

Chapter 19

Giselle was damned uncomfortable about having Bryce find out she'd had sex with a human, especially after the strong stand she'd taken on the subject. But maybe she'd been due for a comeuppance. She might have been way too sanctimonious.

And if the cleaning crew didn't arrive in time, there could be benefits for Luke and Cynthia's relationship. Maybe a dose of humility would help Luke realize he had no business trying to control his little sister's life.

"This is it." Luke parked the car beside a small log cabin with a covered front porch. A couple of wooden rockers sat on the porch, and a rock chimney added to the rustic charm of the place. Large pines hovered close, as if sheltering the cabin.

"Cute." Giselle wouldn't say so and risk hurting Luke's feelings, but she much preferred this setting to the glitz of the Vegas strip. Any werewolf would.

"Yeah, cute. I wonder how they've booby-trapped it. They've had hours to plan this one."

"We could just not go in."

"True." He glanced at her. "But then we'd never know what they did."

"Yeah, okay. I'm curious, too. We'll approach with caution." Giselle thought of the many pranks her brother had pulled as a kid. "Watch where you step."

"That's not reassuring. Anything could be hidden under the leaves scattered on the ground."

"I'm used to the woods." She glanced over at him. "Want me to go in first?"

"No." He blew out a breath and opened his door. "I'm not letting you get doused when I'm her target. Stay here while I check things out."

"Nothing doing." She climbed out of the car, her boots crunching on dry leaves. Ah. Fresh air. Woods. Her favorite environment. She stretched her arms over her head.

He rounded the car and stood gazing at her. "Would it have made a difference if I'd said *please stay put*?"

"Probably not." She lowered her arms and breathed in the pine-scented air as she walked toward him. "But you could try that next time and see. Taking a wild guess, here, but did your father give orders?"

"He was the boss."

"Of the world?"

He blinked. "Of course not! He was the boss of Dalton Industries, and giving orders is part of the job."

"What about your family? Was he the boss there, too?"

"Yes. I can tell you don't approve of that, but for the most part, it was a good thing."

"I'm not passing judgment on him, Luke. He obviously loved you all very much. But a benevolent dictatorship doesn't work these days, especially when a man gives orders to a woman."

He sighed. "You're right."

"But I have to say, meeting you has taught me a lot, too."

"By my poor example?"

She couldn't help smiling. "Yep. 'fraid so. When I finally talk to Bryce, I'll be more interested in hearing his side of the story than trying to convince him to do his duty."

Luke sighed and scrubbed a hand over his face before looking at her again. "I get it, Giselle. I really do. But for a sister to give her big brother space to be his own person is one thing. For a brother to do the same for his little sister, which includes standing by while she struts around half-naked in front of drooling strangers . . . Can you see why that's difficult for me to accept?"

"Yes." She closed the distance between them and slid her arms around his neck. "I can see that what Cynthia's asking of you goes against every protective male instinct you have."

He gathered her close. "It sure as hell does. Thanks for recognizing that."

"You'll have to override those instincts."

"How?"

"I can't tell you how, but I can tell you why."

"I'm listening. Strong motivation is always good."

"Backing off will show that you trust her to manage her own life. After that, you can stop being the authority figure and move on to becoming her friend."

He searched her gaze. "You're a smart lady."

"I am?"

"Uh-huh." He massaged the small of her back. "Ultimately, that's what I want with Cynthia, although I couldn't have put it into words. You just did."

"Probably because you're so close to the situation."

"Maybe, but thanks, anyway. My dad used to say a parent isn't supposed to be a friend, and he was right. But I'm not a parent."

"That's right."

"It's so damned simple, Giselle. *I'm not her parent.*"

Happiness bubbled within her as the sparkle returned to his blue eyes. "Congratulations, Luke. I think that was an honest-to-goodness breakthrough."

"Yep, it is." He beamed at her. "I can feel it. I was thinking like a parent, but it's like a switch was just flipped in my brain. No more parent. Whew."

"Feel better now?"

"Yeah, and about a hundred pounds lighter, too. I don't even give a damn what sort of soaking I'm about to get inside that cabin." He gave her a squeeze and released her. "Let's go find out what they've been up to."

"I'm sure they put some effort into it, whatever it is."

He took her hand as they walked toward the cabin's front porch. "I guess I should be flattered by that."

"I think so. If she didn't care about you, she'd leave town and begin her dancing career somewhere else. Instead, she's campaigning for a job in your casino."

"I still say she has an unrealistic vision of how that will turn out, but at least I'll be there if anything goes wrong."

"And she wants that."

"Apparently." He paused. "Do you hear music?"

She'd heard it long ago, but had decided not to draw more attention to her excellent hearing. "I do. Do you recognize it?"

"I do." He sighed. "She's been in the family vault. I realize it's her choice, but damn. She took a hell of a chance, leaving it playing with the door open and no one here."

Giselle squeezed his hand. "Not such a huge chance. She knows you're right behind her, and this area seems relatively quiet."

"I suppose."

"And you're not the parent."

"No. See, I thought I'd fixed myself, and then I reverted back the minute I thought she'd taken a chance with a video."

"You're getting there, Luke. Don't get discouraged. Habits can be really hard to break." Her heart ached for him. He was so determined to do the right thing, and yet sometimes so confused about what that was. Her issues with Bryce were a walk in the park compared to Luke's struggle to gracefully make the transition after his dad's death.

He'd automatically assumed that he should be the head of the family as well as CEO of the corporation. But there was no head of the family now. His role was cherished brother and friend to his sister.

No wonder he'd been so autocratic with Cynthia in the beginning. "Don't forget that your sister knows exactly which buttons to push to test you and throw you into a panic."

"Yeah, she does." His gaze lingered on her, the light in his eyes warm. "I'm glad you're here, Giselle. God knows what kind of mess I would have made if you hadn't been."

"I won't insult your intelligence by contradicting that statement."

He laughed. "I'm even glad your brother is here. I'm sure he's the one who convinced Cynthia to turn this into a game instead of a vendetta."

"I think he was."

"Come on, then." Still holding her hand, he started up the steps to the cabin's front porch. "Let's find out what our brilliant siblings cooked up for us." Luke hesitated in front of the cabin's rustic wooden door. "We're dry so far, but once we go in, all bets are off. Normally I hold the door for a lady, but in this case . . ."

She slipped her hand from his. "Go for it. Be my hero."

"Do I get a reward for bravery?" He waggled his eyebrows at her.

"Absolutely."

"Excellent. I'm going in." Grasping the knob, he pushed open the door. Nothing happened. "Maybe I have to be inside." He stepped into the room. Still nothing.

"I'm right behind you." Giselle followed him through the door. "It's warm in here. They left the heat on."

"And the video going." Luke walked over to the TV. "This one's from her senior year in high school. She was in a lot of numbers that year."

Giselle moved farther into the room. All the curtains were closed, which made seeing the video easier. Cynthia danced with a group this time. Giselle counted ten girls in identical sparkly outfits of royal blue. The implication that Cynthia wanted to be part of a dancing group again was unmistakable.

For the first time, Giselle saw Cynthia dancing and not simply caught in a still photograph. Bryce had probably seen this video, too, and thank goodness he wasn't romantically attracted to Cynthia. The video showed that the beautiful child of fourteen had become a stunning woman of eighteen. And wow, could she dance.

Giselle drew closer. "She's good, Luke. I'm no expert at these things, but she looks perfectly at home on the stage."

"She always has been." He stood, hands in the pockets of his jeans, his attention riveted on the screen. "You've been right all along. If she doesn't give dancing a shot, she'll regret it. And she'll resent me for opposing her."

"I think so." Giselle slipped an arm around his waist. "As you said, at least she'll be at the Silver Crescent, where you can keep an eye on things."

Luke wrapped his arm around Giselle's shoulders. "No water trick yet. Do you suppose they've rigged it to the DVD, so whoever takes it out gets drenched?"

"Let's open the curtains so we can see what might be lurking in the shadows. After all, I'm a Landry, too. I might be able to figure out what Bryce has set up. That would give me some satisfaction, actually."

"Me, too." He squeezed her shoulder and released her. "But let me open the curtains. That would be a perfect booby trap."

"Good thinking." She stayed where she was while Luke pulled cords that opened the curtains at each window. Again, nothing happened.

But she could see her surroundings much better. Logs were arranged in the stone fireplace as if waiting for the touch of a match. Positioned in front of it were a couch and two chairs upholstered in a green plaid that fit the rustic decor.

The coffee table and two end tables were made from

diagonal slices of a large tree trunk placed on a wrought-iron base. Bark rimmed the edges, but the surfaces were polished and lacquered.

"Nice place," Giselle said. "Cozy."

"It would be if I didn't expect a jet of water to come shooting out at me at any minute." He walked over to the TV and crouched down, examining it from all angles. "I can't see a single thing out of place, but you'd better stand back while I take the DVD out."

"Sure thing." She edged away from the TV. If this was Bryce's grand finale, it could be a doozy.

Luke gingerly extracted the DVD from the player and turned the machine off, along with the television. Letting out a breath, he stepped back. "That was anticlimactic."

"I'll bet they decided not to do a water trick and figured we'd go crazy waiting for it."

Luke nodded. "Makes sense. And that strategy's working. I'm like a cat in a room full of rocking chairs."

"Speaking of rocking chairs, we could go sit on the porch. That setup looks innocent enough."

Tucking the disk in the case lying next to the DVD player, he turned to her, a gleam in his eyes. "I'm not in the mood for innocent."

"Oh?" She'd seen that gleam before. She liked it. It produced a delicious response in her willing body.

"Here's how I see our situation. They want to meet us at eight tonight, correct?"

"Correct."

"And do you think we should go along with their timetable?"

"I do. If they're finally willing to talk, I don't want to scare them off by trying to set up something sooner."

He tossed the DVD on the couch and came toward her. "I happen to agree with that, which leaves us with several hours to fill."

"So it does." She had no trouble reading his mind, and her heart thudded in anticipation.

"Coincidentally, we're all alone in a cute little cabin in the woods. But first I need you to tell me the absolute truth. If you're still sore, then—"

"I'm fine."

His gaze searched hers.

"Really, Luke. I'm recovered. Magic Epsom salts."

A smile tugged at his mouth. "I'd be a fool to argue the point." Heat radiated from him as he stood inches away. Without touching her, he managed to surround her with that heat. "Do you suppose there's a bed around here somewhere?"

She breathed in his virile scent, and a shiver of delight ran through her. "I wouldn't be surprised."

"Then let's go find it." Lacing his strong fingers through hers, he led her toward a doorway on the far side of the living room. "Bingo." He drew her inside.

She gave the room a quick glance although, under the circumstances, she wasn't about to be picky. But it was a lovely setting. The curtains were open. Tall pines outside the window filtered the sunlight, creating a dappled effect on the navy quilt covering the king-sized bed set into a dark walnut frame.

Looking up at him, she allowed the desire she felt to shine in her eyes. "It will do nicely."

"Oh, yeah." Luke gathered her into his arms and backed toward the bed. "Come roll around on the mattress with me, pretty lady. I have the urge to muss you up."

Laughing, she put up a token protest. "Let's take off our clothes first. Then we won't go back looking so—"

"Like we've been having sex? I've stopped caring whether they know or not."

"But—"

"Relax. Have fun. Let me wrestle you out of your clothes. And you can wrestle me out of mine."

"Oh, what the hell." She wrapped her arms around his neck. "Why not?"

"That's the spirit. Hang on. Here we go!" Falling back onto the mattress, he hauled her down with him.

The mattress rolled under them with a sloshing sound. Then what had appeared to be dappled shadows on the comforter began to spread.

"Luke . . ."

He closed his eyes and sighed. "I know. Water bed. And it's leaking."

Chapter 20

The combined weight of Luke and Giselle rapidly pushed water up through the quilt and into the material of his jeans and shirt. "Just slide off me," he said, "and you won't get wet."

"Got it." She eased backward, but the mattress rippled with every move she made.

As the cold water oozed up around him, Luke began to laugh. They hadn't even taken pity on him and left the bed's heater on. He'd been in some ridiculous situations in his life, but this might win the prize.

"Give me your hands." Giselle stood, feet braced on either side of his knees, and leaned forward. "I'll pull you out."

"I don't know." He cleared the laughter from his throat. "I'm pretty heavy. And the wetter my clothes get, the heavier I'll be."

"I'm braced against the bed frame. Your legs are still dangling over the edge. Press your heels against the frame. We can do it." She wiggled her fingers. "Grab hold before you get any wetter."

"Okay." He placed his hands in hers and shoved his heels against the bed frame. He was impressed by the strength of her grip.

"On three. One, two, *three.*" She pulled, and he heaved himself upward. She staggered backward a few steps. His feet hit the floor, and he tightened his hold on her hands. They stayed upright.

She grinned. "See? Piece of cake."

He returned her smile. "Thanks, Wonder Woman."

"Ah, it was mostly leverage. No big deal. So how wet are you?"

"Check it out." He turned around.

"Wow. The back of you is soaked through. You'd better take everything off."

"Great suggestion." He glanced over his shoulder. "Hang on to that thought while I see what's going on with this water bed."

"Well, I hope you know something about them, because I know zero about those things."

"My parents used to have one." He walked back to the bed. "Theirs developed a leak in the middle of the night. I'm sure Cynthia remembers the hullabaloo, which gave her the idea for this trick." He folded back the soggy quilt and the wet sheets.

Just that little bit of pressure caused water to puddle on the plastic surface. As he wiped it away with a corner of the sheet, he could see a tiny pinprick. He wondered how many there were. It might not have taken many.

He continued to roll the bedding out of the way. "Would you please see if there's a plastic shower curtain in the bathroom? And if there is, would you unhook it and bring it in here? I want to strip all this off."

"Sure."

"Thanks." As he exposed more of the mattress, he discovered a few other tiny holes. As he'd learned from the incident with his parents' bed, that would be enough to cause chaos.

When he uncovered the very middle of the bed, he found a sealed plastic bag with a piece of paper inside. "Looks like they left us a love note," he called out to Giselle.

"What's it say?" She came back into the room with a forest-themed plastic shower curtain in her arms.

"I'm about to find out." He wiped his hands on a dry section of sheet before unsealing the bag and taking out the paper. "*My darling brother,*" he read aloud. "*If you're reading this, I apologize for denying you and Giselle some water bed fun. But . . . gotcha, LOL!*

Knowing you, and I do, you're going all paranoid about the potential damage from this stunt. Bryce and I spent hours arranging it, and more hours rigging it up, with permission from the owner, who is in possession of a sizable damage deposit. We put a layer of plastic under the bed to protect the floor. A cleaning crew will come in tomorrow and replace the water bed and frame with the original bed that goes in this cabin.

All the holes are on top, so if you don't disturb the mattress more than you already have, all should be well. Leave everything as is, if you can stand to do that, which you probably can't, but that's up to you, Bro. See you in the penthouse at 8 p.m. Smoochies, Your loving sister and future Moonbeams dancer, Cynthia."

He glanced up. "I'll be damned."

"She sounds as thorough and responsible as you are, Mr. Dalton." Giselle looked at him with a bemused expression. "Still want this?" She lifted the shower curtain she'd been holding.

"I don't know." Folding the note, he surveyed the wet bedding. It had soaked up the water that had oozed out while Bryce and Cynthia had remade the bed to set their trap. If he left it there, it would continue to absorb any other possible leakage, but since all the holes were on top, as his sister had mentioned, there wouldn't be much.

Moving all of it into the bathroom, as he'd planned, would accomplish little except to transfer the sogginess to a different location. "I guess not." Still holding the note, he walked toward her. "But I'll put the shower curtain back up."

"Nope." She stepped out of reach. "I'll do it while you light the fire and start drying your clothes."

"Oh." Thoughts of a leaking water bed and his rebellious sister evaporated in the heat of her gaze.

She winked at him. "Don't tell me you've forgotten about all those hours we have to fill."

His breath caught at the rich sensuality in her voice. "I got momentarily distracted." That seemed inconceivable now, as his heart hammered and his groin tightened. "It won't happen again."

"I doubt it will. Meet you in front of the fire." Her hips swayed provocatively as she walked away from him. His soft groan was greeted with laughter. "Better hurry, Luke. It won't take me long to hang up this shower curtain."

Galvanized by that thought, he headed for the living room. He tucked Cynthia's note in the pocket of his jacket. Then he realized the couch was cluttered with their jackets and the DVD.

He moved it all to a chair, because he envisioned using the couch for the activities they'd been denied on the water bed. But when he examined the couch more closely, he realized it was a futon. Bonus. Releasing the back turned it into the equivalent of a double bed. Not quite the king he would have preferred, but far better than the couch he'd planned to work with.

They'd also want to be near the fire. He set aside the coffee table and pulled the futon closer to the hearth. Next he became aware of how many windows existed in this room compared to the bedroom. If someone were to come up on the porch . . . He didn't relish putting on a show. He locked the front door and closed all the curtains.

Finally he turned his attention to the fireplace and checked the flue to be sure it was open before flicking the butane lighter to ignite the kindling. He couldn't help wondering if the logs in the fireplace, the open flue, and the handy butane lighter had been Cynthia's work, too. She used to love family vacations up in the mountains, and they'd always rented a cabin with a fireplace.

Once the flames began licking at the dry wood, he set the screen in place, got to his feet, and stripped off his damp shirt.

"You can hang your clothes on this. I thought you'd be done by now." Giselle walked in, carrying a wooden kitchen chair. "Whoa, is that a futon?"

"If it isn't, I just broke their couch."

"I'm sure it's a futon. Sure is dark in here, though."

"Think you'll have trouble finding me?"

"Nope. I'll just listen for the sound of heavy breathing."

"Very funny." But true. Now that she was back, he was

primed and ready for action. "Thanks for the chair." He took it from her and positioned it to one side of the fireplace.

"You're welcome. When I went to find a chair, I discovered something else. If we'd followed the urgings of our stomachs instead of our hormones, we would have known that our siblings left food for us in the kitchen."

"You're kidding." He arranged his shirt over the back of the chair. "Do you think it's safe to eat?"

"Depends on whether you believe that her note was written in good faith, but I'd say yes. Their pranks have involved water, not food." She handed him a piece of paper.

Luke quickly read the note.

Dearest brother,
   A bucket of fried chicken and some coleslaw are in the refrigerator. There's ground coffee in a can next to the coffeepot, along with some coffee filters. I didn't leave you any booze because I don't want you drinking and driving. Not that you would, come to think of it.

                    Smoochies,
                    Your loving and talented sister,
                    Cynthia

She kept dinging him for his ultraresponsible behavior. Or was she paying him a compliment? He didn't really know, but she'd demonstrated that she could be just as responsible, as Giselle had said earlier.

Either on her own or with Bryce's urging, Cynthia had made sure her prank hadn't ruined anything, and she'd left food for her victims in case they chose to stay at the cabin. Knowing that, Luke was certain she'd also provided the firewood.

He started toward the chair where he'd put their jackets so he could put this note with the first one.

"I'll take it." Giselle held out her hand. "You still have some wet clothes to get out of."

"I swear you're getting bossier than me." But he smiled as he handed over the note. "Just tuck it in the pocket of my jacket." He nudged off his shoes.

"Done. Nice fire, by the way."

"Thanks. FYI, you're free to start on your clothes anytime, too." He reached down and pulled off his socks, which had stayed dry.

"You don't want to wrestle me out of my clothes, after all?"

"It's not as much fun if we don't have a big bed to roll around on." He reached for the fastening of his jeans. "Besides, I'm getting impatient."

She glanced pointedly at his crotch. "I can tell."

"Are you gloating?" He started taking off his soggy jeans.

"Who, me?"

"Yeah, you." Getting out of the jeans wasn't simple, but he managed it without falling down. He could have used two chairs to hold his clothes, but with some creative rearranging, he spaced them out on one. "You're gloating over the rigid condition of my sexual equipment."

"It's a heady feeling, knowing I'm the cause of such a masterpiece." She pulled her sweater over her head and laid it on the chair with their jackets.

"I suppose I could gloat over your stiff nipples, but somehow that's not as dramatic." Still, he enjoyed the heck out of eyeing the significant dent they made in the white lace cups of her bra. He kept watching as she took off the bra to reveal those pert nipples set against the backdrop of her creamy, plump breasts. His cock twitched in reaction.

Apparently she noticed, because her mouth curved in a saucy smile. "A bit jumpy, aren't we?"

"That was definitely gloating." Shoving down his briefs, he kicked them away. They could dry on the floor. "I want some gloating privileges."

She unfastened her jeans and peeled them off. "How do you plan to get those?"

He stalked over to where she stood. "By finding out how wet you are." He grabbed her around the waist.

She gasped. "My dear sir!"

"Oh, sweetheart, I'm just getting started." He slipped his hand inside her panties, and his fingers encountered all the juicy evidence he needed. "You're as desperate for this as I am."

She held his gaze. "Maybe more."

With a groan, he captured her full mouth and began the amazing process of making love to Giselle Landry. All morning he'd tried to convince himself that sex with her wasn't that much different from sex with any woman. Ah, but it was.

Her soft skin excited him beyond reason. Once she lay beneath him on the futon, he nibbled, licked, and tasted her as if he'd never experienced such wonders before. "Who needs chocolate?" he murmured against her inner thigh.

Her response was a whimper and a restless movement of her hips.

"*Oh*, yeah." Settling his mouth over her slick heat, he feasted with abandon until she bowed upward in surrender and her rapid panting turned into a joyous cry of release.

While she was still quivering from her orgasm, he changed position and eased his aching cock deep inside that welcoming channel. Sweet heaven, but this was good. Cinching himself in tight, he braced his forearms on either side of her head and looked into her eyes. The shadows created by the drawn curtains muted the emerald color of her beautiful eyes, but not the sparkle.

She took a shaky breath and smiled up at him. "Very nice."

"Mmm." He drew back and slid forward again, all the while searching her expression for any telltale wince of pain. "Are you sure you're okay?"

"More than okay." She tightened around him. "Better than ever."

"*Ah.*" He tensed. With a supreme effort, he subdued the climax that threatened to break through his control. "If you get any better, I'm a goner, and I don't want to come yet."

She stroked his back and looked into his eyes. "Then what should I do?"

"Lie still and don't squeeze."

That made her laugh, and her laughter caused a ripple effect that massaged his throbbing cock.

He clenched his jaw. "And don't laugh."

"Sorry." Except she only laughed more, all the while apologizing between bursts of merriment.

"To hell with it." He gave up the fight and began thrusting, deep and fast.

"I like that." She clutched his hips, her fingertips pressing down as she rose to meet him. "More of that."

He sucked in a breath. His whole body was on fire,

demanding release. He lost control and drove mindlessly into her, each stroke bringing him closer to the edge of the seething volcano about to erupt.

"Yes, oh, *yes*!" She lifted up with a jubilant cry.

The ripples of her orgasm touched off the explosion he was helpless to contain, and he surged forward, breathless with the power of the climax ripping through him. The hot pulse of his cock brought a groan of pleasure that vibrated his whole body.

Gradually, the world stopped spinning and he could breathe again. Thankfully, he hadn't collapsed on top of her. Some part of his brain had continued to function and he'd stayed braced on his forearms.

Soft hands framed his face, and he opened his eyes. Beneath him, she seemed as dazed as he was. Slowly, almost reverently, she touched his mouth, his cheeks, and his forehead, as if memorizing his features. He understood the impulse. He'd wanted to do the same, but had been afraid to let his feelings show.

She was braver than he was, apparently. Caressing his face with such tenderness could mean only one thing. She was falling in love with him. Maybe she no longer cared if he knew.

Maybe it was time for him to tell her that he felt the same. "Giselle, I— "

She laid her finger over his mouth and shook her head. "Don't say it," she murmured.

Bracing on one arm, he gently took her hand away. "I don't know why not. We both feel it. Yes, there are issues, but we'll deal with them."

Her smile was the saddest one he'd ever seen. "There are issues that you don't know about."

"So you said before, and we played a silly guessing

game that got me nowhere. Why can't you just tell me what it is? I'm shadowboxing, and I don't like it."

"Then maybe we shouldn't do this anymore."

"Make love?"

She nodded, not even bothering to contradict his use of the term.

"Giselle, I won't stop making love to you as long as you'll let me do it. Are you going to tell me not to?"

She swallowed. "I should, but . . ."

"But?"

"I can't seem to say the words."

"Thank God for that." Leaning down, he kissed away the tears leaking from the corners of her eyes.

Then he pressed his tear-moistened lips against hers. He could tell her with his kiss what she wouldn't let him say out loud. They still had time. Before they left this little cabin in the woods, he'd convince her that no problem, no matter how daunting, was big enough to keep them apart.

Chapter 21

Giselle chastised herself for being weak, but she craved Luke, human though he might be, in ways she'd never craved one of her own kind. She felt so alive with him, as if she'd been suppressing her essential being all her life. With Luke, she could be herself, and he seemed fine with that.

He was more than fine with it, in fact. He loved her. And she loved him back, even if she'd never tell him so. She couldn't have him forever, so she'd make the most of the short time they were together.

With the cabin as their hideaway, they spent the rest of the day making love and sharing the chicken and coleslaw dinner Cynthia had left for them. Because Giselle had dry clothes, she went outside and found the extra wood stored beside the cabin. That allowed them to keep the fire going, which added to the romantic ambience.

She doubted that she'd ever smell wood smoke again without thinking of these hours with Luke. Lying on the futon with him, she gave him an edited version of her childhood because he asked. She knew he sought a clue to the problem she refused to discuss, but she was practiced at evading critical questions. She'd been doing that ever since her parents had allowed her the freedom to mingle with humans.

Although she longed to tell him the truth, she also knew that wouldn't go well. Humans had been taught to fear werewolves, and countless books and movies had added to the misconceptions. Most people believed that Weres were monsters who passed on their beastly tendencies by biting the humans they attacked. On top of that, humans tended to view the concept of shape-shifting with revulsion. Luke praised her beauty when she was in human form, but how would he react if she transformed into a female wolf with a thick coat of dark red fur? Would he love that version of her? Giselle wasn't ready to find out.

Inevitably, the hour arrived when they had to leave if they expected to be at the penthouse by eight.

"I could text Cynthia and change the time." Luke had begun putting on his clothes, which were now dry and smelled of wood smoke. "I think ten works as well as eight."

"No, it doesn't." Giselle zipped her jeans. "Sticking with her time frame indicates we consider her important enough to accommodate her wishes. Once we start fiddling with the time, she could see that as a lack of commitment on our part."

Luke sighed as he put on his shirt. "You're right. But I hate leaving. Nothing's been settled about . . . us."

"Yes, it has," she said softly. "Assuming this four-way discussion goes well, Bryce and I will fly back to San Francisco tomorrow."

He held her gaze. "Okay. Then I'll come up there for a few days."

"That's not a good idea."

"Damn it, Giselle!" Frustration was etched on his handsome face. "I—"

"Don't say it. That won't help. You have to take my word that we have no future."

He stared at her for a few seconds. Then, with a muttered oath, he finished dressing.

They rode back down the mountain in silence, which tore at her, but she had nothing helpful to say. They'd had their idyll in the woods, and now came the tough part—putting those special moments behind them and getting on with their separate lives. He'd expected her to crack and reveal everything. That wasn't going to happen.

Finally, as they stood in the private elevator and it began its ascent to the top floor of the Silver Crescent, he broke the silence. "No matter what happens from this point on, I need you to know something."

"Luke . . ."

"You don't want me to say it, but this may be my last chance, and I damn well will say it. I love you, Giselle."

She gazed at him as her heart broke.

"You won't say it, but I know you love me, too. It's there in your eyes." His voice shook with emotion, and his blue eyes flashed fire. "I don't know what the hell it is that you refuse to tell me, but it better be the sort of secret that would endanger the entire free world if you let it get out. Anything less would be bullshit." He looked at her, obviously waiting. When she said nothing, he turned away. "Okay, then."

She hurt so much she had to clutch her stomach to

keep from doubling over. She'd never wished to be human instead of Were, but heaven help her, she wished for it now.

Luke behaved like the perfect gentleman as he ushered her through the elaborate double doors into the penthouse. Bryce and Cynthia were there, sitting on the butterscotch sectional, sipping from wineglasses. When Giselle and Luke walked in, they both stood.

Reluctantly, Giselle admitted that her tall, red-haired brother and Luke's tall, blond sister made a striking couple. They looked almost like movie stars standing together. But unlike poised Hollywood celebrities, they appeared nervous.

Giselle decided to break the ice. She walked over and gave her brother a hug. "I didn't get to do this yesterday," she murmured. "It's good to see you."

He hugged her back. "Same here, Sis."

Giselle turned to Cynthia. "I've seen you dancing Cynthia, and I just want to say I very much admire your talent."

"Oh." She seemed dazzled by that statement. "Thank you so much."

Giselle's heart went out to her. Although Cynthia was only six years younger, she seemed much more vulnerable than that. She, too, had lost her overbearing father, and she must be feeling an unsettling combination of grief and freedom.

Behind Giselle, Luke cleared his throat. "I've never officially met your friend, Cynthia."

"Guess not." Cynthia seemed to regain some of her poise. "Bryce Landry, this is my big brother, Luke."

Bryce stuck out his hand with an assertiveness that made Giselle proud. "Glad to finally meet you, Dalton."

"Same here, Landry." Luke stood toe-to-toe and eye-to-eye with Giselle's brother. They were the same height and of a similar build. A fight between them would draw even odds.

Giselle prayed there would be no fight. Her loyalties would be hopelessly divided. But after what appeared to be a bone-crushing handshake, the two men separated.

Luke adopted a take-charge attitude. "Obviously we need to talk. I see you both have a beverage. Giselle and I should probably get something, too."

"I'll provide whatever you require, sir." Mr. Thatcher appeared in the kitchen doorway.

Giselle snuck a quick glance at Bryce, to see his reaction to Mr. Thatcher.

Bryce winked at her.

Giselle ducked her head to hide a smile. At the moment, the Weres outnumbered the humans, not that the humans would ever find that out.

"Excellent, Mr. Thatcher." Luke looked at Giselle. "What will you have?"

She considered champagne, because she hoped they'd be celebrating a reunion of siblings, but she wasn't completely confident that would happen. "A glass of wine works."

"Red or white, madam?" Mr. Thatcher asked.

"Red, please."

Luke turned to Mr. Thatcher. "Make that two, please."

"And cheese and bread, please, Mr. Thatcher," Cynthia said. Lifting her chin, she faced her brother. "Mom and Dad always used to have cheese and bread with their wine."

Luke's expression softened. "Yeah, they did. Good call, Sis."

Once Mr. Thatcher left, the four of them stood staring at each other.

Luke took a deep breath. "Let's all sit down. Giselle, the sectional's all yours. I'll get a kitchen chair."

Giselle picked a spot where the sectional curved, so that she was at right angles to Bryce and Cynthia. Luke walked into the kitchen, grabbed one of the chairs, and brought it back, positioning it on the far side of a glass coffee table. Instead of sitting in it, he spun it around and straddled it.

Very macho, indeed. Giselle worked hard not to smile at the tactic, which made Luke seem far more cool than Bryce, despite her brother's attempt to lounge on the sectional as if he hadn't a care in the world. Although one of the males in the room was Were and one was human, their maneuvering for dominance wasn't all that different.

"First of all," Luke said, once again taking the initiative, "I want to congratulate both of you on your inventiveness."

Cynthia's eyes widened. "You do? I thought you'd be pissed."

"I was, until Giselle helped me see that the effort involved was kind of . . . flattering."

Giselle flinched. "I think what Luke means to say is that he appreciates your efforts to help him understand how much dancing means to you." She shot a quick glance at Luke and hoped he'd get the message.

Apparently he had, because he nodded. "Exactly. I hadn't realized before how much you cared about it."

Cynthia sat up straighter. "That's because you're so incredibly dense. I tried to explain this about a hundred times, but you kept blowing me off."

"You have his attention now, right, Luke?" Giselle gave him an encouraging smile.

"Right." Swallowing, he focused on his sister. "If you want a job in the Moonbeams lineup, it's yours."

Cynthia leaped off the sectional with a shriek and nearly knocked Luke out of his chair as she gave him an enthusiastic hug. "Thank you! That's awesome! Oh, my God, I can't believe it! I'm going to be a *Moonbeam*." She began twirling in the middle of the room.

She nearly collided with Mr. Thatcher as he came in from the kitchen, rolling a cart loaded with wine, a crusty baguette, and a mouth-watering assortment of cheeses. "Mr. Thatcher! Luke said I could be a Moonbeam dancer! Isn't that fabulous?"

"Indeed it is, Miss Cynthia." He pretended to be un-affected when she hugged him, too.

But Giselle saw the emotion in his eyes.

Cynthia returned to her seat and exchanged a high five with Bryce. "One project down, one to go."

Luke blinked. "You have another agenda? Please tell me it doesn't have to do with squirt guns and water balloons. My heart can't take it."

"Oh, this one's really simple." Cynthia reached over and patted Bryce's knee. "A no-brainer."

Giselle held her breath and prayed that nothing had changed between Bryce and Cynthia since she'd talked to her brother. She hadn't picked up any girlfriend-boyfriend vibes from them, but she was under a lot of stress. She could have missed the obvious.

Luke's jaw tightened. "So what is it?"

"Bryce and I have talked about this a lot, and we both think you should sell Howlin' at the Moon back to Benedict Cartwright."

Giselle was stunned. She glanced over at Luke, who seemed equally taken aback. But when she turned her attention to Bryce, he gazed at her with a little half smile.

And she got it. Bryce was still loyal to his heritage, and part of that heritage was wrapped up in this bar known to Weres all over the world. By sheer coincidence, he'd become friends with the sister of the human who'd won that bar, and he'd decided to use his influence with her to try to get it back.

That was, she concluded with some chagrin, more than she'd done. She also had influence with the bar's new owner, but she'd never once suggested he might want to sell it back. She doubted he would have agreed, but she'd never put the concept on the table. With Bryce's encouragement, Cynthia had.

Luke had recovered himself. "I'm not selling the bar back to the Cartwrights," he said. "Harrison's behavior might not have caused my father to die, but the stress didn't help any. Dad should have been awarded the Moon in the first place. I had to win it back in a poker game, which is fitting, and now that I have it, I intend to keep it. It's part of the Dalton legacy now."

"But that's not right, either." Cynthia put her empty wineglass on the coffee table. "The Moon is part of the Cartwright legacy, the first thing Harrison Cartwright built in Las Vegas. It has all kinds of sentimental value for that family, but for you, it's only about revenge."

"It's more than that, Cynthia. Every time I looked at that bar, I remembered how our dad fought with Harrison and how he made himself sick over it. It was like a gnawing pain in my gut, a reminder that our dad is gone."

Cynthia's expression softened. "I'm sorry. I didn't realize how much it was hurting you. I should have, but I didn't."

"So you understand why I can't sell it back to the Cartwrights?"

"Yes, but let me ask you something else. How did you feel when I raided the family photo gallery and swiped a DVD from the vault in order to make my point?"

"Truthfully?" Luke sought Giselle's gaze as if drawing energy from it. Then he looked over at his sister. "I hated it. The pictures could have been replaced, but I'm not sure there's a copy of the DVD. Thinking it could have disappeared made me sick to my stomach."

"I'll bet that's how the Cartwrights feel about losing the Moon," Cynthia said. "It's a piece of family history, and now it's gone."

Luke frowned. "Aren't you forgetting something? Dad won the Silver Crescent fair and square, and then Harrison Cartwright put our dad through hell before he finally turned it over. I firmly believe the stress is what killed him."

"That's entirely possible," Cynthia said quietly. "And now you have the bar. How does that make you feel?"

"Great!"

Giselle knew his moods well enough to figure out he was bluffing. And she knew his heart, too. He might have thought exacting revenge for his father and ending his own pain at the expense of someone else was a good idea, but the reality might have proved to be quite different.

"Really?" Cynthia's brow wrinkled. "I find that hard to believe."

Luke's jaw tightened. "Believe it. Having a Cartwright property next to the Silver Crescent has been a pain in the ass, both to Dad and me. Now we own it. I couldn't be happier about that."

"You don't look happy," Cynthia said.

"That's because you don't seem to understand why the Daltons deserve to own that bar."

"I get your motivation, Luke, but you don't have the time to give that place the personal attention Benedict Cartwright gave it. His personality brought in the customers. Unless you find someone with charisma to run it, you could end up with a losing proposition on your hands."

"I hope this isn't leading up to some hidden agenda, like you asking me to hire Landry for that position."

Bryce stood. "Absolutely not." He glanced at Giselle. "In fact, maybe my sister and I should make ourselves scarce and let you two work things out. It's not our business, after all, and we have some things to discuss, anyway."

Giselle got up. "That's an excellent idea. Where do you want to go?"

"If I may make a suggestion?" Mr. Thatcher appeared in the living room as if he'd been summoned, which he most definitely had not. But he'd probably been eavesdropping from the kitchen. "I can escort you both down to the Howlin' at the Moon bar. Even if the two of you have not experienced so much in regard to it, it's a landmark not to be missed."

"I've seen—" In the nick of time, Giselle caught the look Bryce had thrown her way. There was more to this invitation than visiting a Vegas landmark. "I'd love to go," she said, and was rewarded by a big smile from her brother.

Luke stood. "You don't have to leave. Cynthia and I can hash this out later."

"We'll be back." Giselle walked over and touched his arm. "Bryce makes a good point. This is your family business. You and Cynthia need to work this out between the two of you." She held up her phone. "Text me when you've talked it through."

"Trust me, it won't take long." He didn't look particularly happy that she was leaving, but he didn't have much choice. He couldn't order her to stay and participate in the discussion.

"See you soon, then." With an encouraging smile, she turned and followed Bryce and Mr. Thatcher out the door.

Once they were all in the elevator, Bryce glanced at all the wooden surfaces. "Is this thing bugged?"

"Not that I know of," Mr. Thatcher said. "But I advise you to refrain from any conversation for now."

Bryce nodded.

Giselle looked from one to the other. "Are we going where I think we are?"

Mr. Thatcher put a finger to his lips.

Giselle didn't need any more of a hint than that, but she was worried. Even if Benedict was somewhere nearby with the remote, they couldn't chance using it now. She trusted Mr. Thatcher to use the utmost caution when going into the playground, but this didn't feel like caution. It felt downright reckless.

Chapter 22

"You really like Giselle, don't you?" Cynthia kicked off her designer shoes and curled her feet under her.

"I do, but it's not going anywhere." Luke remained standing and began to pace.

"Why not?"

He glanced over at his sister lounging on the sectional, her blond hair loose around her shoulders. Even dressed casually in jeans and a navy hoodie, she was beautiful. She'd always had catlike grace, but he'd refused to see that a dancing career fit her perfectly.

Thank God she wanted to dance here and not on Broadway. Then he caught himself. If she decided to try to make it in New York, he'd be supportive. He was through standing in the way of what was obviously her destiny, at least for now.

Her blue eyes, so like his, focused intently on him. "You don't want to tell me about her, do you?"

"Not particularly, since she'll go back to San Francisco tomorrow and that'll be that. What's the point in discussing her?"

"It's just that I've never seen you so . . . absorbed in a woman before. And you just met her, right?"

"Yeah." He massaged the back of his neck. "That's the crazy part, how fast we connected. I feel as if I've known her a hell of a lot longer."

"Luke, I realize you think of me as a kid who doesn't know anything, but—"

"No, I don't." He stopped pacing to gaze at her. "You're a hundred times smarter than I am."

"You're talking about academics, but you don't think I'm smart about people."

She had him there. "I'll admit I used to feel that way, but my opinion on that score is changing. Tell me about Landry."

"He's just a friend."

"Is he gay?"

She laughed. "No! Why would you think that?"

"Because you're gorgeous! You've had guys running after you since second grade. Why should Bryce Landry be any different?"

"He just is. If you must know, I think he's still in love with his ex-fiancée, and I hope they get back together. Is that your issue with Giselle? She has someone else back in San Francisco?"

"No. At least, I don't think so. She said she didn't, and I can't imagine that she does, considering . . ." He stopped himself before he revealed more than he'd intended.

"Are you referring to the chocolate-covered sex orgy? Is that what convinced you she was unattached?"

He gulped. Damn it, he was blushing. He could feel the heat creeping up his neck. A quick glance at Cynthia confirmed that she was enjoying the hell out of his embarrassment. He couldn't think of a single thing to say that wouldn't make the situation even worse, so he kept quiet.

"We arrived minutes before the cleaning crew." Sisterly triumph rang through every word. "You almost got away with it, but I just knew you two were headed for bedroom games. That scene in the gondola was the clincher. That's why Bryce and I decided to make the leaky water bed our grand finale."

"It was quite a finale, all right." Luke sighed. He'd go through the water bed incident a hundred times if it could be followed by the kind of afternoon he'd spent with Giselle.

"So you're going to just let her go?"

"I suggested coming up to San Francisco for a visit, and she said that wasn't a good idea."

"Hm." Cynthia tapped her finger against her mouth. "So she's a bit of a mystery woman. That intrigues me."

"Look, I don't want you to—"

"Interfere in your life? That's funny, Luke. Makes you uncomfortable, doesn't it? Now you know how I felt."

He blew out a breath. "I was wrong, okay? I'm sorry. And I'm not just saying it. I really am sorry that I treated you that way, as if you didn't know what was good for you."

"I believe you, but I wish I had a recording of that."

"In case I backslide?"

"Exactly." She gestured to the curved part of the sectional that faced her. "Have a seat and stop pacing. I need to think about this Giselle problem, and I can't do it while you're roaming around like a caged lion."

"I'll come over and sit down, but I don't want you delving into Giselle's situation. She's told me to back off and I'll honor that." He walked to the sectional and sank down.

"How noble of you. Did it occur to you that I have a source who might tell me what's going on with her?"

"Uh, you mean Bryce?"

"He's her brother, after all. I could mention that she's throwing up roadblocks and see what he says about that."

"No." The concept made him cringe inside. "It sounds like junior high all over again."

"So you're willing to let her go and never find out why the two of you can't be together? That would drive me crazy."

"I'll deal with it." He didn't know how, but he'd have to. He had no choice.

"I mean, it's one thing if someone dumps you and tells you why. You're upset, sure, but at least you understand the issue. You can get drunk, break a few dishes, and move on."

Luke chuckled. "Is that what you do? Throw breakables?"

"Maybe." She gave him a dimpled smile. "My point is, you won't be able to move on. You'll have that question nagging you forever. *What was the problem? Why did she leave without giving me an explanation?* I guarantee a mystery breakup is the worst kind."

"You've had those?"

"No, but a girlfriend of mine did back at Yale. Some dude walked out on her and refused to tell her why. Two years later she found out he'd had a girlfriend back home with a baby. My friend was *so* relieved. Mad as hell, but relieved. She could finally forget about the creep once the mystery was solved."

Luke couldn't believe he was listening to relationship advice from his little sister, but what she'd said made sense. He *was* frustrated about not knowing the big secret that stood between him and Giselle. Although he'd vowed not to dwell on that, he probably would anyway. He was enough like Cynthia that the mystery would drive him crazy, just like it would her.

"Time is of the essence," she said. "Bryce and Giselle will fly back to San Francisco tomorrow, and the opportunity to investigate will be lost."

"So?"

"We could text them and ask them to come back up here, but I'd rather head on down to the Moon. We can say we finished our discussion and decided to join them for a drink. I'll get Bryce alone, which will be easier at the bar than up here, and ambient noise can make conversations harder to overhear. I could challenge him to a game of pool and find out what's up."

"But we didn't finish our discussion."

She looked at him. "Nobody's here but me, big brother. Tell me the truth. Are you thrilled about owning that bar?"

He met her gaze. Pretending seemed stupid at this point. "No. To be honest, I've considered bulldozing it."

"No!" Her eyes widened. "That would kill Benedict!"

"You sound as if you like the guy."

"Of course I do. I always have. He was nice to me, didn't treat me like a little tagalong. Mr. Thatcher likes him, too."

Remembering that moment at the table when he'd looked into Benedict's tortured gaze, Luke sighed. "I kind of like him, too. But don't you think the Cartwrights deserved to go down?"

"I was angry with Harrison, but he's already dead. I'm sorry, but I never thought Vaughn and Benedict were our enemies. I was sad when the feud started. I liked the Cartwright family. And Benedict loved that bar. I'll bet losing it was the worst thing that's ever happened to him."

"Then he shouldn't have put it on the line."

"I bet I know why he did." Cynthia stretched out her long legs and propped her bare feet on the coffee table. "He probably was sick of staring at the Silver Crescent, and he had even more reason to hate looking at it, because the Cartwrights used to own it."

"I guess that could be true."

"I also bet he wanted to prove himself to Vaughn, just like I've always wanted to prove myself to you." She glanced over at him. "I know how that feels."

"You don't have to prove yourself to me." Emotion tightened his throat. "I'll love you no matter what."

She swallowed. "Backatcha, big brother." She held his gaze for several seconds, and then she smiled. "Wow, we're getting mushy, huh?"

"Guess so." He cleared his throat. "You really think I should sell it to Benedict?"

"I do."

"I don't know if he has the money to buy it."

"Vaughn would float him a loan. I'd lay odds on that. And you won't have the humiliation of the bar losing business under your ownership, which I think it might."

"It might." He hadn't wanted to admit his fear of that happening, but he knew Benedict had been popular with the customers. Building customer loyalty to the new regime would take time he didn't have.

"Have I convinced you?"

He blew out a breath. "Yeah, you have. Don't take this wrong, but you would have made one hell of a lawyer."

"I know." She looked smug. "But I'll make an even better dancer. Ready to go down to the Moon?"

"Might as well. It won't be ours much longer. Once I sell it back to Benedict, we'll have to pay for our drinks, and chances are he'll charge us double."

"You, maybe." Cynthia winked at him. "Me, he likes."

Giselle had a million questions for her brother and a few for Mr. Thatcher, too, but she waited until they'd left the Silver Crescent through the back door. "Let's stop a minute," she said. "We can't go into the playground right now. It's too risky."

"Precisely," Mr. Thatcher said. "I simply wanted a chance to talk with both of you alone and let you know that Benedict and I are scheduled to make our first inspection after closing time tonight. We've arranged to meet at two in the morning. I wanted to offer you a chance to accompany us."

"I'm up for it," Bryce said.

"I probably can't." Giselle expected to spend her last night in Vegas with Luke. She glanced at Bryce. "So you know about how the blocked-off entrance works now?"

"Mr. Thatcher and I had a very brief moment alone when Cynthia was in the bathroom. He had just enough time to tell me about it."

The butler glanced back at the Silver Crescent. "I suggest we move on and actually have that drink at the Moon, in case Luke and Cynthia come looking for us."

"Good idea," Giselle said. "By the way, brother of mine, were you the one who planted the idea of Luke selling back to Benedict?"

He smiled. "I might have been."

She gave him a hug. "Well done. Now let's go have a drink and hope that Cynthia talks Luke into it."

"I sincerely hope so." Mr. Thatcher fell into step on one side of her.

Bryce took the other side. "And if she fails, Sis, I figure you can take a shot at convincing him. You seem to have the inside track."

She had a feeling she was busted, but she didn't know for sure. "Don't start with me, Bryce Landry. Not after you gave me a heart attack when I thought you might be getting cozy with a human."

"The difference is, I *didn't* actually get cozy with a human, while you definitely did."

"You have no proof of that."

Ahead of them, Mr. Thatcher cleared his throat. "I'm afraid he does."

"Oh."

Bryce leaned closer. "Was it good? The chocolate, I mean."

She elbowed him in the ribs.

He grunted. "Easy, Sis. I have to be well enough to travel, you know."

"*Are* you traveling with me tomorrow?"

"I am, and by the way, my camera phone is loaded with pictures of chocolate."

"Bryce, if you tell anyone about this—and I mean *anyone*—I have an entire list of your previous crimes that will go public immediately."

"I won't tell, at least not right away. I value the blackmail potential, so I'm saving it for something really big."

"You'd better be kidding."

He chuckled. "You'll have to find that out, won't you?

Incidentally, there's one surefire way to neutralize the threat."

"I'm sure it involves paying you large sums of money."

"I wasn't thinking about that, but I'll file it away for future consideration. If you want to end my blackmail prospects forever, though, you could mate with the dude."

"*What*?" She came to a halt on the sidewalk outside the Moon.

"All the best families are doing it. Even I can see he's crazy about you and would treat you right. He didn't endear himself to me at first, but the guy's grown on me. I think you'd be happy together."

"You're talking crazy."

"I'm perfectly sincere. I've come to admire the guy. He took my jokes in stride. And I'm not an easy sell when it comes to my little sister's future mate. Yes, he does have a tiny flaw, but—"

"It's not tiny!"

"That's your opinion. Others would differ. Looks to me as if the only obstacle is your prejudice against the concept."

"That is *not* the only obstacle. I'm thinking of him! It would drastically change his life. He'd have to sell his company and uproot himself from a city he loves. Worse than that, he'd have to keep the secret from his sister, and despite what we've been through with those two, they're devoted to each other."

Mr. Thatcher turned around and joined them. "I hope you don't mind if I put an oar in."

"Go right ahead." Giselle looked at her brother. "This fine Were, Mr. Thatcher, has been a second father to Luke and Cynthia. I doubt he'll be enthusiastic about your wild plan to upend their lives."

"On the contrary. I snatched this time for the three of us partly so that I could invite you both to the playground, but also because I was hoping we could discuss this very topic. I've never seen Luke so besotted with anyone as he is with you. I always urge caution in these matters, but . . . I believe he would be happier with you, despite the obvious difficulties, than without you."

Giselle stared at him. "With all due respect, no, he would not. He loves Vegas and he loves his sister. He could never tell her the truth about his life, and that would be cruel to both of them. I wouldn't dream of saddling him with that burden."

"Too bad you won't give him a chance to weigh in on the subject," Bryce said.

Mr. Thatcher's attention was distracted by something directly behind them. "Our conversation is at an end," he said in a low voice. Then he stepped back and waved. "It appears you've finished your discussion!"

"We did!" Luke called out. "What's up with you slowpokes? We figured you'd be on your second round by now."

Bryce and Giselle both turned. She hoped her brother had a reasonable explanation, because she was drawing a blank.

Bryce, her quick-witted riddle maker, came through. "We had some family business to work through, too, and we decided to settle it before we started drinking." He put his arm around Giselle's shoulder and gave her a squeeze. "I gotta say, this is one stubborn female."

Luke laughed. "Don't I know it."

"Stubbornness is in the eye of the beholder," Giselle said.

Cynthia gave her a thumbs-up. "Way to tell 'em, girlfriend!"

Giselle managed a big smile as she watched Luke and Cynthia approach. Tall, fair, and beautiful, they were so obviously brother and sister. She couldn't imagine how their mother could bear to live an ocean away from them.

But that was her choice, and it left them more dependent on each other. No one should come between those two, especially not a female werewolf who'd foolishly allowed herself to fall in love with a human.

Chapter 23

If Luke had doubted his decision to sell Howlin' at the Moon, those doubts evaporated when he stepped inside the door. The place was almost deserted.

Chuck Stevens came forward with a cheerful smile, because that was Chuck's way, to smile in the face of disappointment. But Chuck had to be wondering whether Luke had a strategy to keep the bar business from going into free fall. "Don't know what to tell you," he said. "Business was great yesterday, but today, not so much."

"Don't worry about it." Luke turned to the group he'd brought in, none of whom would be paying customers. "I guess you know everybody except Giselle's brother. Bryce Landry, meet Chuck Stevens. Chuck's the CFO for Dalton Industries."

Bryce reached out and shook Chuck's hand. "My sister's the CFO for the Landry operation up in 'Frisco. Did she tell you that?"

"I don't think she did. She had other things on her mind when we met."

"Like me," Cynthia said. "But all's well that ends well, Chuck. My darling brother's hired me to dance with the Moonbeams, so you'll be signing my paycheck soon."

Luke didn't care if she boasted about that, or that Chuck's eyebrows lifted at the news. His CFO quickly recovered and congratulated Cynthia on her new job. Chuck had been with Dalton for seven years, long enough to figure out that complicated maneuvers took place in a family-owned business.

"So I guess you're all here to celebrate!" Chuck gestured toward the interior of the bar, where only a handful of people occupied a grouping of twenty tables. "Take your pick. I'll get a server right over."

"Thanks, Chuck. If you want to head home, I can handle it for the rest of the night."

"Nah, you have guests. I'm happy to supervise for now. I'm sure business will pick up and we can look into hiring someone."

Cynthia glanced at Luke. "Aren't you going to tell him?"

"Uh, sure." He wasn't in the habit of blurting out his business decisions in such a casual way, but saying something might relieve Chuck's concern that the bar would be a financial drain on the company. "I've decided to sell the bar back to Benedict Cartwright." From the corner of his eye, he caught a triumphant look pass between Giselle and Bryce.

What the hell? Why would either of them care what he did with the bar? Sure, Bryce seemed to have influenced Cynthia to plead for returning the bar to the Cartwrights, but the glance between Bryce and Giselle held more significance than it should, given the circumstances.

Chuck appeared stunned by the announcement. "Sell it back to Benedict? I thought the whole idea was to get it away from that family. Wasn't the poker game a grudge match? Or am I missing something?"

"You're not missing anything," Luke said. "The game was a grudge match, and as you and I were taught in our business classes, revenge is a lousy motivation for a corporate decision. Owning this bar makes no sense for Dalton Industries, but since I got it for free, we can't avoid making a profit when I sell it."

Chuck grinned. "So revenge *is* a good motivation?"

"Only if you know when to stop seeking it. Have our lawyers draw up the papers tomorrow, and set up a meeting with Benedict whenever he's available."

"I'll do that and let you know. Now, find yourself a table and enjoy yourselves. There's no band tonight, but the jukebox works great. And the pool table's open."

Cynthia seemed to be in rare form. "I want that middle table next to the dance floor."

Bryce laughed. "Gonna put on a show for us?"

"I might, but first I challenge you to a game of pool."

Luke should have known she'd remember and follow through on her plan. He'd always been in awe of his sister's brainpower, but he'd never thought she'd employ it for his benefit. Maybe she'd find out nothing, but earlier when they'd come upon Bryce, Giselle, and Mr. Thatcher in a huddle, his instincts had gone on alert.

Bryce had made it sound as if they'd been discussing Landry family issues, but Luke didn't buy it. The moment Mr. Thatcher had caught sight of him, he'd looked startled. Then he'd muttered something to the others. Luke was willing to bet they'd been talking about him.

How Mr. Thatcher figured into all this remained a

mystery, too. But he'd latched on to Giselle immediately, and that was unusual for the reserved butler. When Luke had seen the three of them together, he'd had the oddest feeling, as if they were linked somehow.

That wasn't logical. Bryce and Giselle were brother and sister, of course, but Mr. Thatcher had no connection to them. His family was in England, and the Landrys were based in San Francisco. So why did all three radiate a feeling of togetherness, as if they shared a bond of great significance?

He hoped that Cynthia would make some headway with Bryce and eventually could enlighten her confused brother. If anyone could pry information out of a person, it was Cynthia.

Cynthia and Bryce put in their order before heading off to the bar's pool table. Cynthia chose a Long Island iced tea, and Bryce duplicated her order. It was a strong drink, but Luke had a better handle on his sister's methods now.

By ordering something strong, she'd challenged Bryce to do the same. If Luke had to guess, he'd say that Cynthia planned to nurse hers and catch a slightly drunk Bryce off guard. Then she'd subtly pump him for information.

Luke settled at the table with Giselle and Mr. Thatcher. Giselle, who took the chair to his right, ordered red wine, so he did, too. He wouldn't drink much. He wanted to keep his wits about him tonight. Mr. Thatcher, who'd chosen a chair across the table from them, asked for a gin and tonic.

A bowl of mixed nuts occupied the center of their round table. Luke offered some to Giselle, who took a handful. Then he pushed the bowl in Mr. Thatcher's direction. "I don't think I've ever shared a drink with you," Luke said.

"Normally it's bad form to drink with the hired help."

Interesting. Yet the guy had suggested accompanying Giselle and Bryce to the bar. Luke decided not to mention that. "Seems like a silly rule in your case," he said. "You're like a member of the family."

"I appreciate that. I feel as if I am, but still, you pay my salary. You don't normally pay members of your family."

"I'm about to. Cynthia will draw a salary as one of the Moonbeams. What do you think of that whole deal, Mr. Thatcher? Am I making a mistake?" He discovered that the answer mattered to him. Hired help or not, he wanted this man's approval. He always had wanted it.

"In my estimation, you did the right thing."

"I'm glad you think so." Luke was ridiculously relieved to hear that. "I'm afraid that my dad—"

"Never saw her as she was," Mr. Thatcher said. "Only as he wished her to be. She's been a dancer as long as I've known her."

Luke sent him a look of gratitude. "Thank you. That means a lot to me."

Mr. Thatcher pushed back his chair. "Speaking of dancing, do you fancy some tunes on the jukebox? You and Giselle could dance."

"That's okay," Giselle said quickly. "Leaving you alone at the table would be rude."

"Nonsense. Let's have some music. It would do my heart good to see you dance together."

After he walked over to the jukebox, Luke glanced at Giselle. "What's that all about?"

She flushed. "He's a bit of a matchmaker, apparently."

"I'm not opposed to that, but he's never been into matchmaking before." He gazed at her. "Do you know him from somewhere?"

"No."

He thought it was significant that she didn't ask him why he'd think that. "When Cynthia and I caught up with you three on the sidewalk, I couldn't shake the impression that you'd been talking about me. Bryce stepped into the breach and made up something that sounded like an excuse, but . . . were you talking about me?"

She had a deer-in-the-headlights look, but finally she nodded.

"Why?"

"Like I said, Mr. Thatcher thinks we're good together."

He covered her hand with his. "He's got that right. Bryce is a big boy. Send him back to 'Frisco and stay with me, at least for a while. I know you have responsibilities back home, but you accomplished what you came here for. Don't you deserve a little reward? A small vacation?"

Her green eyes revealed the struggle going on there. "You know I want to stay."

"Then do it."

"That would only make things worse when I leave."

"I'll take that risk."

She shook her head. "I'll leave with Bryce. It's the best for both of us."

Mr. Thatcher returned to his chair. "I don't recognize most of those songs, so you'll have to make do with some old ones, I'm afraid."

The opening chords of "I Will Always Love You" wafted through the bar's sound system. Luke stood and held out his hand to Giselle. "That one works for me."

With a smile that was part frustration and part surrender, she took his hand and joined him on the small dance floor. They had it to themselves. He almost wished they'd been surrounded by other dancers, which would have given them more privacy.

In the spotlight, so to speak, he couldn't hold her as close as he wanted to. He felt self-conscious about pressing his lips to the tender place behind her ear.

But he could talk to her. "Will you spend the night with me?" he murmured against her ear.

She shivered in response. "I shouldn't. I need to make plane reservations tonight."

"We can do that in ten minutes."

"My parents told me to take the corporate jet, but I think that's a waste of resources."

"The corporate *jet*?" He pulled back to gaze into her eyes. "Your family has a jet?"

She smiled. "Doesn't everyone?"

"*No.* I've considered it, but our holdings are all in Vegas. A jet is overkill, unless I want it to impress people."

"Our jet is a necessary expense. We're considering buying another one. We're primarily a shipping company, and we do business all over the Pacific Rim."

"That's impressive. I should have Googled you so I wouldn't be caught by surprise." He drew her closer. To hell with who was watching. "Your company has resources. My company has resources. We can find a way to make this happen. We're good together. You know we are. Don't throw that away."

She continued to smile, but she shook her head. "No can do. It wouldn't work out."

"You are the most maddening woman I have ever met." Pressing his cheek to hers, he danced with her until the song ended. Then he led her back to the table, where their drinks were waiting. He glanced over at the pool table. He needed his resident spy to return with some intel.

As if he'd signaled her on some high-tech personal communication system, she came back to the table, Bryce trailing behind.

"She kicked my butt," Bryce said. "I thought they taught intellectual stuff at Yale, but apparently she majored in billiards."

Cynthia made a face. "I learned the basics in Vegas and polished my game with my college friends. Most of them were math majors, so they understood the geometry involved. They taught me to view the table scientifically."

"That might be true, but I say she was channeling Minnesota Fats." Bryce rolled his eyes. "Just warning you suckers. The girl's got game."

"He exaggerates." Cynthia focused on Luke. "Care to take me on, big brother?"

"Sure. My ego can handle it." Luke stood.

"That's what I thought." Bryce drained his Long Island iced tea. "But she'll humiliate you, my friend. And you won't even see it coming."

Luke didn't give a damn about the pool game, but he hoped Cynthia had information about the woman he craved more than life itself. He chalked his cue and pretended to care. "You can break."

She sent the balls flying, and two landed in the pockets. She lined up for another shot.

"What did you find out?"

She pulled back and sighed. "Wait until I've made my shot, okay?"

At that moment he became acutely aware that she was twenty-two. She was smarter than almost anyone he knew, and beautiful, and a great dancer, and savvy about people when she chose to be. But she was still twenty-two, and living for the moment, which meant getting the number two ball in the side pocket.

Curbing his impatience, he leaned on his cue stick and waited for her to make the shot. She made that one, and the one after that, and the one after that. If she ran the table, they would have no chance to talk. In which case, they'd simply play another game. He wasn't leaving the table without some answers.

Eventually she missed a shot. Not by much, but finally he had a turn. He wasn't going to take it until she gave him some information. "What did you find out?"

"Seriously? Not much."

He groaned.

"No, really. The Landrys are rich, and they have an estate of some kind north of San Francisco. The most I could get out of him—and this was after he'd swallowed most of his Long Island iced tea—was that Giselle was expected to marry a certain type of person, and you didn't fit the bill."

"What the hell? What's wrong with me? I'm healthy and reasonably good-looking. I have money. Maybe not as much as they do, but I can't believe they're focused on that. Giselle and Bryce don't strike me as snobs."

"Me, either."

"So is it pedigree? Are they requiring dudes whose ancestors came over on the Mayflower?"

"I can't believe that's it." She gestured toward the table. "Take your shot."

He sighed. "I'm not here to play pool, and you know it."

"I know, but you have to make it look convincing. Shoot."

He did and, by sheer coincidence, he sank two balls in a row. Then he missed, and Cynthia proceeded to clear the table of every single one of her remaining balls.

Bryce had described the total humiliation very well. Luke gazed at her. "Where did you learn to play like that?"

"As I said, I hung out with math majors. This is a game of geometry and physics. Once you understand the principles involved, all you have to do is execute."

"Okay, I accept defeat. But before we go back to the table, isn't there anything else you can tell me?"

"I know he's really happy about you selling the bar back to Benedict Cartwright. He mentioned that several times."

"Why does he care about that so much?"

"I'm not sure, but he kept talking about the Cartwright family tradition as if that mattered to him. He'd said all that before, when we were pulling our pranks on you, which was why I decided you should sell the bar. But . . ." She looked at him across the pool table. "Do you ever get the feeling that there's some secret society in town?"

"Yes! Have you ever tried to walk into the lobby of Illusions, the Cartwrights' new hotel?"

"No, why?"

"The doorman won't let you in unless you're a registered guest. You can't even enter the lobby *with* a registered guest. Giselle tried to get me in there, and the doorman flatly refused."

"That's weird. Could it be some top secret headquarters?"

"I don't know, but that's a ridiculous level of security, no matter who's staying there. Who restricts access to the damned *lobby*?"

Cynthia rolled the cue ball back and forth in front of her and she seemed lost in thought. "It does make you wonder."

"And there's some kind of connection between Mr. Thatcher and the two Landrys. Maybe they all belong to a secret organization and maybe not, but the three of them have something in common. I don't know what it is, but it's there."

"I absolutely agree. Maybe if you find out what that connection is, you'll find out what's standing between you and Giselle."

"How will I find out?"

"Keep a watch on your lady friend." Cynthia rolled the cue ball across the table in his direction. "By the way, I've invited Bryce to spend the night in my apartment at the Silver Crescent."

"Don't tell me that you're finally going to get chummy with the guy."

"No. He gave up his hotel room once we set off on this adventure together, so now he needs a place to crash and it seems silly for him to book another room. We get along, but he's still hung up on his ex, and although he's sweet, he doesn't do it for me, either. I'm just saying that I'll be able to keep an eye on him. That leaves only Mr. Thatcher. I think he's a piece of the puzzle, too, but I'm not willing to camp outside his door tonight to find out."

Luke rolled the cue ball back across the table in her direction. "You realize we're both talking like we're paranoid."

She smiled. "I know. But that doesn't mean we're wrong."

"But you don't think we're crazy, do you?"

"No, I don't. And whatever's going on, I agree that Giselle's involved in it, so stay alert."

"Do you still think she's the one for me? I mean, all this mystery and intrigue doesn't sound promising, does it?"

"No." Cynthia hesitated. "But I looked over at you two when you were dancing. You move together as if you've been doing it forever. As a dancer, I know how rare that is."

"I'm not a dancer, but I know what you're talking about. We've been able to catch each other's rhythm without really trying."

"Luke, do you believe in soul mates?"

"I . . . I'm not sure."

"Me, either. But if there is such a thing, then she's yours."

Chapter 24

During Luke and Cynthia's pool game, the three Weres had a chance to discuss their plans.

Mr. Thatcher leaned forward. "I don't know how long before Benedict will have legal access to the playground, but shutting it down was such a rushed affair. I feel it's most important to get in there and make sure there are no problems that could prove disastrous."

"It hasn't been that long since the crews left," Giselle said. "It's probably okay."

"But I understand what Mr. Thatcher means," Bryce said. "This is a situation where a little problem could turn into a big one really fast. I really want to take a look at the place, but I just agreed to stay with Cynthia tonight. She offered, and turning her down would seem strange to her after all this."

"You're staying with Cynthia?" Giselle pinned him with a look. "Are you involved with her, after all?"

He sighed. "Not only do you know that I'm not interested in her like that, but it seems that your fascination with Luke is the real problem here."

Giselle recognized that he'd made a direct hit. "You're right. Sorry."

"Cynthia and I are that rare phenomenon—heterosexual friends of opposite genders." A hint of vulnerability flickered in his blue eyes. "And if you must know, I can't seem to forget Miranda."

Giselle felt sorry for him, but he'd done it to himself, and she didn't want to give him false hope. "I'm in no position to comment, but—"

"But you will."

She hesitated, but she was his sister, after all, and sisters were obligated to say the hard things to brothers. "You really screwed up that relationship. I don't know if you can ever salvage it."

He nodded. "I realize that. But she hasn't hooked up with anyone else yet. I checked."

Giselle didn't know if that meant he was willing to return and move into the alpha role or not. She emptied her mind of all expectations as she turned to him and asked.

He put his hand over hers. "I've done a lot of soul-searching in the weeks I've been gone. I had to get some perspective on the situation before I could decide if it was what I wanted or what everyone else wanted for me."

"Before you tell me your decision, let me say that I'll support you whatever it might be."

He grinned at her. "Picked up a few tips from the Luke and Cynthia mess, did you?"

"Yes."

"Good. So have I. What I learned about myself is that family is important to me, too. And tradition. I'm ready to be the alpha."

Giselle took a deep breath and sandwiched his hand between both of hers. "I'm happy that you decided that. Selfishly, I wanted you to, but I meant what I said. I would have been behind you either way."

"That's terrific to hear." He hesitated. "And if Miranda can ever forgive me, I want her to be by my side."

"It's encouraging that she hasn't found another," Mr. Thatcher said. "For both your sakes, I'll hold a good thought."

"Thanks." Bryce glanced at the butler. "As I started to say before, I can probably still go with you tonight. I'm sleeping in a spare room, so if I'm careful, Cynthia doesn't have to know I'm gone."

Giselle shook her head. "I wouldn't risk it, Bryce."

"I'm scheduled to meet Benedict at precisely two," Mr. Thatcher said. "We won't be able to wait for you."

"I understand. If I think there's any chance Cynthia would catch me, I won't do it." He looked over at Giselle. "Sure you won't come with us?"

"I'd like to. But I can't."

"I know. Just teasing you. Enjoy your last hurrah."

"Right." Heat rose in her cheeks. He *would* have to say something in front of Mr. Thatcher. But she also realized he'd kept his comment relatively tame. He could have made it ten times more suggestive.

As luck would have it, Cynthia and Luke returned to the table before she'd regained her composure.

Luke looked at her and raised his eyebrows.

She fanned her face. "Bryce and his jokes. My brother knows how to make me blush."

"It's a talent." Bryce stretched his arms over his head. "I don't know about the rest of you, but I'm ready to call it a night."

Mr. Thatcher pushed back his chair. "So am I. But I've certainly enjoyed the evening."

"You and I will do this again sometime," Luke said. "Maybe not in this particular setting, though. I expect to be persona non grata around here very soon."

Bryce stood. "You might be more welcome than you think. I have a hunch Benedict Cartwright will be happy to have you as an honored customer after you turn over the deed."

"He might, at that." Giselle liked the idea of her brother being a key player in potentially ending the feud between the Cartwrights and the Daltons. His time in Vegas had turned out to be more valuable than she ever would have dreamed.

"I just had an idea, although I don't know if Benedict will go along with it. What if Vaughn thinks Benedict talked me into selling the Moon back to him? Would that get him out of the doghouse and restore some family harmony?"

"That's a compassionate plan," Giselle said. "It's worth a try." But she had a sudden image of a wolf in a doghouse, and she made the mistake of looking at Bryce. Judging from the sparkle in his green eyes, he'd thought the same thing. She quickly glanced away and pressed her lips together. Laughing at this private joke would be a very bad idea.

She would have loved to share the joke with Luke, but she couldn't, and that made her sad. They'd become close in so many ways, yet they still were separated by an enormous gulf. Her heart longed to bridge that chasm and be one with him in all ways, but that was selfish thinking.

"I guess we're all ready to leave, then." Luke took out his wallet and left several bills on the table.

"Hey, are we paying?" Bryce reached in his hip pocket for his wallet. "I assumed it was on the house, but I'll toss in something if it's not."

"The drinks are free, but the server still needs her tips."

"Got it." Bryce threw more money on top of Luke's already large tip. "She didn't have much business tonight, so this should help."

Giselle smiled. Luke and her brother had a similar generosity of spirit. If she thought about it, she might find other traits they had in common. Mentally listing them and imagining a friendship between the two was a pointless exercise, though.

She took out some money she'd tucked in the pocket of her jeans before she'd walked over there and added it to the pile on the table.

"Goodness, I can see where this is headed." Cynthia dug out some crumpled bills and put them on top of the growing stash. "I'm not about to be the cheapskate in the bunch."

"Nor am I." Mr. Thatcher produced a crisp hundred-dollar bill and balanced it carefully on the mound of cash.

Cynthia let out a whoop. "Way to trump us all, Mr. Thatcher!"

The butler smiled. "I always take pleasure in tipping well. Shall we go?"

As before, Mr. Thatcher led the way back to the Silver Crescent's service entrance as if he were the patriarch of the group. For the most part, he filled the role beautifully.

But he wasn't a big-picture kind of guy. He'd focused on the immediate problem—Luke's unhappiness when Giselle left in the morning. He'd serve Luke far better by visualizing the disastrous long-term effects if she brought Luke into her world.

The cheerful group piled on the private elevator together. Mr. Thatcher got off on his floor, and a quick glance passed between him and Bryce before the doors slid closed. When Bryce and Cynthia got off, Bryce winked at Giselle, and true to form, she blushed.

"They beat the cleaning crew up to the suite." Luke tucked his arm around her waist and pulled her close.

"I know they did." She gazed up at him. "Bryce is threatening to blackmail me with the pictures on his phone."

Luke grinned. "I trust you have your own blackmail material stored somewhere?"

"Absolutely. He won't show those pictures to anyone, especially if he wants to get back with Miranda. I'll be a key player in that effort. He won't mess with me."

The doors opened, and he kept his arm around her waist as they walked toward the double doors of the suite. "I doubt anyone messes with you, Harley girl. Which reminds me. You never showed me how to ride that hog."

She looked into blue eyes filled with warmth . . . and regret. "Anyone can teach you. If you buy one, they'll be happy to arrange for lessons. You'll pick it up in no time."

"You know I won't do that," he said softly, holding her gaze. "Every time I got on the damn thing I'd think of you."

Her throat tightened.

"Hey, I'm sorry. I swore I wouldn't get all mushy and sentimental tonight, and now I've made you look very sad."

"I am sad," she said in a husky voice.

"Not for long." He tightened his grip around her waist and smiled. "Come with me, little girl. The big bad wolf is going to eat you up."

It was the wrong teasing remark, and the tears she'd vowed not to cry began to fall.

"Well, damn." He hustled her through the double doors. "I thought that might make you laugh, but apparently not."

She covered her face with both hands. "I'll . . . I'll be . . . okay." She choked back a sob. "Give me . . . a minute."

"I'd give you the rest of my life if I could." He gathered her close. "And I didn't plan to say *that*, either."

His words only made her cry harder. What a fool she'd been to think she could have a fun romp with this funny, gorgeous, generous, stubborn, and thoroughly loveable *man*.

"I'll bet you wish you'd never started this." He nestled her head against his broad chest and rubbed her back.

"No!" Her voice was clogged with tears. "I'm *glad* we've had this." She took a shaky breath. "It's just . . ."

"Yeah. It's always tough when the party's over."

"Are you sorry?"

"Hell, no. I've always figured you'd leave. There was a point when I thought . . . Well, it doesn't matter." He leaned down and rested his cheek on her hair. "But you're not gone yet. I vote we make the most of the time we have left."

She gave a watery chuckle. "As opposed to having me cry the whole blessed time?"

"Something like that. Unless Bryce and Cynthia told you to as a final way to get me wet."

"Oh, Luke." She was half laughing and half crying, but

that was better than totally crying. She drew back and swiped at her eyes. "Can I interest you in a trip to the bedroom?"

He gazed down at her. "You can, but I have no idea what we'll find there. As you recall, I ordered a cleaning crew, not a housekeeper. They might have stripped the bed and left with the evidence."

"At least it won't be a leaky water bed."

"Good point." He hooked an arm around her shoulders. "Let's go investigate our options."

When they reached the bedroom, Giselle's tears gave way to helpless laughter.

Luke released her to go stand at the foot of the bed and stare in disbelief. "It's the *same.* Still effing *white.*"

Giselle stifled her giggles. "If you didn't tell them not to, then . . ."

"But you'd think, after seeing that god-awful mess we made, they'd have asked me if I wanted to keep everything the same." He glanced at her. "Wouldn't you have asked me, if you were them?"

"Maybe they tried."

"Oh." He pulled his phone out of his coat pocket and grimaced. "Three messages. I didn't hear my phone. Did you hear my phone?"

She shook her head. "But I wasn't listening for a phone. I was involved in other things."

He looked up from his phone and his gaze locked with hers. "Me, too." Maintaining eye contact, he shoved his phone back in his pocket as he walked back to her. "And I intend to be involved with those things again. Who gives a damn what color the bedding is?"

"I don't."

"Neither do I." He cupped her face in both hands and

leaned down. "We'll be too busy to notice." And he kissed her with the certainty of a man who knew that his passion was returned.

They undressed each other this time, and it didn't take long. Soon they were rolling naked on the pristine white sheets. They stroked and fondled with the confidence of lovers who've learned which caresses bring the most pleasure.

Giselle banished melancholy thoughts as she reveled in the wonder of loving and being loved by Luke. Sex between them had been good from the beginning, but it had grown richer with each encounter. Tonight she treasured every moment as they writhed on the bed—skin to skin, mouth to mouth, breath to breath. At last they sought the deepest connection, the one they craved most of all.

Each thrust, each tremor, each moan brought them closer to total surrender. As Giselle's body gathered itself, poised for the coming explosion, she looked up into eyes blazing with the same fire burning within her. She could no longer hold back her truth. "I love you, Luke Dalton."

He drew in a quick breath. "Ah, Giselle." His eyes darkened. "I know you do. I know." And he drove home with a triumphant cry, the moment of his orgasm matching hers. They held on tight and rode the whirlwind. Long after the storm subsided, they stayed wrapped in each other's arms.

She would have loved to drift off to sleep that way, but her mind was filled with thoughts of leaving. Sleep wouldn't come. The thought of never seeing Luke again tore her apart.

In spite of all her misgivings, she wanted to be with

him. Mr. Thatcher thought they belonged together. Bryce thought they belonged together. She trusted their insights, but . . . what if they were wrong? What if she revealed her secret and Luke was thoroughly repulsed?

Was it better to leave when he still thought of her as the woman who got away? Besides, if she gambled on him accepting her werewolf nature and lost, they wouldn't have a future, but he'd be stuck with guarding the secret for the rest of his life. What should she do?

"Giselle." His voice was low and intense. "I can almost hear you thinking. Please tell me you're reconsidering."

"I thought you were asleep."

"How could I sleep with all that thinking going on?"

"Oh, Luke. I don't know what to do."

"I do." He sat up. "Stop resisting and say we can be together. Tell me this awful secret, whatever it is."

She gulped. "Once I do, there's no turning back."

"There's no turning back anyway. Like the song says, I will always love you. I couldn't stop doing that if I tried." He blew out a breath. "Just tell me what it is. How bad can it be?"

"Life changing."

"Okay!" He got out of bed and began to pace. "Mr. Thatcher and Bryce are involved, aren't they?"

"Yes."

"I knew it! And somehow it all ties into the security at Illusions. You don't have to say yes or no. I don't know how, but it does."

She trembled. Sitting up seemed like a better way to face this decision, so she did that. Then she decided to get out of bed, too.

He whirled to face her. "I love you!" He practically

shouted it. "Don't shut me out, Giselle. Tell me the truth! Whatever it is, I swear I can deal with it. Nothing's more important to me than being with you. Nothing!"

She could barely breathe as fear tightened her chest. But in spite of the fear, she made a decision. She would tell him.

She wanted him, and he wanted her, and maybe Bryce was right. Luke needed a chance to accept or reject her as she really was. She would take full responsibility for the outcome, but he deserved to know the truth.

He faced her, eyes flashing. "Well? Are you going to tell me?"

"Yes." She gulped for air. Her pulse raced, sending liquid fire through her veins. "I'm . . . I'm a werewolf."

Chapter 25

Luke went completely still. Then, because it was the only logical response, he laughed. "That's a great line, but your timing is lousy. I'm not in the mood for joking around, Giselle." Except her expression was completely serious, which made him nervous.

"I'm not joking. I realize that's a shocking thing to hear, but it's the truth."

He stared at her. Until now, he'd considered her the love of his life. And she was batshit crazy. That wasn't a politically correct description anymore. He didn't know what was PC these days to label someone who was a taco short of a Mexican combo plate.

Sad to say, he still loved her, crazy or not. But she needed help. "Giselle, is there a medication you might have skipped recently? We've been so busy that you easily could have forgotten. Is it in your suitcase? I'd be happy to—"

"I'm not on medication and don't need to be."

Oh, boy. He'd heard of cases like this, where the patient became belligerent. "I'll get Bryce. I'll call Cynthia and tell her to send Bryce down here. I'm sure he knows what—"

"Don't get Bryce. Keep this between you and me for now, please."

"Okay, no Bryce. You and I will handle this together." He tried to stay calm. "How about taking a nice little ride with me? There's a twenty-four-hour clinic within a few minutes of here. You don't have to be scared or anything. I'll stay with you the whole time."

She sighed. "Luke, you're a really good guy. You think I'm psychotic, don't you?"

"That's such a harsh word. You're a little confused about reality, but we can fix that. How about getting dressed? That's a good start." And he'd been so sure that he knew her. Was it possible that she was telling the truth? Nope. Not possible. She had a chemical imbalance, and he would get her some help for that.

"I guess there's only one way to convince you." Dropping to her hands and knees, she stretched out naked on the bedroom carpet, facing him.

"This isn't a good time for sex. I never thought I'd hear myself say that concerning you, but I have my standards. Taking advantage of a disturbed woman is not my idea of acceptable behavior. So if you'll just get up and put on your . . ." He lost track of what he'd been about to say when she began to sparkle.

Okay, this was freaking him out. Normal women didn't sparkle. He'd seen a vampire movie that involved sparkling, but Giselle hadn't announced she was a vampire. She'd said she was a werewolf. He didn't believe in vampires or werewolves, so this couldn't be happening.

A nightmare. He was having a nightmare. He pinched himself, though, and it hurt. Wasn't that the test? He'd love to wake up and find out he was dreaming and his beloved was still in bed with him instead of lying on his bedroom carpet . . . sparkling.

That wasn't all she was doing, though. Along with the pretty lights, she was changing right before his eyes. He rubbed them, thinking that he was hallucinating. Maybe he was the one in need of medication.

Or a good bottle of Scotch. Damnation. The dancing lights faded, and where a redheaded woman with green eyes had been, a wolf now stood. Its coat was a deep red, very close in color to Giselle's hair. And its eyes, although they were those of a wolf, were emerald green.

He began to shake, and his heart was beating double time. His voice was a mere whisper. "Giselle?"

The wolf looked at him, intelligence shining in its green eyes. In *her* green eyes. He couldn't deny the evidence. This wolf was Giselle. And Giselle was this wolf. His brain hurt, but . . . she'd told him the truth.

He dragged air into his lungs. "Okay." He still wasn't registering this. He blew out that same air. "Okay. I . . . I need to think about this. In my wildest dreams, I never . . ." He started grabbing his clothes. "Let me think. I need to talk a walk. Please don't go anywhere."

He pulled on his clothes as the wolf watched him. "Just let me have a little time to sort this out. To adjust. I'll be back. Don't leave." Shoving his feet into loafers, he grabbed his jacket and his keys and headed out, his brain spinning like a carnival ride.

And he'd thought she was crazy. That would have been easier to take. In the elevator, he braced his hands against his knees as if he'd run a marathon. He started to punch the button for the garage, changed his mind, and chose the first floor instead. Driving in his condition—total freak-out mode—was not a good idea.

Ducking out the service door, he started walking, unsure of his destination. He didn't know what time it was, but probably late. The Moon was closed down for the night.

That's where he'd go. He could sit alone in the bar, which still belonged to him. He could pour himself a stiff Scotch, which he really could use right now. And he could think what the hell he was going to do next.

Having a key to the bar in his possession had been a matter of pride. He'd learned the code to the alarm system for the same reason. This property was his, and he'd liked knowing he could go inside whenever he wanted. Like now.

Moments later, he was rummaging behind the bar for the best bottle of Scotch in the house. After he located that, he grabbed a glass and walked over to a table. He deliberately didn't choose the one where he'd so recently sat with Giselle. That little gathering seemed like it had happened years ago.

A werewolf. She'd warned him that her secret would be life changing. No shit. After pouring himself a glass of Scotch, he took a hefty gulp. He didn't plan to get drunk, but he wouldn't mind a little Dutch courage.

He'd need it when he went back to the penthouse, which he would do, and soon. She might be a werewolf, but he loved her. If you loved someone, you accepted them, warts and all. Except this was a little more significant than a wart.

The clock behind the bar registered two thirty in the morning. His life had changed forever about twenty minutes ago. For some reason he thought he should remember the time and date that his entire worldview changed.

Now that the initial shock was past, he had a million questions. All he knew about werewolves came from Hollywood, and they usually got that stuff wrong. He hoped they got it wrong. Otherwise, he might need a lot more Scotch.

He'd nearly finished his first glass and was debating whether to pour a second when he heard a noise. No, not just a noise. *Voices.* They came from the hallway that led to the restrooms and the kitchen. Good God, was he about to start hearing voices now? Or seeing ghosts?

More likely, he was lucky enough to be here when somebody was breaking into the place. That would cap his evening off nicely. Screwing the top on the bottle of Scotch, he took it with him as a potential weapon and started down the hall.

Yeah, this was weird. The sound of male voices came closer, but not from either of the bathrooms or the kitchen, which would be logical if someone was messing around in here. The voices came from behind the wall at the end of the hallway.

Although the conversation was muffled, Luke thought there were at least two guys, maybe three. Standing there waiting to see what happened might not be the wisest course of action since he was outnumbered. But after watching Giselle turn into a wolf and then downing a glass of Scotch, Luke was in a what-the-hell mood.

If ghosts walked through that wall and came toward him—and at this point anything was possible—he would hightail it out of there. Even if he threw the bottle of Scotch, it wouldn't stop a ghost.

Whoever was behind that wall, they were about to

run smack into it if they were real people. Then he heard a familiar accent. A familiar *British* accent. Mr. Thatcher?

He thought the night couldn't get any weirder until the wall started moving. While he stared, no doubt with his eyes bugging out of his head like a cartoon character, the wall swiveled, allowing three men to walk through the opening.

"Yikes!" Bryce stopped short, and the two behind him, Mr. Thatcher and Benedict Cartwright, plowed into Bryce.

For a moment, the hallway was silent except for the sound of everyone gulping for air.

Luke found his voice first. "What in damnation is going on?"

The three men looked at one another as if each hoped that one of the others would come up with a good story.

Luke tried again. "Where did you come from? What's behind that wall?"

Bryce swallowed. "Well, it's complicated."

Luke studied Bryce, whose coloring was very close to Giselle's. Same basic genetics, which meant . . . He mentally slapped his forehead. She'd said that Bryce would support her story of being a werewolf.

"Perhaps we should all sit down," Mr. Thatcher said.

"Not yet." Luke focused on Bryce and decided to try some fishing. "I know about your sister, Landry."

His eyes narrowed. "Who told you?"

"She did."

"When?"

"About thirty minutes ago. And I figure, since you two are related . . ."

"Where is she?"

"Right here."

Luke turned to find Giselle standing behind him—the Giselle he'd first met, a long-legged, gorgeous redhead in jeans, boots, a sweater, and a leather jacket.

"You didn't lock the front door," she said. "I had a hunch you might be in here." She glanced at the bottle of Scotch. "Drowning your sorrows?"

"No. Celebrating the fact that I finally know what's going on with you." He gestured at the three men standing at the end of the hall. "And I'll take a wild guess that you're all the same species." He fixed his gaze on Mr. Thatcher. "Including my butler."

Giselle glanced at Bryce. "You suggested that I tell him, so I did. I even put on a demonstration, after which he ran out of the suite as if his tail was on fire."

"I did not." Luke frowned. "It was a shock. I had to be alone for a little while."

Giselle held his gaze. "Alone except for a bottle of Scotch. That doesn't reassure me as to your state of mind about all this."

He saw bravado in her green eyes, but it was hiding a layer of hurt. "I'm sorry. I should have stayed."

"Cut the guy some slack, Sis." Bryce walked forward and hooked an arm around Luke's shoulders. "Give him some time to get used to the idea. It's not every day that a man finds out he's in love with a werewolf."

A gasp of surprise made them all freeze.

With a soft oath, Giselle whirled around as Cynthia walked toward them. "Where did you come from? I didn't hear you!"

"I was back in the corner, listening. I went up to the penthouse to tell Luke that Bryce was gone, and I took the fire stairs like I always do. I saw Luke charge into the elevator. He looked upset, so I followed him. When he came in here, I slipped in behind him. I was ready to say something, but then he grabbed the Scotch, which told me he wanted to be alone. I tucked myself into a corner, not sure what to do." She paused for breath. "A werewolf, Giselle? Really?"

Luke groaned. "It's a joke."

"I seriously doubt that, big brother." Cynthia crossed her arms. "And I'm not leaving, so you might as well fill me in."

"Nobody's leaving." Benedict Cartwright stepped forward for the first time. "We obviously have a major security breach." He pulled out his phone. "I can have a Cartwright security team here in five minutes, or . . ." He paused to glance around the group. "We can all sit down, have a drink, and figure this out among ourselves."

"I choose Option Two," Bryce said. "Anybody else want to voice an opinion?"

"Definitely Option Two," Luke said. "Don't call anybody, Cartwright." He glanced around at the assembled group. "Let's have a seat in the bar. Drinks are on the house."

"And I'm mixing 'em," Benedict said. "You may be a better poker player, but I'm a hell of a lot better at bartending."

Luke looked him in the eye. "That's for sure, Cartwright. You belong here, and I don't. I'm going to sell this place back to you. I finally figured out that was the only sensible thing to do, with a little help from my friends."

Benedict almost smiled at that. "It's good to have friends."

Giselle had held it together so far, and she was a pro at

presenting a calm facade, but she couldn't guarantee how long she could keep it up. She'd risked everything to reveal her Were being, and Luke had run out on her. Bryce had told her to give Luke some time to get used to the idea, but what if he never did?

As everyone left the hallway, bound for a table in the bar, she stayed behind. So did he. He came toward her, and she tried to gauge his expression, but her darned eyes kept tearing up and she had to blink the moisture away.

"Giselle."

"Yeah?"

"Please forgive me for running out on you like that."

She sniffed. "It's okay." Close up, she could see from the look in his eyes he was sorry. "My brother's right. It's a shock to hear it, and I—"

"So you do forgive me?"

She nodded.

"Thank God." He cupped her face in both hands, touching her for the first time since he'd watched her shift. "Because I love you so much." He brushed at her damp cheeks with his thumbs. "And I feel like an ass for hurting you and making you cry."

She swallowed. "You don't have to say you love me to make me feel better. I'm not who you thought, or *what* you thought. If this doesn't work for you, then I'll—"

He cut her off with a kiss, a tender kiss that she would cherish forever, no matter what happened.

Then he lifted his head. "We have lots to talk about. I have lots to learn. But never doubt that I love you with all my heart."

She gazed into his eyes and knew that it was true. They would love each other forever. But that didn't mean they'd be together forever. She sensed he was reserving judgment on that. She couldn't blame him. He had no idea what he was getting into.

"Let's go in and have Cartwright mix us a drink." With an encouraging smile, he laced his fingers through hers as they walked out of the hallway.

He kept her hand tucked in his as they ordered drinks at the bar and walked over to the spot where the others had pushed a couple of tables together. He made sure they sat close together, and his firm grip reassured her that he wasn't repulsed by what he'd seen when she shifted. He just needed to know more, which was fair.

As they sat down, Cynthia was busy peppering Bryce with questions, questions Luke probably had, as well. But she knew he'd have some personal ones that he wouldn't ask in mixed company.

In the meantime, Bryce was doing a bang-up job of correcting Cynthia's misperceptions about werewolves, and possibly Luke's as well.

She leaned toward Bryce. "Can you see better than a human?"

"Not during the day, but my wolf night vision is awesome."

Cynthia appeared transfixed by that notion. "Do you hunt?"

"No. Yuck."

"Is that just your preference? Because I can sort of picture you—"

"None of us hunt, at least not in modern times. Centuries ago, that might have made sense, but now it's a lot less work to go to the store and buy the food."

"But you could hunt if you wanted to."

Bryce shook his head. "I'd be terrible at it. I'd have to

be taught, and since nobody hunts anymore, the skill has died out."

"I'll bet, if you were really hungry and—"

"Hey, Sis, can we drop the subject?" Luke flicked a glance at Giselle. "She was a bloodthirsty little kid. Loved gory movies."

"Still do." Cynthia laughed. "While you, on the other hand, are the biggest wimp on the planet. I'd look over at you and you'd be all hunched down and not watching."

Giselle smiled at him. "I'm the same way. Been teased about it all my life."

"A round of drinks, coming up!" Benedict appeared with six glasses on a tray and dispersed them before pulling up his own chair. "So, how's the discussion progressing?"

"Let's see." Bryce held up one hand and ticked off the subjects. "We've talked about the political structure of werewolf packs."

"And you're going to be the Landry alpha, Bryce." Cynthia picked up her cosmo. "That's supercool."

"Ah," Luke said. "So the alpha is the equivalent of a CEO."

"Bryce will be the CEO," Giselle said. "And the alpha."

"Vaughn's the alpha for the Cartwrights." Cynthia glanced over at Luke. "Remember how we talked about the suspicious nature of the security at Illusions? You couldn't get in the lobby because you're not the right species. It's a werewolf-only hotel."

Luke nodded. "It's all beginning to make sense to me now. The Silver Crescent used to be a werewolf hotel, didn't it?"

"Yep." Benedict sipped his drink. "You can't imagine how long the renovations took."

"Thus the stalling on signing over the deed." Luke sighed. "That paints your father in a whole new light."

"I'm a little worried about this security breach," Benedict said, "but it's kind of nice to be able to set the record straight. My dad made a mistake betting the Silver Crescent, but he wasn't trying to drive your dad crazy. He had a Were community to protect."

"You don't have to worry about the security breach," Cynthia said. "You can trust Luke and me. Right, Luke?"

"Yes." He squeezed Giselle's hand. "I'll guard this secret with my life."

"Whoa." Bryce looked impressed. "I like the sound of that, Dalton. I think you'll be just fine."

"So will I." Cynthia glanced around at the group. "I'm sitting with my new friend Bryce, my childhood friend Benedict, my second father Mr. Thatcher, and Giselle, the woman—or Were, whichever I'm supposed to say— my brother's in love with. All of you are very important to me. I'll do the protecting-with-my-life thing, too."

"That shouldn't ever be necessary," Benedict said. "But thanks. The council will be glad to hear it."

"Council?" Luke's grip on Giselle's hand tightened.

"The Were Council," she said. "They'll have to review this situation and determine what's the best course of action."

He looked at her, his gaze wary. "Meaning what?"

"Depending on their evaluation of your trustworthiness, you might just be monitored for a brief time."

"Yeah, but you don't have to worry about it," Bryce said. "Giselle's on the council."

"Besides that," Cynthia said, "Bryce was telling me

before, when you and Giselle were kissing in the hallway, that if you mate with her, you'll be totally accepted. And once I pass the trustworthiness test, which I so totally will, then I'll be accepted, too, because I'm your sister." She smiled at them across the table. "See how this is all working out for the best?"

Giselle stifled a groan. She'd just dealt with a brother who'd balked because he felt railroaded into a situation. She couldn't imagine Luke being overjoyed about the corner he'd just discovered himself in either.

Chapter 26

Luke felt Giselle tense and he could guess why. She didn't want him to feel manipulated into something before he even understood it. Most of all, she wouldn't want him to think everyone was pushing him into a relationship that involved a lifetime commitment. That lack of choice was the very thing that had driven her brother to take a long Vegas vacation.

But Luke didn't feel manipulated, even though Cynthia had made it clear what she thought should happen. Instead he felt challenged, and in a good way. Giselle might have different DNA from his, but the more he thought about it, the more that fascinated him.

As for the world she lived in, he understood it better than she might think. It was the world of commerce, the world he'd grown up in and been trained for. The Cartwrights and the Landrys might each be a werewolf pack, but they were business oriented and apparently successful at it. No wonder his father and Harrison had become friends. Except for the werewolf thing, they had led similar lives.

He was beginning to see a grand new adventure spreading out before him, and that was exciting. If he could share that adventure with Giselle, the most fascinating female he'd ever known, he would be a happy man. Being accepted into her circle sounded great to him. He wasn't clear on what the deal would be with kids in that scenario, but she'd said she couldn't get pregnant, so that might not be an issue.

So far, though, nobody had bothered to explain a more immediate mystery, so he decided to ask the obvious question. "What were you three werewolves doing behind that revolving door?"

Benedict grinned. "I wondered when you'd get around to that."

"Well, I just did. Care to explain? Especially since I still own this bar, and that means I own the revolving door and probably whatever's behind it."

"I'd be happy to tell you," Benedict said. "In fact, this is going to make my life a whole lot easier."

Luke gestured across the table. "Proceed."

Benedict launched into an explanation that sounded almost as unbelievable as the existence of werewolves. Luke found himself glancing down at the floor. Beneath his feet was something he never would have imagined in a million years.

Cynthia's eyes widened. "All that stuff is underground? And no one knows?"

"The werewolves know," Benedict said.

"I can't believe the secret hasn't gotten out." Luke continued to wrestle with the concept. "Somebody hears a rumor and somehow gets past security to check it out. In human form, everybody looks the same."

"Yes, but they don't smell the same," Giselle said. "I

knew the minute Mr. Thatcher walked into your suite that he was Were. And vice versa."

"So a human wouldn't pass the sniff test? Is that what you're saying?"

Benedict nodded. "That's the time-honored way we tell Weres from humans. Because you're right. Any human walking in here right now wouldn't have any idea we're from a different species."

"Well, obviously, I want to see this place." Luke finished his drink. "Shall we go?"

"Me, too!" Cynthia swigged the last of her cosmo. "I wish I could see it all working, though, with the stream and the waterfalls in operation, and the forest sounds, and the moon. I think the moon is genius, considering the name of the bar."

Bryce looked over at Benedict. "Can you see any reason not to turn on the water? We fixed that small leak. It would be good to test the system, though, and make sure everything's working right if the playground will open again soon."

Benedict's gaze registered approval. "Good thinking, Landry. And for the record, I appreciate your help and friendship over the past few days."

"Glad to be of service."

"How about turning on the lights and sound system?" Cynthia asked. "I'd love to get the full effect."

Bryce turned toward Luke. "It'll run up your utility bill, man. And you're the one on the hook for that until you sell the Moon to this dude." He angled his head toward Benedict.

"What the hell." Luke shrugged. "My little sister wants to see the show." He glanced over at Giselle and smiled. "So do I, come to think of it."

Cynthia left her chair and came over to kiss his cheek. "Thanks, Bro."

"The controls are in the locker room," Benedict said. "Follow me."

"I want to see how you activate everything," Bryce said.

Cynthia headed off right behind them. "I knew you two were cool, but I had no idea how cool."

Luke caught Giselle gazing after Cynthia with a flicker of concern in her eyes. He shared that concern. Cynthia might think this werewolf stuff was fascinating and cool, but knowledge of it would have a cost. He wanted to know what that was.

He looked over at Mr. Thatcher, who was finishing his gin and tonic. "We need to talk."

Cynthia popped back in the room. "Aren't you all coming? I thought you wanted to see this, Luke."

"I do. You go ahead and get things started. I'll wait here with Mr. Thatcher until you say it's ready for viewing."

"Same here," Giselle said. "Come and get us when it's all at its spectacular best."

"Don't worry." Cynthia flashed them a smile. "I will!"

Once she was gone, Mr. Thatcher squared his shoulders as if preparing for a blow. "If you choose to fire me, sir, I completely understand."

"I'm not going to fire you, Mr. Thatcher, but I need to know from you and Giselle what happens next. I run a large business, and when we have a security issue, we fix it. I've heard a little about a council and some monitoring, but that seems too simplistic and easy. What's the real scoop?"

Giselle put a hand on his arm. "You and Cynthia are in no danger. I promise you that."

"Certainly not!" Mr. Thatcher looked horrified at the idea. "I would lay down my life for you and Cynthia. Not that it will be necessary," he added quickly.

"That's what I need to know." Luke fought to stay calm. "Personally, I can take care of myself, but if anyone plans to harm my sister, there will be hell to pay."

"They won't," Giselle said. "You have my word."

He turned to her and found love and certainty in those green eyes. He was vastly reassured. "Then if we're not going to be killed, how will you deal with us? We know the secret. Surely we're considered a security risk."

"That's right." She met his gaze without hesitation. "That's why I was so determined that you wouldn't ever know. But . . . then Bryce said something to me that I wasn't able to forget. He said if I never told you, I was taking away your ability to choose whether you wanted to be with me or not."

"Thank God for Bryce." He gave her hand a squeeze. "He was right. And I'm fine with whatever has to go on with me. It's Cynthia I worry about. I know I'm not her parent, but this is different. She was swept up in this by accident, and I want to make sure she'll be safe."

"She will be. We'll work through it together."

"Great. Just tell me how."

"I'm not sure yet."

Mr. Thatcher cleared his throat. "If I may offer some thoughts . . ."

Luke glanced over at the man—no, the *werewolf*—he'd considered a second father. To think he'd always considered Mr. Thatcher a little on the dull side. "Please do," he said. "I'm counting on you to help me sort this out."

"I haven't had much time to ponder this, but one thing I know—you and Cynthia are completely trustworthy. I've watched you both grow into adults who keep your word."

"So that's all I'll have to do? Promise not to tell? I find that hard to believe."

"It'll be more complicated than that," Giselle said. "But having three werewolves vouch for your character will go a long way with the council. It's not as if you're the first two humans to find out about us, and we've managed to keep the secret for centuries."

"This council has sole discretion to decide what's to be done with us?" Luke didn't appreciate having his fate or Cynthia's in the hands of others, especially a different species from his own.

"That makes it sound like some kind of kangaroo court," Giselle said. "It's not. It's a reasonable group. And, as Cynthia said, I'm on it."

"That could make a difference. I hope. Unless you're going to be in trouble for revealing the secret to me, and, by accident, to Cynthia." He gazed at her. "I'll say it was all my fault. I hounded you until you told me."

"No, no." Mr. Thatcher waved both hands. "Don't do that. If anyone needs to be the sacrificial lamb, I'll volunteer. I knew the two of you were falling in love, and I didn't do anything to stop it. In fact, once I realized that Giselle might consider changing her views, I encouraged it."

Luke gazed at him. "What views?"

"We can talk about that later." Giselle clearly wanted to change the subject.

He decided to let her do that, but he'd get back to it sometime later. He wanted to know her *views* and how he fit into them, or how he didn't.

"Nobody's to blame for this except me," Giselle said. "I'm the one who chose to reveal the secret. Bryce encouraged me, but I'm the one who—"

"What's that?" Bryce walked into the room. "Are you trying to pin this rap on me, little sister?"

"Never." Giselle slipped her hand from Luke's and stood. "I'm glad you urged me to tell Luke. He deserved to know."

"I'm grateful." Luke stood and walked over to shake Bryce's hand. "This is a lot to take in, but far better for me to be on information overload than to have no information at all. And no Giselle."

Bryce nodded, his gaze understanding. "Obviously I agree with that. I didn't expect Cynthia to be a part of all this, but maybe that's a good thing. She's on the inside with you now, instead of on the outside. Given how close you two are, I think in the long run this will make things easier."

"Hm." Luke regarded Bryce with new respect. "Good thought. I hadn't considered that."

"I told Cynthia the council will probably require that she and her brother sign a nondisclosure agreement," Bryce continued, "and there could be—"

"You've been discussing this with her?" Luke heard his tone of voice. Way to have a knee-jerk reaction. He backpedaled immediately. "I mean, good. I'm glad you talked to her about it."

"Actually, *I've* been discussing it with *him*." Cynthia came up behind Bryce and peeked over his shoulder. "I wasn't born yesterday, big brother. I realize we're now in the category of those who know too much, so I asked Bryce how werewolves handle a case like ours. I don't relish getting eliminated. Do you?"

"Uh, no, I don't." He reminded himself that Cynthia's brain was always working, so naturally she'd figured out the possible consequences of this caper, too. Maybe someday, twenty years from now, he'd shed the last of his protective behavior. Then again, maybe not.

"The way I look at it," Bryce said, "Mr. Thatcher can vouch for you and Cynthia, and Benedict can add in his two cents, since he's known both of you for a long time, too. The council could impose some monitoring for a year or so, but that might be it."

"*Might*?" Luke frowned. "I don't like these vague terms. Give it to me straight. What's the worst that could happen?"

Bryce eyed him. "You mean if they decided you pose a definite security risk?"

"Exactly. Let's say they don't trust me, or Cynthia for that matter, despite what you all say. What would they do? Kill us?"

Bryce sighed. "No, you have to get that out of your head. We don't kill. But we might need to contain you."

"Aha! I knew it. You'd have to catch me, first, though. And my little sister can run like a bat out of hell."

"Oh, we would catch you. But don't worry. It's not like we have a prison with a dungeon or anything. It's more like staying at the most luxurious resort in the world."

"As if that makes it better," Luke muttered.

"But it won't happen!" Cynthia said. "We have three great character references. If you'll just let me do the talking, we'll be fine."

From the corner of his eye, Luke saw Giselle cover her mouth as if hiding a smile. Okay, so his little sister was cute and sassy while he was the gloom-and-doom guy in the bunch. But despite all the insights he'd gained recently, he couldn't turn off that basic urge to keep Cynthia safe. That had been imprinted on him when he was ten, and it wasn't changing. At this point, he wasn't entirely convinced that he could keep her safe, and worry churned in his gut.

"I think we've beat that subject to death," Bryce said. "How about a tour of the werewolf playground? That should cheer everybody up!"

Luke doubted it would make him any more cheerful, but he was curious. "Let's do it." He gestured for Giselle to go ahead of him.

She leaned toward him as she walked by. "It'll be okay. I promise."

"Hope so." He believed she'd do everything in her power to make it so, but she couldn't possibly have complete control over what would happen.

As he started to follow her, Mr. Thatcher touched his arm.

He turned around, and the butler motioned him closer. "There is that perfect solution, the one Cynthia mentioned," he murmured.

"I've been thinking about that." They wouldn't marry. They would *mate*. The term had a primitive ring to it that both excited and alarmed him.

"I urge you to think about it."

"It's tough to get my mind around it, Mr. Thatcher. It's a radical concept. And most of all, I . . . I don't know if she would want that." *Or if I do.* He might have been thinking about it before, but now that he knew she was a different species, he didn't feel as if he knew her as well as he had imagined. It wasn't that he didn't love her, but knowing she was a werewolf gave him pause and made him want to know more before he made any decisions.

"Ask her."

Chapter 27

Giselle was dying to know what Mr. Thatcher was saying to Luke. But instead of meandering and using her sharp hearing to eavesdrop, she walked briskly down the hallway to the locker room. Her footsteps echoed on the wooden floor, which helped to block out their conversation.

Luke and the butler had a long-standing relationship that had suffered a major shock. Discovering she was a werewolf had obviously been difficult for Luke to accept, but adjusting to Mr. Thatcher's new identity could be even tougher. She had no right to intrude on their discussion.

When she walked through the door at the end of the hallway and entered the locker room designed for Weres to store their clothes, Luke and Mr. Thatcher were still in the bar. Benedict, Bryce, and Cynthia stood waiting for her at the opposite end of the locker room, at the entrance to the playground.

"We wondered if you'd ever get here," Cynthia said. "Of course you've seen it before, but my brother hasn't. I'd think he'd be dying of curiosity. Where is he?"

"He and Mr. Thatcher are having a talk."

"Oh." Cynthia glanced at Giselle. "Partly about you, I'll bet."

"I don't know. Maybe."

"You should have hung back to listen. I would've."

"Hey!" Bryce pretended to be shocked. "Don't forget I have to vouch for your sterling character, missy. Don't be announcing to me that you're a habitual eavesdropper."

Cynthia shrugged. "I'm a little sister. We survive by eavesdropping. Am I right, Giselle?"

"You're right, but in this case, it felt wrong. What do you think they might be saying about me?"

Bryce traded glances with Cynthia before he faced Giselle. "Probably the same thing Cynthia and I talked about while we were activating the systems. I filled her in on the new trend of Weres mating with humans."

"Yeah, and I think that's awesome." Cynthia's blue eyes sparkled. "You and Luke should totally do that. I've never seen him so crazy in love. So unless you hate his guts, you two should—"

"I don't hate his guts." Giselle had to smile at that. "The opposite, in fact."

"You love his guts?" Cynthia laughed. "Don't mind me. I get like this sometimes."

Bryce laughed. "Sometimes? How about twenty-four-seven?"

"All right, so I'm a nutcase." Cynthia rolled her eyes. "But seriously, Bryce and I think you and Luke are perfect for each other, and we should know. I'm Luke's sister and Bryce is your brother. We know you two better than anybody."

Giselle was impressed with the logic of that statement. It was absolutely true that Bryce knew her better than anyone, and so far he hadn't given a thumbs-up to any of the werewolves she'd dated. "But Luke is happy here," she said. "I don't want to uproot—"

"He's not happy!" Cynthia blew out a breath. "He's a damned martyr. Hooking up with you would be so good for him. He needs to learn to delegate instead of carrying the whole shebang on his admittedly broad shoulders. He could even delegate to *me*."

"I thought you wanted to dance."

"I do, and I will, but I can multitask. I wish you would take my brother up to San Francisco and make an honest man of him, Giselle. He can still be CEO down here if that floats his boat, but I favor an absentee executive, if you get my drift. Eventually I'll be running this company, anyway, so he can gradually get used to that."

Giselle couldn't help smiling at the audacity of this twenty-two-year-old woman. "I believe you will be the CEO one day. But what about Luke? What's he destined to do with his life if you take over Dalton Industries?"

"I see him turning into a country gentleman, maybe buying a winery in Napa. Admitting he's not the Type A he's trying to be here in Vegas. And being blissfully content with you in that lovely pastoral setting."

"Really?" Giselle stared at her. "I thought he liked the hustle and bustle."

"He thinks he should because our dad did. In case you haven't noticed, he's been trying very hard to be Angus Dalton 2.0."

Giselle burst out laughing. She was still laughing when Luke and Mr. Thatcher came into the locker room.

Luke gazed at her. "What's so funny?"

"Your sister. She cracks me up."

"Glad to hear it. Maybe she wants to do standup comedy instead of dancing with the Moonbeams."

"You just gave me an idea, brother of mine." Cynthia executed a quick little soft-shoe. "A dancing standup comic. I'm going to work on that."

"I'll buy a ticket," Giselle said.

"There you go." Cynthia shot her a look of solidarity. "I have my first member of the audience."

"You'll fill the seats," Bryce said.

"I'll second that," Benedict said with a grin. "Guaranteed. But how about we take a stroll through the playground, now that everyone's here?"

Giselle nodded. "Let's do that." Her heart felt lighter knowing that Bryce and Cynthia believed in a happy-ever-after for her and Luke. But they could believe that till the cows came home, and if Luke didn't want anything to do with werewolves, she would lose him.

If so, she would let him go easily, without drama. He would never know that her heart would be permanently broken. Cynthia and Bryce had only confirmed what she already knew—Luke was her soul mate. No other would do for her.

Bryce and Cynthia went through the swinging door, designed so that a wolf could open it without difficulty. Mr. Thatcher gestured for Giselle to go next, but she hung back.

"After you, Mr. Thatcher. Luke and I will bring up the rear." She didn't know if he wanted to walk with her or not, but they'd had so little time to speak privately since she'd shifted into wolf form. They should give themselves a chance to talk, however it turned out.

"Good idea," Luke said. Before they went through the door, he took her hand again.

She considered that a positive sign. He'd had a lot to assimilate in a short time, but obviously he wasn't ready to give her the old heave-ho, or he wouldn't have laced his fingers so securely through hers.

They stepped through the door onto an overlook, and his fingers flexed. She wasn't surprised that he'd react that way. The view was breathtaking, especially considering they were underground.

Cool, pine-scented air wafted up to them, along with the sound of rushing water and the hoot of an owl. A full moon shone intermittently though clouds scudding across a starry sky. Through the artistry of the playground's creators, they stood on the edge of a canyon high in the Rocky Mountains on a moonlit night.

"I'm heading down," Benedict said. "Watch your step. This place was designed for werewolves, who have excellent night vision. But if you walk carefully, you should be fine. The path is wide enough for two creatures, either Were or human."

Giselle took a deep breath, drawing in the wonder of the place, the same wonder she'd felt when she'd come here years ago. In the midst of a city teeming with noise, lights, and crowds, this retreat existed for the Weres who longed for an escape into a serene forest. The playground was an engineering marvel and a sanctuary for those of a different species. No wonder werewolves everywhere had mourned its loss when a human had gained possession of their special place.

"I can't believe this," Luke murmured. "I can hear crickets."

"Werewolf scientists collaborated to make it as authentic as possible, given the technology at the time. It's updated whenever new designs become available. As we walk along, you'll hear rustling in the leaves to simulate the movement of night creatures like raccoons and skunks."

"How about animatronics? Any fake birds or animals here?"

"As I understand it, the builders decided that would be an insult to visitors. Our sense of smell would tell us immediately the creatures weren't real. The sounds provide a more convincing illusion."

"Makes sense, now that I know more." He glanced at the winding path. The others were already several yards in front of them. "Want to take a walk in the woods?"

"I'd love to."

Luke started down the incline at a leisurely pace. "I like that we don't have to worry about snakes."

"They say Harrison Cartwright wanted to create a place where the participants didn't have to worry about anything and could simply enjoy the ambience. It's an anxiety-free zone, and werewolves don't have many of those."

"Are Cynthia and I the first humans to see it?"

"I can't say for sure. I'd love to tell you that's true, because it would make this moment even more special, but I doubt you're the first humans in here. Aidan and Roarke Wallace of the Wallace pack each have human mates, and I have to believe at least one of those couples has been here on vacation."

"Is their father the one who's president of your council?"

"He is." She brushed past a pine branch that extended into the path. "Did Mr. Thatcher mention him?" Her stomach tightened. This anxiety-free zone no longer was. Now they would talk about the central issue between them, the one that could bring them together or tear them apart.

"He did mention the guy, and the situation with his two sons. I . . . was startled to find out that werewolves and humans were . . ."

"Mating?"

"Yes." He pulled her to a stop on the path, a place shadowed by tall pines. Their needles carpeted the ground, and a stream flowed nearby, its rippling music adding to the sense of being deep in the midst of a wilderness. "How do you feel about that?"

So it was out on the table, the question that had plagued her ever since she'd fallen in love with him. Her answer had been easy in the beginning. Because he hadn't known that werewolves existed, she'd vowed to keep that knowledge from him so that he'd never have to make such a painful choice.

She faced him. "I'll tell you the truth."

"I hope so." His eyes flashed in the semidarkness. "I expect no less from you, Giselle."

"I've never lied to you."

He was quiet for a moment. "I guess not. You just didn't tell me everything. Now I want to know it all, beginning with how you stand on this mating business."

"I've always been firmly opposed to it."

He exhaled. "Then why did you tell me? Why did you make it seem as if you wanted to be with me, no matter what the difficulties might be? I don't—"

"I was against it until I met you."

The silence stretched between them. Finally he spoke, his voice strained. "And now?"

The dam broke and her tears flowed. "Oh, Luke, I've tried to give you up, but every time I think of living without you, it's as if this big black hole is swallowing me, and I can't . . . I can't . . ."

"Me, either," he said softly. "Me, either, my love." And he pulled her close, tucked her head under his chin, and rocked her back and forth as she cried.

"But I'm asking you to change *everything*."

He chuckled. "Everything changed the minute you walked into my office demanding to know what information I had on our rebellious siblings. I haven't been the same since."

"But I'm a *werewolf*, Luke. That means if we have offspring they could be human or Were. Can you live with that?"

Now he was totally confused. "I thought you couldn't have kids."

"I can have them. I just can't get pregnant until I'm mated to someone. It's a Were thing. But you and I could have offspring. They'd just be . . . mixed. Could you deal with that?"

He hesitated for a brief second.

"Look, if you can't, I respect that, Luke. I completely understand."

"Hang on, Giselle. I can absolutely deal with that. It's a startling concept, especially after I'd thought you couldn't have kids, but the one thing I can't live with is being separated from you. So there you have it."

"You'll have time to think about these things. I'm not demanding your answer now." She was determined to get everything out in the open. "Here's another issue. I'll want to shift now and then and run through the woods. Will that gross you out when I do it?"

"Nope. I'm sort of jealous, if you must know. And by the way, demonstrating that ability was the gutsiest thing

I've ever seen in my life." He kissed the top of her head. "What if I'd freaked out and called 911? What if I'd tried to kill you?"

"I trusted you. I knew you wouldn't harm me."

"Exactly." He pulled her closer. "Just as I trust you and know you'd never harm me, either. I can't imagine what mating with a werewolf means really, but if the alternative is giving you up forever, the choice is ridiculously easy."

She hugged him tight. "Mating with me means you won't have to be locked inside that resort-style prison."

"That's good to know. I wasn't too pleased with that scenario."

"And Cynthia will have privileged status as your sister, so unless she starts acting crazy, as if she's about to broadcast our presence to the world, she'll have complete freedom of movement."

His muscles relaxed, and he sighed. "Good. That's so good. I can be very happy knowing that my sister will be okay."

"She'll be okay whether we mate or not." Giselle lifted her head to gaze up at him. "Don't make that the deciding factor, Luke. No matter what happens between us, I will fight for Cynthia with all I have. So will Bryce. So will Mr. Thatcher. She has champions among us. She's well protected."

The shadows hid his expression, but his warmth radiated around her. "You *would* fight for her, wouldn't you?"

"Damn straight I would. I'm loyal to you, and that means I'm loyal to your sister. Werewolves have a very strong sense of family. Besides, she's a kick. I really like her."

"She likes you, too." He gathered her close and gazed

down at her. "She asked if I believed in soul mates. I said I didn't know. She told me if there was such a thing, you were mine."

Her breath stalled. "And what do you think?"

"I think she's onto something." He leaned down, his mouth nearly touching hers. "Will you be my mate, Giselle? My soul mate?"

She was like a balloon full of helium, ready to fly, but she didn't want to leave this place, this man, this moment. "Yes," she whispered. "Because, you see, I already am."

Not long afterward, while Luke was in the midst of a deep kiss that would inevitably lead to more than a kiss, he became aware of approaching footsteps.

Apparently the rest of the party had finished exploring the playground and were walking back up the path. Then the footsteps stopped, as if all four had realized they'd come upon an intimate scene, one they didn't want to interrupt.

Luke stopped kissing Giselle long enough to turn his head and hold out his hand. "Whoever has the remote to that revolving wall, give it to me, please."

"Right on." Seconds later, Benedict placed the remote into Luke's outstretched palm. "Don't lose it, dude."

"Thanks. I won't." Luke shoved it in his jeans pocket. "We might be a while. You can all go home."

"Don't forget to close up," Benedict added.

"We won't!" Giselle promised from the depths of her sweetheart's embrace.

"Yeah, like she's really focused on that," Bryce said. "Not."

Luke chuckled. "Don't worry, Bryce. I'm the responsible type. Ask my sister. And besides, I still own the place. See you all in the morning."

Then he went back to kissing the love of his life, who also happened to be a werewolf. As he was beginning to understand, that was going to make this love affair one hell of an adventure. And it would begin now, very aptly, in the middle of a make-believe forest.

Dear Reader,

I've loved cavorting with my sexy werewolves, but every once in a while a girl likes to try something new. In my case, it turned out to be three novellas gathered under the banner of *The Perfect Man*. Haven't we all dreamed about such a guy and wondered if he really exists?

Well, so have three close friends—Melanie, Astrid, and Valerie. In college they were sorority sisters, and now they're working girls living in Dallas, a city known for billionaires and cowboys. Over margaritas at the Dallas hotspot called Golden Spurs & Stetson, the three friends fantasize about their ideal mate. Is he one of the city's sought-after bachelor billionaires? Or is he a virile, chaps-wearing cowboy? If the sky's the limit, maybe he's both!

I've had great fun throwing these sassy ladies into situations where they come face-to-face with hot guys who challenge them to rethink their vision of what constitutes the perfect man. The series was published as three e-book originals last summer, and the response was wonderful! But these stories were meant to be told together, so now you can get them all in one volume.

This September, come join me in a hunt for the perfect man. Believe it or not, I found three excellent candidates, and I dare you not to fall in love with each of them. I sure did!

Warmly,
Vicki

Read on for a look at

The Perfect Man

Available September 2014 from
Signet Eclipse.

"To Paris!" Melanie Shaw lifted her margarita glass and grinned at her two best friends in the world, Astrid Lindberg and Valerie Wolitzky.

"To Paris!" they both echoed as they touched the salted rims of their glasses to Melanie's.

Melanie sipped her full drink and set it down carefully in front of her. Good tequila should be savored not gulped, and Golden Spurs & Stetson served the best margaritas in Dallas. "I still can't believe we bought plane tickets today. We're actually going." She gazed across the round table at Astrid, her petite blond friend whose family had more money than God, and Val, a sassy redhead who was one of the best young lawyers in Dallas. "I mean, *Paris*. Do you realize we've dreamed about this since college? I can remember sitting in the sorority house late at night talking about this trip."

Astrid smiled. "Me, too. And it always had to be just us experiencing it for the first time together. Edward couldn't understand why I refused to go with him last spring. He didn't get that I was waiting until the three of us went."

"That's what I love about you," Melanie said. "You could have flown to Paris anytime, but you waited for us."

"Of course I did! Besides, I'd much rather tour Paris with you two than Edward." Then she blinked. "Did I just say that out loud?"

"'Fraid so." Val studied her over the rim of her glass. "You do realize that half the women in Dallas want your guy. Good-looking billionaires don't exactly grow on trees."

"I know." Astrid sighed. "I just . . ."

"I think Astrid prefers a Stetson-wearing man." Melanie winked at her. Astrid had defied her wealthy family's wishes and become a large-animal vet, a job that put her in constant contact with cowboys.

Astrid picked up her margarita. "Okay, I'll admit that Western wear gives a guy a certain rugged appeal."

"Doesn't it, though?" Melanie had been raised on a ranch and had dated cowboys almost exclusively. Her current boyfriend, Jeff, wasn't particularly adventurous. For instance, he had no interest in going to Paris. But he sure was pretty to look at. "I'll take a broad-shouldered cowboy over a billionaire any day."

"Why settle for one or the other?" Val glanced across the table. "As long as we're dreaming, why not order up a billionaire cowboy for each of us?"

"The best of both worlds." Melanie nodded in agreement. "The perfect man. Why not?"

Astrid raised her glass. "Billionaire cowboys for all. It's no more than we deserve, right?"

"Right!" Val said.

Laughing, they finished their margaritas and ordered another round. Tonight, with their long-awaited trip to Paris finally becoming a reality, nothing seemed impossible.

Also available from

Vicki Lewis Thompson

Werewolf in Alaska
A Wild About You Novel

As the founder of Werewolves Against Random Mating, Jake Hunter abhors the idea of Weres mating with humans. Yet he can't help admiring his beautiful neighbor across the lake, Rachel Miller, who is known for her artistic wolf carvings—which all look a lot like Jake.

As Rachel gains fame for her carvings, rumors circulate that the two are involved. Not wanting to infuriate his proud clan, Jake keeps his distance from his comely neighbor. But when Jake shifts to save Rachel's life, their lives will collide with an intense passion, one that could change everything they've ever felt about themselves—and each other…

"Humorous and romantic."
—*USA Today* (on the series)

vickilewisthompson.com

Available wherever books are sold or at penguin.com

facebook.com/ProjectParanormalBooks

S0524

Also available from

Vicki Lewis Thompson

Werewolf in Denver
A Wild About You Novel

When blogger Kate Stillman takes on political bad boy
Duncan MacDowell in a public debate on werewolf
segregation, she is confident she can handle the challenge.
But she soon finds herself attracted to the sexy Scottish
founder of WOOF (Werewolves Optimizing Our
Future)—who happens to prefer dating human women.
Yet what hope do they have when their future together
depends on Kate losing her argument?

**"Devour…Vicki Lewis Thompson's books
immediately." —Fresh Fiction**

vickilewisthompson.com

Available wherever books are sold or at
penguin.com

facebook.com/ProjectParanormalBooks

Also available from

Vicki Lewis Thompson

**THREE DOWNLOADABLE INTERMIX
NOVELLAS AVAILABLE NOW**

One Night With a Billionaire
The Perfect Man

Melanie, Astrid, and Valerie may be best friends, but they have
very different ideas of what kind of man is more fun—one with
a pocket full of cash or a guy with spurs on his boots?

Tempted By a Cowboy
The Perfect Man

The sisters of Gamma Delta Rho just can't agree whether the
perfect man is rich or rugged. But can a cowboy ever prove
he's worth his weight in gold?

Safe In His Arms
The Perfect Man

Valerie and her sorority sisters are constantly debating what
makes the perfect man—but how do you find "the one" when
you can't even face a first date?

Available wherever books are sold or at
penguin.com

facebook.com/LoveAlwaysBooks